A screech split the air: a Wa...

hard. Atlas Bear.

"Awaiting instructions," Atlas Bear radioed us.

"Weapons free," Neena said.

"Hey, I'm down here–" I started to say.

A too-brilliant light erupted from the airship's ventral hull. Tracer bullets streaked across the night, slammed into the containers next to me, and raced along the deck. I felt each impact in my boots, like hammer blows. And the sound was more pain than noise.

Firelight spilled out from the rents Atlas Bear's bullets had torn in its sides. And it was getting brighter by the second. Just the kind of day I'd been having.

The container had a good sense for dramatic timing. It waited just long enough to let me curse before exploding.

MARVEL HEROINES

OUTLAW
RELENTLESS

TRISTAN PALMGREN

ACONYTE

FOR MARVEL PUBLISHING

VP Production & Special Projects: Jeff Youngquist
Associate Editor, Special Projects: Caitlin O'Connell
Manager, Licensed Publishing: Jeremy West
VP, Licensed Publishing: Sven Larsen
SVP Print, Sales & Marketing: David Gabriel
Editor in Chief: C B Cebulski

Special Thanks to Jordan D. White, Gail Simone,
Mike O'Sullivan, and UDON Studios

© 2021 MARVEL

First published by Aconyte Books in 2021

ISBN 978 1 83908 074 6

Ebook ISBN 978 1 83908 075 3

This novel is entirely a work of fiction. Names, characters, places, and incidents are the products of the author's imagination or are used fictitiously. Any resemblance to actual events, locales, organizations or persons, living or dead, is entirely coincidental.

Sales of this book without a front cover may be unauthorized. If this book is coverless, it may have been reported to the publisher as "unsold and destroyed" and neither the author nor the publisher may have received payment for it.

Cover art by Joey Hi-Fi

Distributed in North America by Simon & Schuster Inc, New York, USA
Printed in the United States of America
9 8 7 6 5 4 3 2 1

ACONYTE BOOKS

An imprint of Asmodee Entertainment Ltd

Mercury House, Shipstones Business Centre

North Gate, Nottingham NG7 7FN, UK

aconytebooks.com // twitter.com/aconytebooks

To those on the outside looking in and those on the inside reaching out.

PROLOGUE

"Inez," my dad always told me, in a voice a little too serious for what he must have thought of as telling a joke, "never grow old."

He would say this as he was coming back from the pasture with a hitch in his step, hiding a limp. Or after grunting loud as a steer as he pushed himself off his recliner to make Elias and me dinner. Or when I found him sitting in that same recliner at six in the morning, heavy rings under his eyes, unable to sleep.

I nodded solemnly. He acted like he was waiting for me to crack a smile, but I never did.

He only called me by my first name when he was serious about something. Otherwise, it was always a nickname, something nice and embarrassing. I'm not even sure he realized the difference. But I sure did.

Even as a kid, I never figured I would grow old. Not in the sense that I was immortal. Just in the sense that I wouldn't make it.

I don't remember when I started thinking that.

But I definitely remember why.

ONE

I didn't figure I should be going out on this job, not as exhausted as I was. But that inner voice of caution was too easy to ignore. The fact was, I'd been in worse states before. Hell, I've even been shot – more than once, on the same occasion. And you know what I did afterward? I got right up and kept fighting.

Because that was the only thing I *could* do. Because nobody gave me any other choice.

Easy enough to get back in that mindset. All I had to do was tough it out again. I'd come out of it eventually. Always had before.

This is one of the many troubles with being a mutant. Anything medical in general. Aging, especially. It's hard to find an old mutant, if you follow what I'm saying. Nobody understands our bodies, not really. Not even us.

I just wish I weren't so tired all the time.

I hadn't had to deal with that before. Not like this. Aging has been on my mind a lot lately. There was no other way to say it other than that I'd been dragging. Every morning when my alarm went off, I felt like I'd fallen asleep only five minutes before.

'Course, a good fist fight has a way of waking me up. Adrenaline will soothe over a lot.

I had just started up the narrow, corrugated stairs when he passed me by. Crew-cut man, olive skin, big bundles of muscles. Didn't think much of him. I'd blustered my way past a dozen like him on this job already. I was on my way to the container ship's bridge, focused on my destination.

Something must've tipped him off. He took a look at me as I passed. Then a quick double-take. He reached for his belt, where he had a radio handset.

Even tired, I've still got my reflexes.

I'm no stranger to pain. I've got my favorites. The sweetest kind stems from my knuckles and radiates down into my bones like heat from a fireplace. Better than coffee, bacon, and pancakes. *Almost* as good as Neena's puppy[1] pushing his nose into the side of my neck at three in the morning whenever I stay over at her place.

The goon staggered into the bulkhead. The back of his head slapped it with an audible metallic *bang*. Satisfying.

'Course… another good way of waking up is a punch on the chin.

I didn't see his counterpunch coming. He followed up the first punch with a second, harder, in the center of my forehead. Stars swam over my vision. Good training, this man. I was fully awake now.

If the rest of his training was as good as his fighting skills, he'd be calling for help soon. Couldn't let that happen. Couldn't

---

[1] His name is Pip – and by "Neena," Outlaw is referring to the mutant merc more popularly known as Domino. –Ed.

take the time to be staggered. I followed up with a hard punch to his gut, just below his ribcage. It knocked the wind out of him. Just in time, too. His mouth was already open, halfway to calling for help.

I had some unfair advantages over him. Big and bulky as he was, he was just an ordinary person.

Me? I'm a mutant.

Pardon my manners, they're usually atrocious. My name is Inez Temple, but most folks call me Outlaw.

My next punch lifted him right off his feet. I knocked him clear up to the shoulder-width landing halfway between this deck and the next. He crashed into the bulkhead and dropped with a gasp. I'd felt something *snap*. For his sake, hopefully just ribs.

Not that I had much sympathy for A.I.M. agents.

The acronym stands for Advanced Idea Mechanics, which is an awfully dull way to say "evil superscientists." They're a bunch of scientists with plenty of brainpower but no hearts. Their latest play for power was designing a bunch of nasty weapons to distribute to nasty folks worldwide. That was what this container ship was carrying. They were going to sell them to any terrorist organization, militia, or criminal group who meant to use them, and then swoop in afterward and take advantage of the chaos.

I stepped up to where he was silently lolling and writhing, grabbed the back of his head, and cracked it against the deck. He went still. I tried my best not to kill him, but with head injuries there was no guarantee. Mutant strength is a little hard to control.

There used to be a time when I wouldn't have thought twice

about introducing him to his maker, but Neena and Rachel have been trying to be better about that kind of stuff lately. And what do you know? Their attitude has rubbed off on me.

Still – sometimes it wasn't easy.

OK, a *lot* of the time it wasn't easy. But I was learning.

At least this man was still breathing. No guarantee as to his long-term prospects, but it was better than what I once would have done. He wouldn't have extended the same favor to me – not unless it was to preserve me to dissect in a lab somewhere.

I searched him quickly. He had an ID card, a radio, and a phone. I pocketed the card and smashed the other two. He didn't have any weapons. Most of the crew didn't go around armed, probably to avoid drawing attention. For the same reason – and to fit in among them – I'd had to come unarmed, too. I usually carried a pair of Colt revolvers everywhere I went. I didn't feel like myself without them.

I hate wearing clothes other than my own. I hate espionage, subtlety, and sneaking around. I was aboard the cargo container ship the *Little Miss Ironsides*, disguised as a member of her crew. Ugly navy-blue jumpsuit, zipper in the front, and a cap with the ship's name, logo, and just enough shade to hide my face. Or at least hide my face from a distance. My hair was more of a problem. My long blonde braid ain't exactly seagoing regulation. I had tucked it into the back of my uniform, inconspicuous as possible.

On a commercial ship, I might not have had to worry about keeping appearances shipshape. But this wasn't just a commercial ship. Not by a long shot.

This crew was military, and their uniforms just as much a disguise as mine. They were A.I.M. soldiers. It was weird to see them out of their garish yellow beekeeper uniforms, but they wanted to make sure that, if the US Coast Guard or anyone else laid binoculars on them, they looked nice and innocent.

Here's a long mission briefing cut very short: the *Little Miss Ironsides* was powering right toward Boston Harbor. The cargo containers on its deck were full of not-so-nice weapons that A.I.M. intended to sell to other not-so-nice people. My friends and I had been hired to stop them. We'd split up to take different parts of the ship.

I looked around for some place to stash the body. All the hatches in this corridor were closed.

The fog in the back of my head hadn't quite dissipated. I'd studied this ship's schematics in the mission briefing along with everybody else, but, in my exhaustion, the details vanished. I couldn't remember where I was.

I didn't hear any shouts or pounding bootsteps. No one had heard the bangs. Or at least no one had been alarmed by them.

I closed my eyes, tried to focus. Imagined the blueprints of the ship splayed out on the table in front of us at Avengers HQ. Tony Stark's hairy wrist as he pointed out target after target. Me biting my tongue, trying not to say anything that would get us into trouble. My best friend Neena had been standing beside me, arms folded, with the rest of our little posse – including Black Widow, trying not to look too wistful at being back in Avengers HQ after so long away.

Focusing on the senses usually helped me pluck whatever else was missing out of my memory, but not this time. The deck schematics were a blur.

I had other problems, anyway. Even if I found a safe place to stash Sleeping Handsome here, it would only be a matter of time before someone noticed his absence. We were on a harsher timetable now.

I unclipped my own radio from my belt. "Hard wind blowing in," I said. Code for *trouble brewing*. At least my memory hadn't fogged that over.

Neena's staticky voice answered me: "Don't pay it any mind."

Decoded version: she was running into trouble, too. Even more decoded: it was only a matter of time before our cover was blown anyway. I should focus on getting into position rather than on hiding the evidence.

She didn't elaborate on the cause of the trouble.

The number of grimy bootprints on the corrugated deck said that this was still a high-traffic area. One of the hatches had a window. I peeked in, and saw a brightly lit, compact chef's galley. It was empty. No guarantee that anyone wouldn't come in, of course. But it was somewhere to deposit the body. I dragged him into the galley and left him behind a counter.

When I came back out I still saw no one, heard no one. I exhaled, tucked my cap tighter over my head, and carried on.

Seeing the galley had stirred my memory. I still didn't remember the cabins around me, like I should have, but now I knew I was about a deck below the bridge.

I hadn't slept well the night before. Now, I've gotten pre-mission jitters before. In this business, the best way to tell who's *really* tough and who's just faking it is to see who will admit to getting them. But it wasn't jitters that had kept me up. I didn't know what it was, but it had been going on for a couple nights.

Well – maybe more than a couple.

This kind of tired was new to me. It wasn't a forty-eight-hour-stakeout tired, nor a running-so-hard-you-want-to-puke-up-your-guts tired, or even a spent-all-night-clubbing-two-nights-in-a-row tired (gotten more and more used to that one since I joined Domino's posse). This was a deep-in-your-bones tired, a weariness more akin to an ache.

And here's something that never happened to me before: sometimes, I couldn't remember falling asleep. I wouldn't wake up in my bed. I'd find myself waking up on a couch, or a floor, or even the back seat of my rental car, with no memory of having decided to go there.

And then there were the dreams. Dreams of places I'd never go again. My childhood home in Texas. My father's grave.

I didn't want to talk about it. Talking wasn't gonna fix it. I sure didn't want to see a doctor. I just had to grind through.

My destination was up one more staircase. The hatch was even labeled "Bridge," just to make me feel like a panicky idiot. I breathed out, pushed the bill of my cap down to hide my face, opened the hatch and stepped through.

It wasn't much to see. If 'bridge' makes you think *Star Trek*, prepare to be disappointed. Commercial container vessels like this don't have the big, complicated electronics. The cabin on the other side of the hatch was more like an elongated closet. It was as narrow as the corridor outside, quite a bit shorter, and crammed full of junk. Boxy old control stations, fresh from the 1980s. Backlit white square-shaped buttons, rows of switches, and five greenscreen displays on old CRTs.

The view was good, at least. Big-paneled stormproof windows lined the front wall. Last time I'd seen outside, everything had been coal black. (That had been hours ago, when my little stealth pod had nuzzled up to the *Little Miss*

Ironsides like a feeding piglet.) Now the horizon was a fierce orange. Only it was still three in the morning. This wasn't a proper dawn, but light pollution. Orange pillars of light spiraled from the horizon and reached up into an overcast sky. We were getting close to the port.

There were no seats. This was a place where big, faceless corporations put people to work. The real captains of container ships were investors and executives, not the schmoes who lived and suffered on these crates. At least, that would've been the case if A.I.M. hadn't bought the ship. But I had a suspicion that A.I.M.'s hierarchy wasn't all that different. The big boys at the top were nowhere near here. They sent their grunts and goons to take the risks and do the dirty work, and took all the profits and glory if it paid off.

Case in point: the only other person here, a middle-aged Japanese man, didn't look anything other than tired. A real middle-manager type. He didn't wear a disguise, though. The windows must have been tinted on the outside because he was in his bright yellow A.I.M. uniform. The only thing missing was his face-obscuring helmet, like a radiation suit's, which was hanging from the back of his neck.

"You all have work you need to do," he said, sounding bored. "And get a new cap. That one's too small. It won't hide your ugly face from anyone with binoculars."

Now that had just been unnecessary. "Sorry, skipper," I said. "Just looking for supplies. Know where I can find any rope around here?"

"Dumbass." He hiked a thumb toward one of the rear hatches. "Supplies are right back there. You should know." After a moment's consideration, he asked, "Why?"

I've never been able to stand a bully. "Just have to tie someone up is all."

He needed a second to put that one together. By the time he did, I'd already crossed the distance between us.

He wasn't much of an obstacle. Didn't think his heart was in the fight, really. By the time he caught his breath after the sucker punch, I was halfway through hogtying him.

His feet smelled something awful, which made it too bad for him that his sock was the best gag around. Not that I was feeling too broken up. "Nothing wrong with my face," I said, surprising myself with how irritable I was. Exhaustion left me brittle. I left him shoved in a corner, steaming mad but unable to do anything about it. After securing all the bridge's hatches, I studied the ship's controls.

I wasn't much of a sailor. I liked swimming well enough, but, tell the truth, ships made me a little seasick. Still, our pre-mission training had been thorough. Our employers – a combined task force of members of the Avengers, Stark Industries security, and old S.H.I.E.L.D. hands – had the deck plans for this model of ship on file. Pictures, training manuals, everything.

The ship's controls fogged in front of me. They jumbled together, as complicated as they were meaningless. Levers, dials, blinky screens. Nothing made sense.

I closed my eyes and took a breath. This had to be nerves. If I could just wait it out, I'd be fine.

When I opened my eyes, everything straightened out again. I knew what I was looking at. The ship was on course toward port. It wouldn't need much manual steering until it got closer in.

My part of the operation was simple: change the ship's course subtly enough that no one noticed.

See, the thing was, for this operation to get as far as it had A.I.M. had to be convinced everything was going perfectly. A.I.M. wasn't dumb. They knew how many people would stop their operation if they could, and so they had built failsafes. There were explosives in the containers. If A.I.M. became too suspicious, they could obliterate everything.

We needed to get the weapons A.I.M. was shipping. Then the eggheads could study them and develop countermeasures before A.I.M. cooked up anymore.

So, we'd left the buyers alone, for now. The A.I.M. crew had checked in with them all along their trip, getting the right code phrases, making sure their sale was still good to go. It had only been here, at the handoff, that our employers could get into a strong enough position to attack without tipping A.I.M. off first.

All this led to a second problem: the good guys couldn't afford to let A.I.M. get anywhere near the buyers. Too much risk of those weapons getting loose. Nor did we want to get into a firefight in a public harbor with gaggles of civilians around. Even at night, ports were busy.

So my job was to get this ship pointed toward a private pier where our employers had a reception party waiting for them. If I did my job well, no one on the aft decks would notice until it was too late.

In short – too many damn acronyms on this job. The important thing was that this was the first big job my team had taken at the behest of the Avengers. The biggest good guys in the world don't often trust mercs like us. To say we've got checkered pasts would be a bit of an understatement. For some of us, it's more black than white. But, lately, Neena had been making more of a play to get into the heroism business. And I was backing her on that, all the way. I'd spent enough of my life sitting out on the sidelines while the world spun out of control. If we pulled this job off, it could open up opportunities for us down the road.

'Course, having a former Avenger like Black Widow on our team helped those odds, too.

Black Widow was with her old teammates, the Avengers, at the pier. Neena, Rachel, and I were the only ones aboard right now. They had their own jobs. Rachel[2] was mining key corridors and hatches to cut the A.I.M. goons off from different parts of the ship once the trap was sprung. And Neena should've been in place among the containers, there to stop anyone who clued into the ambush and tried to destroy the cargo. I say *should* because I still didn't know what Neena's message meant.

If something went pear-shaped, the only other person who could get in a position to help was Atlas Bear. She was a Wakandan exile, but she hadn't left Wakanda empty-handed. She brought along her heavily armed airship – which was waiting with our employers at the ambush site. Mr Stark was there, too, heading up the operation.

I studied the container ship's controls and mapped them out onto what I'd learned during the mission briefing. There were always differences between the instruction manuals and reality. The labeling on the backlit buttons had worn off with years of use. But they didn't swim around anymore, and, before long, I

2 Rachel is more popularly known to the rest of the world by her callsign Diamondback. –Ed.

found what I was looking for. Rudder and engine controls, and the screens to help me shift the ship's bearings oh-so-slightly.

It was delicate work. Delicacy isn't my strong suit, but I can manage, and I did it fine then. I flattened my boot heels against the deck, to feel for any shifting. If I noticed anything, I'd been too aggressive. But there was nothing. I'd done my job well enough. Nobody would know about the course correction unless they were paying attention to the instruments, and the instruments were up here.

After a while, I had to kick the hogtied man to keep him from getting too loud through his gag. Not very heroic of me, but sometimes the ends really do justify the means.

Someone had left a pair of binoculars on a ledge underneath the front windows. I scooped them up. Our bearing had shifted subtly, and we were headed toward one of the darker parts of the harbor. Good. I radioed the code phrase – "Two o'clock and all's well" – and waited.

No answer. If everything was going all right, there wouldn't have needed to *be* an answer. But Neena's last message stuck in my craw. Something was going sideways somewhere, and she couldn't tell us what it was. Not without giving away the game.

I hate waiting. I gripped the sides of the control console tight enough to leave finger dents in the plastic. The *Little Miss Ironsides* crept closer to the shadowed pier.

The tension started to get to me. It wasn't fear, not exactly. But being on edge all the time takes a toll. Something on the bridge was ticking. *Click click click.* It took me too long to identify that it was coming from an analog clock in the corner. It played my nerves like a bow on a violin.

That deep-behind-the-eyes tiredness was coming back. The thing about that kind of tired is that knowing about it doesn't help you fight it. I gritted my teeth and bit the inside of my cheek. That didn't help. I leaned against a bulkhead, took my cap off, and rubbed my forehead.

I don't know how it happened. Last I knew, there was no one else on the bridge.

Something sharp and heavy smashed into the back of my neck, right above my shoulder blades. It would have struck my head if I hadn't bent to massage my forehead at that moment.

My breath *woofed* out of me like a horse bolting from the barn. It didn't want to come back in. I crashed into the side of the workstation ahead of me. The fog in my head cleared. I reacted without thinking. I levered my foot around, lashed it out.

The kick found nothing but air. My assailant caught my leg and twisted. My combat instincts caught up just in time. I grabbed onto the side of the console. The leverage let my other leg stay on the ground. I swung my elbow backward.

My jab landed in something soft. Could've been a cheek, could've been a throat. Couldn't tell. By the time I managed to right myself and turn, my attacker was stumbling away.

I should've been cued in by the hogtied captain going too silent. He'd gone rigid, his breath tight. He'd seen whatever was coming up behind me and tried not to give it away.

My attacker was another goon in an A.I.M. costume, a woman. Like the bound and gagged skipper, her hood was hanging from the back of her neck. Short-cropped hair dyed black, and a muscular frame. She stumbled into one of the workstations.

The deck underneath us rumbled. Somewhere far to the aft of the ship, the engine sound cranked up. *Damn it.*

"Outlaw!" my radio barked. The clipped voice sounded like Iron Man himself, Tony Stark – though, through the static, it was hard to be sure. Whoever he was, he was breaking code protocol. "What the *hell* are you–?"

My attacker was clutching her face, but I saw her eyes dart to my radio. I *saw* the gears in her head clicking together.

She lunged for another workstation. Rudder controls. Before I could stop her, she grabbed a lever and jammed it all the way over to the right.

Now, a container ship is damn big. Even a "smaller" ship, with minimal cargo, took a lot of power to move. There was never any danger of the ship knocking us off our feet. But we did feel the *clank* of all that metal shifting. The hull groaned as the rudder shoved through water much faster than it had been intended to. And we also felt the change in direction – a shift deep inside our guts.

And if we could feel it, everyone else on this ship could, too. A shout echoed from somewhere down a nearby corridor.

I snarled. The change in the ship's momentum put a wobble in my step, but it did the same to her. By the time I was on her, she didn't have enough balance to dodge or duck. I threw myself at her, and we crashed to the deck in a tangle.

For a while, nothing else but the fight mattered. I was on the attack – where I preferred to be. We struggled for a while, but only because my balance was off. I was the mutant. My abilities included superstrength. I clamped my hand over her face. She tried to bite my fingers, but I was so ticked off I didn't even feel it. I drew back my fist and slammed it into her forehead. She went limp against me. I dropped her to the deck.

And then the rest of the world caught up with me.

My radio was squawking and hissing like a bird chasing a snake out of the nest. Mr Stark wasn't the only one who'd dropped code protocols. A cacophony of voices was trying to speak over each other at once.

"Outlaw." Neena's voice. "Inez… what's happening?"

Rachel's voice: "–No alarms yet, but it's only a matter of–"

Then Mr Stark again: "All teams, stand by for immediate action!"

"I'm taking this into–" It took me a while to place that voice. Atlas Bear's. There was a deep, throaty rumbling in the background.

What a damned mess.

The hatch behind me was hanging open. That was how my attacker had gotten in. But I'd secured those hatches right after I'd taken out the captain. Those things were so heavy, and the wheels that locked them so clunky, that I should've heard if someone had opened it.

Somehow, somewhere, I'd screwed up. I couldn't quite piece together what had happened. It must have gone down in that moment when I'd lost my concentration.

I snapped up my radio, and had to wait several seconds to find a space where I wouldn't be speaking over somebody else. "Bridge is under control. Engine problems."

"Get that ship back on course," Mr Stark growled.

"You know it's too late for that," Neena said.

She was right. I wrenched the rudder controls back to where they were, but ships like this turn big and slow. Once they'd committed to a course change, they had a hard time going back. Even if I got us to the correct pier now, we wouldn't come in at the right angle.

Heavy bootsteps clomped down the corridor my attacker had come from. More than one pair of them. Two men, one with a ponytail and the other shaved flat, burst through the door. They were still in their commercial crew disguises. The one with the ponytail looked around frantically. His eyes locked on me as his partner saw the woman I'd taken down.

Well – I was the one who'd been itching for a little more action. Always look on the bright side of life, Dad used to say. Usually when he wanted to needle me.

Catching people by surprise is a nice little stress reliever. The man with the ponytail had half a second to see me coming at him, but even if he'd had longer, he couldn't have expected mutant strength. My first punch cracked his jaw, spun him around and lifted him right off his feet. He crashed into his partner just as his partner was drawing his sidearm.

There wasn't much room to maneuver. They didn't have anywhere to go to get away from me. By the time they toppled to the ground, the fight was pretty much over. From then on, it was a matter of mopping up and knocking out. By the time I returned to the ship's controls, though, we'd swerved farther off course.

No way to hide from the crew that something was wrong. My gut curdled. I didn't know how I'd gotten things so screwed up.

The guilt would have to wait. We were going to beach if nothing changed. So I did the only thing I could. I cut the engines.

Rachel's voice crackled over the radio: "Two of them are headed toward the forecastle." That was where, while on scouting, Neena had determined the self-destruction switch for the ship's cargo had been placed.

"I've got them," Neena answered.

Even through layers of bulkheads, I heard the sharp reports of two sniper shots, one a second after the other.

Then the radio erupted again. "Get that airship back down–" Mr Stark started to say.

"Protect the weapons," someone else interrupted. It sounded like one of the Stark Industries eggheads. "We need to capture them. *Capture–*"

To fit in with the mostly unarmed crew, I'd had to come without any of my guns. I grabbed the weapon off the man who'd tried to draw on me. It couldn't be something as conventional as a Glock. Nooo, nothing's ever as simple as it should be. A.I.M., stuck-up techheads that they were, had to make everything a gizmo. This pistol had no trigger. Just a shiny black bar. Fingerprint scanner. Damn thing was biometrically locked. Of course.

I kept it anyway. Just habit. When things went bad, I felt naked without some kind of weapon.

No point in staying here. With the engines shut down, it would take time and coordination to start them up again. If the A.I.M. crew found the former and had the ability for the latter, we were sunk anyway. I charged out the hatch my attackers had come from.

The walkway I emerged onto was high up on the bridge castle, and it would have given me a good view if my eyes had been adjusted to the night. The deck lights highlighted flashes of color. This ship wasn't as full of cargo as a lot of container ships coming in from overseas, but there were still enough things below to make a labyrinth of reds and greens and blues.

Neena was watching the front of the ship, where she thought the self-destruct switch was. She'd taken the sniper role on this mission so, unlike me, she'd been able to come armed. The problem was that all these containers meant that there were plenty of corners and shadows she couldn't cover.

My eyes gradually adjusted to the dark. From here, I saw at least three people running through the containers, headed toward the forecastle. No matter where Neena was, she wouldn't have clear shots at them all.

A narrow steel staircase zig-zagged down the side of the bridge castle. Steel support struts fastened it to the hull. I grabbed the closest strut and started sliding. A story off the deck, I leapt. The landing staggered me, but not so much to keep me from catching up with the closest A.I.M. goon.

I couldn't make out his features in the shadows, but he sure was startled to see me. I no longer fit in, anyway. I'd forgotten my cap back on the bridge.

He was at the edge of a short row of containers. He was armed, though his gun was holstered. Instinctively, I drew on him.

He took a short, quick breath, raised his hands in surrender.

That must've been why I'd taken it. To bluff. Yeah – sure.

By the time he saw the fingerprint scanner and figured out my problem, it was too late. The pistol was hurling right at his forehead. *Clonk.*

Bootsteps reverberated through the deck. Like an acquaintance of mine is fond of saying, it was clobberin' time.

The next A.I.M. goon fell to a sucker punch from behind a corner. I ducked around another container just in time to see another of them fall to a *crack* from Neena's rifle. Belatedly, it occurred to me that it was a good thing that I'd forgotten my cap. Without my hair, there was little to distinguish me from any of the other crew.

A screech split the air. It was somewhere between a train whistle and a banshee. I winced, but recognized the sound. A Wakandan airship, aerobraking hard. Atlas Bear.

As soon as I rounded the next corner, I saw it. A sleek, rounded shadow cut across the sky, studded with projecting fins and blades. In silhouette, it looked like a descending spider. Its shadow dropped against the skyscrapers.

"Get that airship *back*," Tony Stark demanded, for what must've been the third time.

Atlas Bear ignored him. "Awaiting instructions," she radioed us.

"Weapons free," Neena said.

"Hey, I'm down here–" I started to say.

A too-brilliant light erupted from the airship's ventral hull. Tracer bullets streaked across the night, slammed into the portside hull, and raced along the deck.

I felt each impact in my boots, like hammer blows. And the sound was more pain than noise. It was incredible. Like firing a pistol next to your ear inside a concrete bunker, over and over.

I dove to the deck just as a tracer bullet streaked overhead and punched into the highest of the two containers stacked beside me. When I opened my eyes again, the gunfire had moved on, but the light had only gotten stronger.

Firelight spilled out from the rents Atlas Bear's bullets had torn in its sides. And it was getting brighter by the second. Just the kind of day I'd been having.

The container had a good sense for dramatic timing. It waited just long enough to let me curse before exploding.

TWO

"All right," Tony Stark said, his armored elbows propped on the debriefing room's table. "Let's hear it."

Rachel, Neena, and I started talking all at once. After several exasperated moments, I cut over them with the truth: "It was my fault."

My dad taught me not to lie. And I've mostly held true to that. Kinda. I've told plenty of lies, but I've never been *dishonest*. If you catch my drift. The lies I've told have all been a mercenary's lies – there to serve a purpose. If I'd lied here, it would've just been to make myself look better.

They knew the problem had started on the bridge, anyway. So I had to tell them. About the hatch that I'd been sure was secured. That, if it *had* been secured, I should've heard open.

Lots of people stood around us in the debriefing room. Most I'd never met. Only Mr Stark, Neena, Rachel, and I sat at the table. Mr Stark's people – Stark Industries scientists, Avengers support staff, and old S.H.I.E.L.D. agents alike – were behind him. The other main members of the Avengers were still out on assignment.

The rest of the posse was here, too – standing behind Neena, Rachel, and me. The posse was all scraped and bruised up. No serious injuries, but anybody looking at us could tell how near a thing it had been. My chest still hurt when I breathed in, and the shockwave had hit me hours ago.

Rachel set her hand on my shoulder. But I looked Mr Stark right in the eye when I spoke. He'd taken his helmet off, but this was quick enough after the battle that he'd left the rest of his red-gold suit on. Maybe because he hadn't had time to change. Maybe just to show it off.

"We got your shipment," Neena told him. "Most of it."

Mr Stark looked at her, eyebrow raised.

"Half of it," Neena said.

He didn't shift a muscle.

"We got enough," Neena said. "I checked the manifests and the surviving cargo myself. We got at least one of every weapon. That's all your scientists should need to reverse engineer everything."

"Technically true," Mr Stark answered. "But if you've never told engineers or scientists that they have to reverse engineer something, but they're not allowed to take something apart to study it because we only have one of them – well, now's your chance, because they're right here."

The angry-looking folks behind Mr Stark took their turn to erupt at us.

I groaned, massaging my forehead. I wished I had my hat to hide my eyes. My head was still spinning. I wanted to blame the explosion and shockwave, but the truth was this was the same type of tired that had weighed me down on the bridge. If anything, now that the adrenaline had faded, it was worse.

Sometimes I hate being so darn honest. It'd be nice to be able to lie to myself about how I felt, at least. Thanks bunches, Dad.

My memory had gotten jarred around by the shockwave. I was still trying to piece it together. The explosion on the *Little Miss Ironsides*'s deck hadn't knocked me out. But it had stunned me, put me into a state of strange awareness where I saw and heard everything around me as if through a fog. Sparks drifted through the air like the aftermath of a fireworks show – debris falling back to the ship. Flaming shards of twisted steel littered the deck. Something hot had struck my elbow, burnt and blistered it.

My ears were ringing so loudly I couldn't hear anything. When I could, I pulled myself to my feet, grabbed my radio, and told Atlas Bear to stop shooting. I couldn't hear squat, but she could. No more tracer bullets flashed by overhead.

Next important thing to verify: how fast the fire was spreading. A fire on a container ship loaded with potentially volatile weapons wasn't gonna stop just because we wanted it to.

I scanned for lifeboats. I'd taken note of them while coming aboard the ship, but forgive me for being a little disoriented. If we couldn't stop the fire, then we would have to try to save as many people as possible. A.I.M. folks included.

I hate getting involved in fights with acronyms. The bloodshed is too depersonalized, too abstract. Give me the heat and the hate of a personal grudge any day. When people get involved with acronyms, it seems like they lose part of themselves. It starts to get clinical, and not very fun at all.

Evil as A.I.M. is, it's also a big organization. The big names at the top need plenty of muscle, goons, and pen-pushers. Most of the people on the *Little Miss Ironsides* probably fit that description. Not all of them could be true believers. Some people come from hard luck backgrounds and will do whatever they feel they have to do to get their paycheck. I know what that feels like.

Sure, we'd hurt and killed people coming aboard, but that was business. They'd do the same to us. Not saving people from a burning boat would've been… just nasty.

We couldn't help the true believers. But the ones on the border – well, they might be a little more willing to talk if we got them out of here.

A sharp yellow light reflected off the edges of the next containers. The deck rattled an instant before the sound clapped my ears. Nothing worse followed – this time. Sooner rather than later, this was going to end in a chain reaction that would take out most of the ship before we could blink.

The smart thing would have been to leave.

Now, I don't want to say you can't be smart to be mercenary. You have to be awfully clever. But there are certain kinds of smart it doesn't pay to have. The kinds of smart that would have you think twice about choosing such an awfully violent profession, for example. I don't often make what other people might call smart decisions.

I staggered back in the direction I'd come from. Found the man I'd clobbered with the thrown pistol who was rocking on the ground, cradling his forehead. I grabbed his hand, yanked him to his feet. His eyes widened when he saw my face, but all I did was point toward the nearest lifeboat. He seemed to get it. Truce accepted. He turned, and, dizzily, started walking.

All around the sides of the boat, crew were running toward the lifeboats. They paid no attention to me, or anything but the fires. Some of them had dropped their weapons. Others still had them holstered. I hoped the ones who'd kept their weapons were smart enough not to fight when our employers came for them. But that part of the op was out of my hands.

Had to focus on what I could control. Pick up the pieces.

I crossed my arms and glowered at the debriefing table. None of this was going anywhere I liked. The weight of the stares was too much.

But it wouldn't have been right of me to try to get away from it or deny what had happened. Had to cope with what was.

Neena stared down Mr Stark. She wasn't going to give up sticking up for me. But it was a rearguard action.

Mr Stark told her, "And you were the one who gave the order for weapons free."

"If I hadn't, we would have given them time to organize a defense, and to hit the kill switches in the containers. Then we'd have nothing, *and* you'd have lost a lot of your people in a firefight that didn't need to happen!"

All true. But she was only doing her job – taking responsibility, as team leader, for anything and everything that happened under her watch.

"Not everything goes perfectly in every op," Rachel added. "That's one of the advantages of working with us. When things go sideways, we're flexible enough to finish the job."

It was hard not to notice that the other members of our

team were being pretty quiet. They stood behind us. I sure felt the weight of *their* stares, too.

I suppose some introductions are in order.

Our names get a little complicated. In this business, if you don't have a callsign or code name, no one takes you seriously. Like I said, my name is Inez Temple – but I've been Outlaw since the days when I was freelancing.

So: here's Neena Thurman. Better known to the outside world as Domino. A real mercenary's mercenary. Just about every merc looks up to her in one way or another. Even Deadpool, though he'd have to be in a real pinch to admit it. It used to be she was in it for the guns and money rather than the heroism, but lately that's changed. Like me, she's a mutant. Her powers don't tend so much toward brawn, though she's got plenty of that.

No, she's got something beyond cool. Her power is *luck*. And if your first reaction is to say, "Luck isn't a super-power," you haven't seen her in action. I've watched someone pull a gun on her, have it jam immediately, get it kicked out of their hands, bounce off the ceiling, and crack them in the head. All in the space of half a second.

She's the leader of our little posse. And my best friend. She's jagged on the outside but, once you get on her good side, she's sweet as peaches. I'd say that if anyone wanted to hurt a hair on her head, they'd have to get through me first – but Neena can take care of things herself. I might still kick them in the head to teach them a lesson, though.

Then there's Rachel Leighton. Her other name's Diamondback. She's been with us since the beginning of the group. She used to run with a gang of ne'er-do-wells called the Serpent

Society, though she has her regrets about that now. She's our explosives expert. She dresses better than anyone else I've ever met. She's always got an appropriate get-up for any mission, and is deceptively combat-capable, too.

Any stereotypes you might have about country folk and fashionistas might make you think we wouldn't get along. Forget them. Rachel's a gem. I love her. We might not have gotten along so well on first blush (happens an awful lot to super folks the first time they meet), but, after that little battle was out of the way, we clicked like pineapple and Canadian bacon on pizza. Not everybody's favorite, but definitely mine.

The others and I weren't quite on a first-name basis yet, even if we knew what they were. They were newer to the team.

I already mentioned Black Widow. Aka Natasha Romanoff. She's the biggest name on our team, and sometimes it's hard to shake the feeling that she's slumming it with us. See, she used to be an Avenger. She left that team around the time when she needed to fake her own death and joined our posse when we were saving the world from the Creation Constellation. (It's *complicated.* Things in this business usually are. I may have nearly ascended to godhood and gotten humanity destroyed by the Celestials, but I got better. Honest.)[3] She needed a new home to drift into, and we gave her one. Neena, Rachel, and I got the impression that there was some kind of emotional tangle that kept her from going back to the Avengers. She never denied it, but she never wanted to talk about it. She looked mighty uncomfortable here. Tony Stark tried to meet her eye, get her to acknowledge him a couple times – but,

---

3 The superlative *Hotshots* Vol. 2! –Ed.

from the way he looked away quickly, he never found what he was looking for.

I'm not sure we'll ever feel comfortable with Black Widow as a part of the team until we know she's here to stay. We're not a rebound super hero team. We're mercs more than we are heroes. For the most part.

Atlas Bear, or Shoon'kwa, joined up with us not long after her exile from Wakanda. She has precognition. It's made a real Cassandra out of her. She can *see* the future, but only bad futures. Catastrophes that will happen if she can't stop them. She'd been booted from Wakanda because she'd tried to do too much about those bad futures. Things the Wakandans thought were impolitic, like killing. She'd gotten a *little* gentler since joining us, when we showed her some ways to fight the future without terminating every source of possible trouble, but her abilities and her exile left her understandably sour.

Her mood was dark most of the time, but she saved her darkest looks for Mr Stark. It was hard to forget the disdain in her voice when, in the middle of that last battle, she'd ignored his orders. She seemed to think she had a beef with him, which was weird, because he'd never shown any sign of recognizing her.

Finally, there's White Fox. Ami Han. She's a Korean special agent, and, though she looks human enough from a distance, she can disabuse you of that notion pretty quick if she wants to. She's a shapeshifter – the last of the *kumiho*, a kind of magic multi-tailed fox. She linked forces with us during that Creation Constellation fiasco, too, and has been fighting at our sides ever since. Like Black Widow, she has other loyalties, too – but, unlike Black Widow, she is open about them. She still worked for South Korea's National Intelligence Service.

So far, none of her loyalties had conflicted. I wasn't sure, right then, that I could say the same thing about Black Widow and the Avengers.

"You got the weapons," Neena told Mr Stark. "You've got A.I.M. prisoners to interrogate. Some of them might even be helpful since we saved them. I don't see your problem."

"The problem is that I've got a bunch of hotshots screwing things up, who took things into their own hands while leaving the rest of us to sit here, and who treated the plan like it was just a means for them to try to show off."

"You've got a bunch of hotshots," Neena said, measuredly, "who saw where a plan was falling apart and salvaged a situation that, if anyone less flexible had been in charge, would've ended in disaster."

"If you don't think this was a disaster, I'd love to see what you think success is like."

"A success is when you achieve your mission's goals," Neena told him.

"She's gotcha there," I said.

From the intensity of the hostility shifting toward me from all sides of the room, I probably shouldn't have drawn attention to myself. Tough. I meant what I said.

Dad tried to teach me not to cuss. That lesson didn't really take. In times like that, it felt dishonest to hold them under my tongue.

There had been a crane on the *Little Miss Ironsides*'s deck. A big, yellow monstrosity on tracks. I shot a glance between it, the ship's deck, and the water. It didn't take me long to put this stupid, dangerous idea together.

"It looks like you all are in trouble," Atlas Bear radioed.

"We're in trouble," Rachel confirmed.

Atlas Bear's airship could be whisper-quiet when she chose, but not during combat. That was when she switched on the noisemakers, made it as loud and intimidating as an oncoming train. Its thrusters roared as the airship hovered on a curtain of gray exhaust. The A.I.M. crew flinched away from it.

The airship angled toward the bridge castle. "Get to the top level," Atlas Bear said. "I can extract you from there."

"Already there," Neena said.

"I'm on my way," Rachel chimed in. "Give me thirty seconds."

I didn't chime in. I bolted across the deck, paying no heed to the few crew hustling about. Even if someone recognized me as an intruder, only people with a death wish would try to stop me now. I doubted anyone serving as deck crew, bad guys or not, would be so committed to their bosses' cause.

'Course, I'm always capable of being surprised. But I wasn't this time.

The deck jolted. It felt almost like the ship had run against something. An explosion like a cannon shot popped my ears. I couldn't tell whether this one had come from the containers above deck, or the engine room below. Either seemed like bad news.

"Inez?" Neena asked.

I didn't have enough breath to answer. That was my excuse, anyway.

I clambered into the crane's cabin and slammed the door behind me. Just in time. The deck rattled. A fraction of a second later, the sound of another detonation rattled the plastic windows. They *pinged* and *thumped* as debris rained down on them like hail. I sat facing the now-scratched and burnt windshield, and tried not to think about how far along the fires had gotten.

"Inez," Neena said. "Talk to me. Tell me you're all right."

Finally, I answered. "I'll be all right."

For a moment, the crane's controls swam in front of me, just like the ones on the bridge. I've never done any construction work before. (One of the reasons I became a merc was to get *out* of that kind of thing. The bigger reason was – well, it's hard for a mutant to fit into civilian life. Trouble and hate come to us like ants to strawberry jam.)

This time, the fog cleared on its own. Most of the controls had obvious functions. And, while I was sure I was missing some nuances, I didn't need to be precise. And I sure didn't need to be *safe*.

The controls were locked. A glowing pad on the right wall had a slot keycard reader and an instructional image of a disembodied hand holding an ID card. I grabbed the card I'd stolen from the A.I.M. goon, swiped it through – and what do you know, it worked.

Its motor started. A deep, guttural rumble like a tiger's purr shook the seat. The controls were labeled in Chinese, but there were plenty of self-explanatory pictographs. Joystick on the right for lateral controls. Joystick on the left for height.

Bright yellow firelight reflected along the sides of the nearest containers. There were no longer any crew near me. I could have sworn some of the firelight was green. Who knew what kind of materials A.I.M. was shipping in these containers?

A cluster of multicolored containers, two layers high, sat close to the edge of the deck. I had no idea if A.I.M. color-coded by the containers' contents, but there was at least one of each color here.

Good enough for what I needed.

I yanked the control lever and swept the crane arm to the side. The metal arm shrieked in protest. It wasn't designed to move this fast, or so carelessly. I drove the crane arm into the stacked containers like the arm was a wrecking ball. It smashed into the containers hard enough to dent them both. Their restraining cables snapped. Three of the containers tipped over the side and crashed into the water. Another clung to the side, teetering uncertainly, and for a moment I thought I'd have to waste time trying again. Then its cargo shifted and it, too, plunged into the sea.

The containers were reasonably airtight. They would float for a while. Maybe. Most likely. If they didn't, the Avengers and S.H.I.E.L.D. were resourceful. They'd have divers.

Probably.

From her position atop the bridge castle, Neena couldn't have missed what I was doing. The radio squawked. "Fire's spreading," she said. "Get the hell out of there, and up here!"

"Come on down here with me, and we'll both be fine," I answered. Neena's luck power was a sight to behold sometimes. I'd seen her survive frag grenades because all the shrapnel miraculously missed her.

"That's not how my luck works, and you know it," Neena said. "It protects *me*. It doesn't protect people around me."

More containers stood by the opposite side of the hull, just within the crane's reach. If I had enough time, I could get to them, too. Give the Stark Industries eggheads some more toys to pick at.

I glanced at Atlas Bear's airship. A big, sleek, black-and-violet beetle hovered over the bridge castle. If this whole ship was gonna blow, the airship was still too close. I hoped Rachel was right when she'd said she'd only need thirty seconds to get there.

"Y'all had better go," I told them. "I'll find my own way out."

"Inez..." Neena started.

"Trust me."

While we spoke, I was wrenching the crane arm over to the last containers. My first strike hit at just the right angle. It sent one tipping forward into the others. Another four of them broke through their restraining cables and crashed into the water. I couldn't see the impact from this angle, but I heard the splash.

THREE

"My own way out" turned out to have been a frantic sprint to the side of the boat and an undignified dive overboard. I'd hardly splashed in when the water above me roiled with the biggest explosion yet. The bubble trails of white-hot debris speared through the water. Some of Neena's luck must've rubbed off. None of it struck me.

I swam my way over to one of the A.I.M. lifeboats, and "convinced" them to stay put and stay calm until they were picked up for capture. Didn't take more than one or two punches. We coasted in the light of the fire.

The container ship was a flaming wreck, but still afloat. The bridge castle was intact. The people I'd left in there would be shaken, but fine so long as they got out in time.

Mission accomplished, right? All's well that ends well.

In the debriefing room, I resisted the impulse to squeeze the water out of my ponytail. Damn thing was still damp.

Once we'd gotten back to Stark Industries' local offices, I'd retrieved the backpack I'd left with them. My clothes, my real clothes, and my hat were in there. We hadn't been given the time or privacy to change before being dragged into the debriefing room, but just having them near made me feel better. I wasn't far away from being myself again.

I didn't say anything through the rest of the interrogation. Didn't figure I had to. I'd already said everything I needed, and that only made things worse.

The temperature in the rest of the meeting cooled after that. I shouldn't have been surprised. Nothing we said could change the bare facts. We'd accomplished the mission's objectives, and we'd done it in a way that made everybody unhappy.

The people on each side of this table just placed different weights on one over the other – or so I told myself. I was still in good with the posse, the people who counted to me.

I really wanted to believe I was still in good with them.

One last interesting thing happened. As I stood to go, I caught sight of Atlas Bear's glower. It was even darker than usual, and it was fixed on Tony Stark.

She paused long enough to grab Mr Stark's attention. He furrowed his brow. "What?"

"So many of the ways I've seen the world die start with you," she told him.

This was the first time I'd seen Atlas Bear and Mr Stark in a room together, but Mr Stark would've been briefed on all of our abilities. He knew who Atlas Bear was, and what she could see.

It wasn't long ago that she would have tried to kill him because of what her precognition had just showed her. He would have known that, too.

If he had any questions about what she'd said, she didn't give him time to ask. He watched her, brow still creased but lips hanging open, until we reached the door.

The tension seeped out of my shoulders. Most of it, anyway. I didn't know that I could ever relax in a place like this. Beige walls, cubicles, and stark white fluorescent lighting. The kind of place that was about as cheery to me as a prison. At least prisons were upfront about the fact that they wanted to crush your soul. I've spent more of my life in the county lockup than in any office, and, honestly, I don't know that I'd swap. At least what got me in that lockup was having fun. The only thing that lands you in an office is the awful desperation of job-hunting.

The Stark Industries folks didn't have anyone see us out of the building, but they wouldn't need to. They'd have cameras everywhere, and they'd be watching. All their more sensitive places were locked up, anyway. Neena's posse may have been their partners, but that didn't mean they trusted us. Even bunched together in the elevator, we stayed quiet, each of us stewing in our own frustrations.

Outside, the sunlight bit my eyes. The last time I'd been outside, it had been a dead night – as dead as nights ever got under the nauseous sodium-orange haze of Boston's light pollution. But that had been before the debriefing. Time had slipped away from me. Now – hell, I didn't even know if it was morning. The skyscrapers blocked the sun.

We'd gotten more than a block away before we collectively decided it was safe to talk. It was like a breath came out of us all at once. The others all started speaking.

"How could you have let–" White Fox demanded.

"I don't like that man," Neena said. "Every time we've met, he's–"

"What an amateur mistake–" Black Widow said.

"– Engine controls slip like that–?" White Fox continued.

"– Hateful mess that was," Rachel was saying. "Let's not do any of that again–"

Too much going on all at once. It took me too long to realize that at least half their anger, especially the half coming from the newer members of the team, was directed at me. Atlas Bear was silent, but, when I turned, that dark stare was aimed right at me.

Maybe I wasn't in so good.

If we were going to do this, I wanted to do it properly. I reached into my backpack, felt the folded-up brim of my Stetson. It sprang out like a puppy chasing a squirrel through an open gate. I planted it over my hair. There. Now I was the only one of us not squinting into the sun… and I felt more like myself.

"Run us through this again," White Fox told me. "How'd anyone get that close to the engine controls? Why didn't you see them?"

"You heard me well enough in the debriefing." She just wanted to drive it home.

"Either you didn't hear them come in through those big, heavy hatches," White Fox said, "or you didn't check the bridge before you secured it."

It would've been easy to think that White Fox was just trying to get under my skin. And maybe that *was* part of it. But, like the rest of us, she cared a lot about this job. Super heroes and supermercs tend to be on the perfectionist side. Deep down in her bones, she wanted to get it right. It wasn't just the team's reputation on the line. It was hers, too. Belong to the wrong team, and people in this business will remember that for ages. Hell, a lot of people still needle Rachel for having belonged to the Serpent Society, no matter how many years and about-turns ago that was.

Usually, I relished a good argument. But what she was saying wasn't wrong. I had no comebacks.

In her position, I'd have been pretty upset, too. The defense we'd offered during the debriefing – that we'd still gotten what we wanted in the end – was immaterial next to the fact that I'd screwed up to begin with.

I was glad I had my hat to hide my eyes.

"It's going to be a long time before we get any work with the Avengers or Stark Industries again," White Fox said.

That was fine by me. I would never forgive Tony Stark for pushing the Superhuman Registration Act. I would work with him to hurt a bigger bad like A.I.M., and because Neena said so, but I wasn't going to lose any sleep over anything else. Not that it would have been wise to mention this now.

"The Avengers hate working with mercs, anyway," Black Widow said. "Tony Stark is a little more flexible, but the other Avengers… they still wouldn't have…"

"Still *what*?" Neena demanded.

White Fox sighed. "You know what she's trying to say."

"You don't think we would have gotten the offer at all if you weren't on the team," Neena said.

Black Widow just looked at her. She knew what would happen if she said *yes*. But she still wanted to say it.

We were treading into some truly dangerous waters. To Neena, the idea that she was coasting on someone else's reputation, that this wasn't *her team*, was a deep cut. She'd break up this team before she'd let either of those things be true. She'd almost done it before.

Black Widow shifted the subject, but only a little. "You want to move up in the world. You want to get better jobs, to work with the big boys. That's fine. But think about whether what you brought to the table before will be good enough now."

"We've always been the best in the business," I said. "Even when you were with the Avengers, you knew that." There were only a few mercs that could rival us, and most of those weren't team players. Like Deadpool.

"You know," Black Widow said, "most of the teams I've worked on have had some member shakeups over the years. Keeps them fresh and vital. On top of their game."

"Natasha," Neena warned. First time I'd heard her call Black Widow by her name.

It wasn't that I thought nothing could get past my armor. I know I've got chinks in my scales. I just thought I knew about all of them. Turns out I didn't.

My nails bit into my palm. I couldn't talk about it. I couldn't tell them how tired I was. I couldn't tell them how often I'd been dreaming of home, in Texas. A house I'd promised myself I'd never have to go back to. And I certainly couldn't tell them about how I kept waking up in places I couldn't remember falling asleep in. They'd think I was falling apart.

Neena and I were best friends, but we were in a deadly business. If she thought I couldn't hack the job, or that I would put the rest of the team at risk, I couldn't stay on it. Sentimentality can only get you so far in a firefight.

"I just messed up, is all," I said. I'd made plenty of mistakes in my life. With few exceptions, none of them had been such productions.

Black Widow didn't say anything else. But she didn't need to. She'd planted the idea, and now White Fox picked it up. "Whatever it was, it cost us a lot," White Fox said. "And it could have cost us a lot more."

"Just lay off, you two," Neena said, but there wasn't much force in it.

"I mean it. We want to move up in the world, right?"

Neena didn't answer. Any answer would have been a trap.

White Fox said, "We're going to have to think long and hard about the kind of attitudes we're going to leave behind. 'Just messing up' won't cut it as an excuse when we're working with teams like the Avengers."

"You want to kick me out of the team, you can just say so," I told her.

"*Never* going to happen," Neena cut in.

I was used to sticking up for myself. All my instincts were going into fight-or-flight drive. And I didn't really have a "flight" mode.

"You want to talk about this in private?" I growled.

White Fox tightened her jaw and ground her teeth. "Natasha and I aren't 'after' you, Outlaw. But it would be a good idea to think about what we want as a team, and if we're going to be able to get it, acting like we are."

"I'll tell you what *I'm* after," I said. "Things used to be an awful lot more fun. When it was just Neena, Rachel, and me. Before we started opening the posse up to spies and hangers-on."

I'd stepped over the line. I hate to say it, but I meant to. I didn't know how to get back.

I also didn't know if I'd counted on Neena to keep breaking in, cool things down. She didn't. Rachel was silent, too. The sound of footsteps beside me didn't stop, but it diminished. A couple people must've stopped walking. But not Black Widow.

She was looking right at me. Even with the brim of my hat hiding my eyes, I could feel it. While I'd been arguing with White Fox, she'd been smoldering the whole time.

"That's your whole gimmick, isn't it?" Black Widow asked. "Always chasing the past. You know, I used to think that outfit of yours was just a costume."

"That's not fai–" Rachel started to say. I cut her off.

"I used to have a lot more fun on my own, too," I said.

I was halfway across the next block before I realized I was walking away. I walked facing down, my hat blocking the view in front of me. I didn't care. I strode briskly, fists clenched, and, if there was anyone in my way, they swiftly got out of it.

What stuck with me the most was that Neena didn't say anything. She'd stuck up for me at the start of the argument, but that had been it. After I'd chimed in, doing what I'd *thought* was defending myself, she'd fallen silent.

Good old Inez. Show her a tough situation she can't punch her way through and trust her to always make things worse.

There was nowhere else for me to go after that. But I sure couldn't follow them.

City hotels are so damned expensive. It wasn't that I didn't have the money. Last few jobs before this one had paid well, and even Mr Stark had coughed out our paychecks (sans bonuses) for this operation. But it was the principle of the thing.

It took a long walk to find a hotel that fit my standards. I'd hoped the exercise would give me a chance to cool down, but it didn't. The Princeps Hotel was a mean little building, dark gray and humorless, nestled up against the side of a much better-looking one. When I got to my room and turned on the AC, the air started to move, but I sure didn't feel any cooler.

That could have just been me, though.

I was the worst kind of angry. It wasn't rage, or hate, or anything that could've been turned to some kind of use. No, I was what my dad, God rest his soul, called *sullen.*

And I was still tired. So tired. It was all catching up to me.

And it wasn't going to leave me alone.

I don't remember falling asleep. That was the terrifying thing. One moment, a fog seeped over my head. And the next...

I had a dream about the best horse I ever knew. One of the only things I still missed from home, Wheezer. She was a palomino with a mane the color of sun-bleached sand. The name, happily, wasn't accurate these days. She'd been born prematurely, had breathing problems. Dad didn't think she'd survive long, and he wouldn't have had the time to spend all day nursing her regardless.

But I wouldn't let her go. I had to feed her like an orphan foal, keep the bottle held low, to make sure she wouldn't aspirate it. I set my alarm to wake me up every two hours overnight – a big step for a kid who slept until noon every weekend. She lived in the cleanest stable that ranch ever saw. I wasn't going to let any pneumonia get her.

She pulled through. Tough little foal. I didn't feel comfortable naming her anything at all until she was over it. Calling her Wheezer was like a little private joke between us, a reminder of how we'd triumphed. Taking care of her was an accomplishment; the first thing I ever did I could be really proud of. She and I had both come out of the womb a little bit off.

She was past her prime as a riding horse now, but she was still living comfortably at Dad's old ranch. My brother Elias took good care of her. I trusted him that far, at least. Elias had a soft spot for animals. It was the one thing we'd had in common.

My dream didn't last all that long. I was riding Wheezer. The sun had baked the two of us, and I was drenched in sweat. Somehow, I was more tired than Wheezer. Even with my mutant endurance, I ached. It was like the exhaustion of these past few weeks had crept into my memories.

And the second I thought that, I knew for sure I was dreaming.

A pair of angry car horns jolted me upright. Suddenly, I was soaked through. Cold water pattered off the brim of my hat. It drenched my pants and squeaked in my soles. For a moment, I wondered if I'd stumbled into the shower, turned it on, and fallen asleep.

That would've been bad enough. This was worse.

Headlights sparkled through the rain. They were so bright they stung to look at, and the horn so loud it smarted to hear. My world spun. I was out in the open. Boston's skyline circled the horizon, a crown of jewels half-lost in the downpour. The cold cut straight to my bones. For a moment, I got it confused with the cold I'd hoped to get out of the hotel room's AC. But that must've been hours ago. It had been daytime then, and this was deep night.

The cars honking at each other moved on, leaving me alone in the cold and the dark.

I was sitting on a metal park bench, soaking in the water. The street in front of me fogged over, went gray and blurry.

The skyline was familiar, even in the dark. I'd been in Boston enough times to know the general layout. I should've been able to piece together where I was. But my mental map of the city was just as scrambled as everything else in my head.

I breathed into my hands, smelling for alcohol. Nothing.

But I found something in my palm: a paper receipt. It was drenched in rain, and most of the numbers were unreadable.

The muscles in my legs were tired, strung out, as if I really had been riding Wheezer all night.

I waited for my memory to clear, help me remember how I'd gotten here. It never did. All I could do was sit, cold and shaking.

FOUR

One thing you might've heard about me is that I have a nickname. "Crazy Inez." People call me that when they want to get under my skin. They do it because it works.

First time I got the nickname was when I was a kid. I had a temper problem in school. And outside of school. And... well, just about everywhere, really. Later, when I became a merc and some of my enemies started poking into my background, the nickname came back up and started going around. I hated it now just as much as I did then.

Of course, as soon as those types found out how I reacted to it, that just made word go around faster.

I hated to think, even for a moment, that I wasn't in control of myself.

Shut up. I know it's ironic. That's not the point. Or maybe it is the point. I don't know. Funny how, even when we know we're doing something self-defeating, it's still hard to bring ourselves to stop it.

However I'd gotten to that park, I didn't have my hotel keycard with me. I had to beg the hotel's night auditor to let me back in. She was *real* thrilled about that. Honestly, if I'd had the presence of mind, I would've acted drunk. At least that would've given me an excuse. But I was too shaken up to think straight. I was half-tempted to knock the hotel room door down and just walk inside. Probably would've ended up spending the night in jail.

One of the reasons I knew I hadn't been in my right mind was that I'd left my change of clothes in my backpack. I'd gone out in my jumpsuit disguise. Only thing I had on that I *wanted* to have on was my hat. I carried that into the bathroom, hung it on a shower hook to dry. One scalding-hot shower later, I was more awake.

After I got back in my own clothes, I felt a bit more like myself. Snug jeans, low-cut shirt, and a tan leather vest. Nothing too flashy. My hat was uncomfortably damp, but not so much that I'd go without it.

I'd dropped the receipt tape on the room's desk. Even dried out, most of it was still unreadable. The top of the ticker read "United States Post Office."

I couldn't remember having gone to the post office any time in the past week. I had no idea where this had come from.

The raw pleasure of being myself again only lasted so long. There was nobody else here to see it. And the tired was always there, creeping up on me.

At least that dream had been better than the nightmares I'd had lately. They'd taken me back home to west Texas. A single-story, ranch-style home out in the middle of nowhere. Crinkled, rocky hills rumpling the horizon. A crimson dawn sky. Scraggly desert brush tangling around my feet. There were silhouettes of people everywhere. Dark, indistinct forms –

every time I looked at one, it seemed to melt away into nothing, merge with the shadows of sunrise. I couldn't find a single one of them. But I knew they were there.

The nightmare was no less troubling after waking up. It made me think too much about home. After Dad died, my brother Elias was the only family I had left. And there were times when I didn't care to think of him as family. Dad had split the property between us in his will, but I'd been happy to let Elias buy my share off me. Taking care of land wasn't suited to my lifestyle. And the less time spent around Elias, the better.

I'd promised myself I'd never return. There wasn't much of a draw for me there. Just memories.

I pulled my phone out of my backpack. I hadn't turned it on since I'd gotten back from our mission. I braced myself for a million texts and voicemails.

No messages at all. That felt much worse.

Neena was at the top of my contacts list. Time to rip off the bandage.

I didn't know what time it was. I hadn't looked when I'd turned my phone on. My mind had been elsewhere. But, when Neena answered, she sounded fresh as ever. I kinda knew she would. After every job, if it's been anywhere close to success, she takes the rest of us out for a night on the town. If they'd done that this time, it would've been without me.

"Yeah?" Neena asked.

"You know who it is, Peaches," I said. Neena had different ringtones for all of us. Mine was a snippet of Ennio Morricone's score from *The Good, the Bad and the Ugly*. (Do I have to tell you which part?)

"Uh-huh," she said. "So what do you want?"

She was gonna make me say it. She could be like this when she wanted to punish someone. It was more than a trifle annoying, but, I had to admit, it was keeping me honest.

"Look, you know what the hardest thing in the world for me to do is," I said.

"Admit that's not your real hair color," she said.

"That's a low-down, dirty blow," I said. And worse because it was true. "And no."

"Walk on past an open bar."

She was having fun, but there was an edge to her voice. I groaned. "It's *ask for help*."

A pause. When she spoke again, her voice was different. "Tell me where you are, and I'll be there."

It took me a moment too long to remember the hotel's name. That fog again. After we disconnected, I sat on one of the beds and willed my hat to dry faster. I was already cold, and it just made me colder, but I wasn't taking it off. I didn't want to suddenly find myself someplace without it. It was still pouring outside.

I was getting tired again. Couldn't let myself get tired. Last time I'd done that, well, apparently, I stopped being myself for a while. It made me think of Dr Jekyll and Mr Hyde.

In spite of my best efforts, I'd started to doze again before the knock at my door. I jerked upright and opened it. Neena was soaked through, too, and none too pleased about it. Unlike whoever I'd been when I'd walked outside, she'd been smart enough to bring an umbrella. It hadn't helped. The wind was driving the rain sideways. She stalked inside, looking as stormy as the weather.

Like me, she'd changed into something more like herself: a leather jacket with a buttoned vest underneath – plenty of pockets for hiding keys, gadgets, and small weapons.

She looked at the rumbling AC unit, and then me, her eyebrows raised. No wonder I was so cold. I'd forgotten to turn the damn thing off. I really *was* falling apart. "I fell asleep with it on," I said, lamely.

"You're not usually tired at this hour," she said.

"Yeah. Well. This hasn't been a usual kind of day."

"No such thing in this business," she said. "And we've had plenty of worse days. Just gotta get through them."

I went to the closest bed and sat, trying to play it nonchalant. "So – hit me with it. What'd the others say after I left?"

She pulled out the desk chair, leaned against its back, and smirked. "I did drag an apology out of Black Widow."

"That must've taken some doing. Sorry I missed it. What'd she say?"

"She said she was trying to test you," Neena said. The smile vanished. "See what you thought of your own performance in that mission."

"I've been in this group years before she came along," I said. "I don't need to pass any tests."

"She didn't think you *did* pass."

I shouldn't have needed to defend myself. One of the problems with talks like this is that I kept feeling like they were *beneath* me. I've been with Neena and Rachel since the start. I should've felt safer in this group than anywhere else.

"Are you here to drag an apology out of me?" I asked.

"No. I'm here because you said you needed help."

She said it looking squarely at me and didn't give me any pause to look away. Not without looking like I was avoiding the question. Damn her.

"Your hat's all wet," she said. "You go anywhere tonight?"

"I don't know where I've been tonight."

She frowned. She didn't have anything to say to that. It had just made her plain worried.

I had no choice. I had to spill it. I told her about my exhaustion. The bone-deep ache in my muscles. The fact that sometimes I couldn't remember falling asleep and woke up in places I couldn't remember getting to.

I didn't need to say I couldn't go to a doctor. She knew it, too. Hell, she lived it. I didn't trust doctors. Few mutants did.

Once doctors found out you were one of *them*, things only went in a few directions. Some doctors said they couldn't help you. Some said they didn't *know* how to help you, but didn't put much effort into trying to find out, either. Some were plain afraid of you, like being a mutant was contagious.

Some would tell you that you should try to be *normal*, to fit in with 'normal' folk, and that the stress of being different was to blame for the way you felt. Some would treat you like a laboratory animal, poking and prodding at anything that made you different. Some would treat you like a criminal, ask you if you were there because you wanted to get drugs – and that was double true if you were looking for any kind of mental health care.

Mutants have a long history of being wary of doctors, and for good reason. The doctors we deal with from the non-mutant world range from outright cruel to, at best, callous. We all remember experiments – government-sanctioned experiments – that exposed mutants to diseases just to see what happened next.

I hadn't been to a doctor regularly since I was a kid, before my dad or I really knew what I was. Since then, I've only ever gone for emergencies, like that time I got shot.[4] And even then, it was deeply unpleasant. I got out of the ER as soon as I could. It was more my mutant endurance and over-the-counter antibiotics than any doctor that got me through that ordeal.

Neena had been through the same things, but worse. She'd grown up in a cage, "raised" by doctors and scientists trying to understand mutants in any way they could except by treating them like human beings. She and I were the only mutants on our team. Most of the others were plenty different from the 'human norm,' but she was the only one who spoke my vocabulary.

So I never mentioned doctors once to Neena, but they were part of the conversation all the same. These problems were like tonight's rain – omnipresent, impossible to ignore, but not worth talking about at the same time. If that makes sense.

Neena waited for me to finish. She didn't ask anything asinine, like how long it had been since I'd had a vacation. (Only three weeks. We'd taken a week off after that thorny job in Chicago.) "How long has this been going on?" she asked.

"A couple weeks now–" No, I couldn't keep lying about it. I wouldn't have just been lying to Neena, I'd have been lying to myself. Living in denial. "–A couple months. A little

---

4 Way back in *Agent X #5!* –Ed.

bit when we were in Chicago to find those missing twins.[5] And then again when we went to New York for the Latverian Embassy job. And then… it was quiet for a bit. I thought it had gone away. Only it came back worse than ever when we got to Boston."

Neena arched an eyebrow. "And you were just hoping it would stop happening?"

I lowered the brim of my hat over my eyes, as though that would make this easier to talk about. "I didn't know that there was anything else to do."

"What made you decide to say something now?"

"What do you think? We got through that last assignment, but I screwed up bad." I still didn't know how that woman had sneaked up on me in the bridge. Whether she'd been there and hiding all along, or if she'd opened that heavy hatch without my noticing, it didn't speak well of my abilities.

"And *that's* what made you decide this wasn't going to go away?" Neena pressed.

"No." She was riding me hard because she knew she had to before I would admit this. "Deep down, I knew this wasn't going away."

I'd just thought I could… well… cope with it. Like I've coped with everything else.

A big hard-to-ignore part of me still wanted to do that.

"What made you change your mind?" she asked.

"This was the first time I'd screwed up in a big, bad way," I said, spreading my arms.

---

5 In *Domino: Strays*, a Marvel prose novel by the fine people behind this one. –Ed.

She tightened her lips. "Yeah, but you still didn't talk about it until now."

A good best friend will know exactly how, and when, to get underneath your skin. That didn't make it any less galling. "I can't take the risk of it happening again and going worse, OK?" I said. "Especially now that you are all watching me for it. And Miss Cloak and Dagger, especially."

"So you're talking about it because Black Widow went after you for it?"

"Well, I wouldn't put it quite like that–"

"So it sounds like she did you a favor."

I was prickly as hell and counted it as a minor miracle that the only thing I said to that was, "Maybe." If everybody did me favors like Black Widow's, there wouldn't have been anything left of me. I'd have been scraps of meat dangling from the tip of someone's witty repartee.

We were silent for a long moment. This whole damn thing was so ridiculous. I'd gotten everything tangled up. My health. My body and mind. My job. And now my relationships with my friends and partners. Until today, the problem had seemed so small.

Then Neena grinned.

She wasn't doing it unkindly. I couldn't help but do the same. I had no one but myself to blame for all this. How many hoops had I made us jump through just to get everything on the table? I could've opened up and talked about it weeks ago. I think she understood why I hadn't, but… still…

It was either laugh or do something worse, something I hadn't done in ages. Not since Dad died.

"Damn, Peaches," I said. "What am I gonna do?"

"You tell me."

I rubbed my hands together. "What if I'm too old to keep doing this?"

"What kind of thinking is that? Especially since I'm pretty sure I'm older than you."

We didn't know that for sure. The scientists who'd raised Neena never divulged her birthday.

"Anybody who calls you old is calling me old." She leaned over, gave my shoulder a hard poke. "So don't do that. I'll beat you up."

I swatted her finger away. "Fine. 'Worn out,' maybe."

"I'll do the same thing. You're avoiding the question, by the way. What *are* you gonna do about this?"

"Yeah, I'm good at avoidance."

Neena wasn't going to let me deflect again. "I think you already know what you have to do. It's why you called me."

"I called because I wanted help," I said.

"I'm not equipped to help with something like this," she said. "None of the posse are."

I shot her a dark look. I'd avoided the D-word so far. "I'm not going to see a doctor."

"There are people you could go to," Neena said. "People who *actually* know a little bit about mutants."

"Yeah? Who knows a damn thing about us?"

Neena just raised her eyebrow and waited for me to come to the obvious conclusion. "Other mutants," I said. *Of course.*

"Not just other mutants," Neena said, waving to the window as if to remind me of the whole world out there. "The X organizations. I've got trustworthy contacts."

"I don't like going to *any* doctor," I grumbled.

Neena wisely ignored me. "We're not used to asking for help from them, but they've got no reason to turn us down."

"I've gone to them for help before," I said. "Didn't like the way that turned out."[6]

"Do you want to get help?" Neena asked. "Or not?"

I have a pretty good stink eye, but Neena met it without flinching. Not her first time facing it down.

"Or do you want to keep going forward like you are, hoping something's going to change?" she asked.

The second option was what I was accustomed to doing. Frankly, the urge was so great that, even after screwing up on this last job, I'm not sure I could've fought it. If Black Widow hadn't said what she had, I would've tried to keep plowing forward. But I'll give Black Widow this: she'd made it clear I couldn't go on ignoring it.

"I'll go," I said, miserably.

Neena cracked another smile. This time, though, it was from relief. I wondered what she would have done if I hadn't agreed.

To this day, I don't know. And I don't want to know.

"We'll do better than that," she said. "Atlas Bear can take you right to the New Charles Xavier Institute."

"That your way of making sure I go?"

She shook her head. "You've given your word. You've done so much work for this team. This is the least we can do for you. And I promise that, no matter what else happens, it's not going to be the last."

---

6 There will be more about this later so don't feel like you're missing out, but for those of you who like to read ahead, Inez is referring to the events of the *X-Men: The 198* miniseries! –Ed.

I'd actually been counting on a nice, long solo trip to get my head in order. I massaged my forehead. "Just... give me time, Peaches. I'm not set to leave right away."

I hate doctors. Always have. Even if they're people I trust, I don't want to be examined. I don't want to be poked and prodded at and dissected on someone's clipboard.

I'd committed myself now, though. I'd looked Neena square in the eye and told her that I would do it. I couldn't back down from that.

But I also didn't know when – and if – I came back to her, I'd be the same person I always was. Or if the doctors would take more from me than I'd already lost.

FIVE

Once you travel Wakandan air, it's hard to go back to anything else. Even as the atmosphere boiled and roiled around us, Atlas Bear's airship slipped through the air as smooth as syrup.

I stayed in the back most of the time, on the pretext of sleeping. I hadn't planned on *actually* dozing, but somehow, I managed it. I set a glass of water on the table beside my bunk and by the time I woke, not a single drop had spilled. I spent some of my time in the cabin staring at the surface of the water, looking for the slightest vibration. Nothing.

I wished traveling with Atlas Bear was so easy.

I couldn't stay in my sleeping quarters all the time. That would've looked like I was avoiding her. Which I *was*, but I always try to work some plausible deniability into my excuses. So I headed out.

She was up in the control cabin, ensconced in a cocoon of control consoles and holograms. This five-hour flight was supposed to be boring – we got it cleared with all the normal air traffic authorities for once – but she kept her eyes rooted on all the sensor and threat detection displays. I didn't think she'd moved a muscle, except to look from one hologram to another, while I was in the back. A talent like hers makes it easy to always be thinking of the ways in which things could go wrong.

The two of us were alone. This was my medical leave; I didn't want any of the others tagging along. All I needed was Shoon'kwa, our pilot. I sat in the seat next to hers. A co-pilot's, I guessed – though I'd never seen anyone other than Atlas Bear handle this craft. All its consoles were dark, deactivated.

Up here, the windshield was a bubble, surrounding us. Cirrus clouds billowed their icy breath across the glass. I planted my hand against it, expecting to feel a chill. I hardly felt anything.

"Please don't do that," Atlas Bear told me.

I pulled my hand back. Honest, the fingerprint smudges were *hardly* noticeable.

Atlas Bear let out a long-suffering sigh.

"Don't you have, I don't know, cleaning robots to take care of things like that?" I asked.

"I have Windex," Atlas Bear said.

"Oh."

After another moment, *I* sighed. "Tell me where it is. I'll take care of it."

"You're my guest. It wouldn't be right of me to let you do housecleaning."

A groan escaped my throat. I massaged my forehead. "Just let me do something right."

To my surprise, Atlas Bear looked over at me with a little smile on the corner of her lips.

"I get it," I said. "You're teasing me."

"You seemed like you needed it."

"Yeah. Maybe." I folded my arms behind my head, leaned back in the co-pilot's seat. "I can tell you one thing I *don't* need right now is to be knocked down another peg."

Atlas Bear returned her attention to her controls. She didn't ever relax her vigilance for long. I felt a little privileged that I'd seen even a bit of that. "Yes, well. We all have to stay on our toes," she told me.

It's a measure of my comfort with people in this profession if I think of them by their given names rather than their handles. Atlas Bear's real name is Shoon'kwa. She joined the posse a while back, before Black Widow and White Fox. I've known Atlas Bear long enough that, honestly, I should've started to think of her as Shoon'kwa by now. I know Neena and Rachel both do.

Maybe I resented new people coming onto the team. I missed the old days, when it was just Neena, Rachel and myself. Atlas Bear joining us had presaged the others, and all the changes they'd bring.

But it wasn't fair of me to hold that against Shoon'kwa.

"I appreciate the ride," I told her.

"No airports where you're going," she said. "I don't think anything but the X-Men's 'copters and jets go near the Institute."

"Could we not call it the 'Institute?' It's hard enough taking myself to see doctors without making it sound all ominous."

"*The Institute*," she intoned, like she was shining a flashlight under her chin.

"Aren't you playful today."

"All my life, I've had to be a quick learner," she said. "I learn from the people around me."

"Easy to forget sometimes that you're a teenager."

"I didn't used to have time to make jokes with people."

"You also didn't have many people to make them *with*," I pointed out.

"Did you hear what I said to Tony Stark?" she asked.

I nodded.

"So many bad futures stem from him," she said. "Not just associated with him, mind you. Directly *caused* by him." She took her eyes off the controls again to look toward me. She wasn't smiling this time. "With that many of them – I would have been paralyzed by rage. By fear. I wouldn't have been able to control it. I would have tried to kill him. Part of me is still convinced that would have been the right thing to do."

The first time the team had met Shoon'kwa, she'd hired Neena's posse for hit jobs: to kill people she had perceived as threats to the world's safety. Each time, we'd double-crossed her by saving the person she'd sent us to murder and found another way to defuse the crisis.[7]

Those crises had been real. Shoon'kwa's precognition never lied to her about that. But it also never showed her any solutions. Just an endless cavalcade of world-ending disasters. Tough place for a kid to be. Tough place for anyone to be, really, but she was a teenager. Scared the common sense right out of her. In her terror, the only thing she could think to do was end each threat violently. Take whoever was responsible down and make sure they'd never get up again. That kind of thinking had gotten her exiled from Wakanda.

---

7 From a story starting in *Domino* #7. –Ed.

"Glad you didn't try it," I said. Mr Stark had been wearing his Iron Man suit at the time. I appreciated not being vaporized.

"It takes discipline," she said. "Fear is a monster. And it makes us monsters."

"Or just makes us useless." I chewed the inside of my lip.

She glanced to her controls, just to check them, but otherwise kept her attention on me. "It's a lot harder to manage yourself when you're operating alone," she said.

"Believe me," I said. "I know."

If Black Widow hadn't gone after me as hard as she had, I'd probably still be trying to deal with everything alone.

And if Shoon'kwa and I hadn't talked, I'd be feeling a lot more miserable than I did now.

I still didn't feel great about where we were going, though. *The Institute.* Shoon'kwa had gotten the tone right.

In a way, I hated going to the X-Men more than a non-mutant doctor. The last time I'd come to the X-Men, it was as a refugee.

It's a long story, and I'll try to keep it short.

The biggest hassle about being a mutant is that somewhere, someone is always hunting for your blood. It's never not true. All kinds of human-firsters, super villains, super jerks, and just plain people with super chips on their super shoulders will come gunning for you. Even if you keep your guard up, even if you keep your identity as a mutant secret, and even if you think you know who your enemies are – you can always be blindsided.

And that's how it was for the majority of mutantkind, not all that long ago. Two alternate realities came crashing together, changing both of them, each of them yoked to a madwoman.

People called it M-Day. I didn't see it all go down. I had only left home a few years before, and was just getting my start in the mercing business. The only thing I knew for sure was that, afterward, there were a lot fewer mutants in the world than there used to be. The people were still *around*, still alive, but they'd been robbed of their identities. They'd been changed, against their will, to just being humans.

A *lot* fewer. Down from millions to hundreds. One hundred and ninety-eight, to be exact.

There was no other way to say it than a genocide.

By some combination of luck and circumstance, I was one of those one hundred and ninety-eight mutants to remain who I was.

A lot of people who hated mutants, sensing the weakness of those of us who remained (and fearing we'd find some way to revitalize ourselves), closed in for the kill.

I'd been working alone at the time. After three assassination attempts, I realized I had to run. And it seemed like there was only one place to run to. Xavier's School for Gifted Youngsters.

The X-Mansion advertised itself as a safe haven for all the remaining mutants. Refugees welcome. There was still protection in numbers. Most of the X-Men had retained their powers, and they were some of the canniest, most powerful mutants in the world.

So they said. So I'd hoped. They could put us behind walls, but they couldn't keep us safe.

The X-Men had allied with government forces that, in the end, turned out just as eager to put us down as anyone outside the walls. Killers and assassins found us inside and outside the walls. The guards turned out to be there to pen us in as much as "protect" us. Hell, the government wanted to put *chips* in our bodies to track us if we ever left.

It got so bad that the rest of us had to stage a breakout, just to get away from the people who'd pledged to protect us.

The X-Men eventually came to their senses and rebelled against the snakes they'd let inside their walls. It took them a mighty long time to come around to what had happened. A lot of it wasn't their fault. But a good part of it was.

I never wanted to go back to them. Neena trusted them more than me. She was friends with lots of them. She had a long history, deep-knit ties, et cetera, et cetera. She rarely gave me specifics. As part of the X-Force, she did a lot of things she can't talk about, and even more I was sure she didn't want to.

The last time I'd gone to them for help, though, I'd ended up having to break my way out. It's hard to forgive that sense of betrayal. It didn't matter that there were extenuating circumstances. They should have done better. Not just by me, but by everyone else who'd trusted them.

I had nothing against the individual members of these organizations. Met plenty of them, before and after. Some good people, some not-so-good, just like everywhere else in the world. I didn't have problems with any X-Man, but with *The X-Men,* so to speak. I didn't believe that they could do what they'd promised: keep mutantkind safe. They just didn't have it in them.

They were too willing to trust. Too willing to give second chances, and to stake the lives of others on those chances.

I wouldn't have said this to Neena because she might have taken it personally, what with her being friends with lots of them. But, the truth was, I didn't have much trust in my heart for their type. Not anymore.

At my request, Atlas Bear hadn't flown me to the place I'd been before. The Jean Grey School – formerly the X-Mansion – would've been a shorter trip, but it was tangled in all my bad memories. I wouldn't have been able to look at it without seeing remnants of the refugee camp's walls, or the empty yard where all our tents and housing had been set up.

But the X-Men had split up – or were branching out, or schisming, or whatever. I didn't stay up to date with the politics. There was more than one school for me to go to.

So we were headed somewhere I'd never been before. The New Charles Xavier School for mutants, all the way up north in Canada – not as many people I had a bad history with there.

The clouds had gotten thinner, icier, since we'd left Boston. There was no snow on the ground, not this early in autumn, but I didn't need to be able to read Shoon'kwa's holograms to know I'd get goosebumps stepping outside. We descended, spiraling toward a cluster of silver buildings. Solar panels glinted sunlight among the hills.

"You sure you're going to be fine outside in *that?*" Shoon'kwa asked, with a glance at my clothes.

My outfit was not exactly subtle, nor suitable for cooler weather. I didn't even like to button my vest, let alone wear something heavier than jeans. "I don't get cold," I lied. "It's a mutant thing."

Shoon'kwa looked appropriately skeptical, but she didn't say anything else.

Look, everyone in this business has their style. So did I. I can rattle the names of twenty people who wear more impractical costumes off the top of my head.

"If you need me to go anywhere else," Shoon'kwa said, "I'll be here."

I looked at her a moment. "Thank you," I said, and meant it.

The airship's boarding ramp struck dirt. Thanks to the all-encompassing bubble windshield, my eyes were already adjusted to the light outside. Two people were waiting for me. The first was a young man who looked like, if I reached behind his ears and rubbed, he'd squeak. He wore, incongruously for where I'd found him, a full suit and tie. His red goggles were a little more on-brand for an X-Man, though. He had them on his forehead, where they kept his locs at bay. And a woman not much older was with him. Dyed black and silver-white hair, same colors but a shorter style than Neena's.

Neena had called ahead. Let people here know I was coming. One less thing for me to do, or to find an excuse to wriggle out of.

"You're Outlaw?" The young man looked at his clipboard the way I'd seen doctors do before, as an excuse to keep from making eye contact with me. Great.

"Not many other people likely to be dressed like that, don't you think?" the woman beside him said, and then to me: "I'm Tempus."

"Triage," her partner added.

I raised my eyebrow. "Triage? Isn't that a little on the nose?"

"Hey, look in a mirror," he said, surprising me. Maybe the kid had guts after all.

At least I knew for sure what the kid wanted to do with his

life, to give himself a callsign like that. I decided to tease him a little more. That was better than thinking about why I was here. "Are you both doctors?"

"I'm the doctor," Triage said.

His partner didn't speak. I gave her a pointed look.

"I'm his friend," Tempus said. "I'm tagging along. Learning medical skills. Every X-Man needs to be a polymath."

"I don't *need* any tagalongs." The fewer people involved in this, the more comfortable I would be.

"She's helping," Triage said, firmly.

Hearing his tone, I let it rest. These two were friends. I understood that. I'd been in similar enough positions when Neena or Rachel had brought me along on their jobs, or vice versa. I didn't want to put effort into separating them.

But then Tempus had to open her big mouth again. "Besides, trainees should always work in teams." Triage winced and massaged his forehead.

Trainees? I looked around. No one else had come out on the landing strip.

"They're handing me over to a student doctor?" I asked.

"Hank McCoy's busy saving the world," he said, with a glare at Tempus. "And we're just doing an intake evaluation."

"You don't even have anybody with you to hold your hand."

"I've got more experience than you might think," Triage said. He reached toward my hand, and then stopped. "May I?" he asked, as if he was still working on how to deal with patients.

"When I talked about holding hands, that wasn't an invitation."

The speed at which his cheeks reddened confirmed just about everything I was thinking about him. He had no idea how to deal with someone like me. At least if I was here, I was going to have a little fun.

"I- I have a healing ability," he stammered. "This is how it works."

"Out here? In the cold?" The air was crystal clear and sunny this morning, but that didn't do anything to stifle the bite of the cold.

"It'll only take a moment," he said. "Unless you're uncomfortable…"

Fast learner. He'd figured out how to press my buttons in record time. The last thing I wanted to do was show weakness to a stranger, let alone someone who was going to doctor me. He and Tempus were probably acclimated to this cold. "Try it," I said.

His touch was warmer than it should have been. Like there was energy passing between us. For a long, awkward moment, we were breathing in synch. In and out, at the same time. I wouldn't have been surprised if our heartbeats were in rhythm.

He let go. "I can't feel anything obviously, um, not functioning. You're exhausted. I can tell that. I can clear out some of the fatigue toxins, if you'd like."

Great. They'd sent the trainees out because they figured this would be *easy*. Or psychosomatic. All in my head. Just another strung-out mutant, pushed past her limits. "Is that your final diagnosis?"

"No," he stammered. "Let's get you inside so I can get a better look at you."

I wish I knew how much he and Tempus believed me. But the last thing I was ever going to do was ask. They wouldn't have told me the truth, anyway.

SIX

What was left of my sense of humor shriveled up the moment I saw what he wanted to do with me. "Oh, *no* you aren't," I said.

He and Tempus stood in front of a heavy, room-sized beige machine with a hatch on one end that reminded me of a submarine's torpedo tube. I'd seen devices like this before, though I'd never had to get in one. It was a full-body scanner.

"Claustrophobic?" Tempus asked.

"It's not an irrational fear if it's *entirely justified*," I told her. "Not letting anybody trap me."

Triage was trying to hide his impatience. "The hatch won't be shut while you're in," he said. "You can come out at any time. Not that you *should*, but you could."

"Aren't you, you know, gonna put a stethoscope on my back and listen to me breathe, or something?"

"We already went over your symptoms," Triage said. "It took us *ten minutes* to learn *three things* about them. I'm not letting you drag this out any longer."

"I'm just helping you develop your bedside manner. Working with difficult patients." Putting off the inevitable.

"I've had plenty of difficult patients," Triage muttered. He ran his hand across the side of the machine lovingly, like it was a pet. He had his natural healing ability but was receiving plenty of conventional medical training, too. "This is important. I helped develop it. It's a multifunction vascular, muscular, and neurological scanner specifically tailored for the most common physiologies exhibited by mutants."

"I'm learning it, too!" Tempus piped in.

"Wow," I drawled. "You must be real proud."

"The more mutants we can get in the scanner, the more we can learn about all the different ways the X-gene can express itself," Triage said. "We can learn more about, and maybe develop cures for, all kinds of disorders that affect mutants but not humans."

"Mutants *love* to be scanned and prodded and studied." I folded my arms and felt a lot smaller than I should have.

"Do you need some time?" Tempus asked. All the playfulness had left her voice, but then she said, "I can give you time. That's my mutant ability, you know. Freezing time."

If there was one thing I wanted to do less than get examined, it was be frozen and helpless while they did it. Even if I wouldn't be aware of the time passing. "Let's just get it over with," I said.

They had me lie on a foam-cushioned tray, with a little rise on one end to suggest, but be nowhere near as comfortable as, a pillow. It was reminiscent of comfort without actually *being* comfortable. I sighed, laid down, and let them slide me into the machine, head first.

The scanning chamber was at least brightly lit. Strips of light ran along the top and bottom corners, while tinted black glass hid most of the scanning equipment from me.

I've never been in a CT scanner or anything like it, but I imagined they were a lot more claustrophobic than what I had to get through now. This chamber was huge. It would have had to be, if it was going to cater to mutants. This machine could fit anybody up to the size of Colossus. Even then, it wouldn't work for every mutant.

They still made me take my hat off to get inside. I had to repress my urge to debate this, get argumentative. That wasn't going to make me feel any better. I reclined my head onto the cushion and tried not to think. I couldn't keep that up for very long, though.

"Is my insurance gonna cover this?"

"You have insurance?" Triage asked.

Of course I didn't. Not many mutants did. Not many companies would take us. Even if you lied and said you weren't, you were just begging one of them to find out and disqualify you when you needed it.

"We're in Canada," Tempus said. "Things are a little more enlightened here."

That prompted another eyebrow rise. I knew plenty of mutants who came from Canada, and I hadn't had to pry much to find out how Canada had treated them.

"About most things," Tempus added. I wondered if she wasn't watching me on camera, hadn't seen my expression.

"Mm-hmm."

"The scan won't work if you're talking all the time," Triage said. "Just lie back and keep quiet."

"Lie back and think of mutantkind," I said.

Tempus made a *ppffft* sound. Triage sighed, but wouldn't let me tweak him. Too bad. I was looking for something –

anything – else to think about other than the machines whirring to life around me.

As Triage had promised, the hatch remained open. I could look toward my feet and see him out there, fiddling with the equipment.

Silence from outside for a while. Then Triage and Tempus muttering together, at the corner of the room. That made me nervous. Next time I tried getting a rise out of them, they ignored me.

I hate feeling like I'm trapped. The weird thing was, I never was claustrophobic as a kid. I didn't mind crawling in and out of the rocky pits and crevices around my father's ranch. Now there may have been a *teensy* bit of post-traumatic stress response. A lot of that stemmed from the time I came to the X-Mansion as a refugee.

The claustrophobia hadn't just come from the high walls and the guards. It was everything that happened afterward. After we busted out, we had to go on the run. (Neena was with us; in fact, she'd led the escape. But this was before we'd formally teamed up.) All told, about a hundred or so mutants had busted out of the walls the government had put up around the X-Mansion. Escaping landed us in a whole heap of other trouble. She'd found us a place in the Nevada desert to hide: an old weapons bunker, locked away under virtually unbreakable heavy doors. Since we thought we could control the doors, it seemed like the perfect place to hole up.

While Neena is the luckiest person I know, she can't actually control her luck... and her luck doesn't look out for anyone but her. And, as it happened, she'd led us into a trap.

I've met a lot of mutant-hating humans in my time. There's

little more soul-scarring, though, than a mutant-hating mutant. One of the refugees that had come along with us, a New York kid named Johnny Dee, hated who he was.

To the very, *very* little extent I'm willing to be fair to him, his abilities weren't the easiest to live with. His X-gene had "expressed itself," as Triage would say, in the form of another living organism growing out of his chest like a conjoined twin. It was an ugly, pitiful little thing. A big toothy maw with grasping tentacles but no functioning brain – at least not that anybody had managed to figure out. It had a talent nearly as repulsive as it was: feed a piece of a person's DNA in that maw, and, in a little bit, it would spit out an egg that contained a palm-sized doll of that person. A cute little puppet.

Johnny Dee could take that puppet and use it to seize control of that person. Even hurt them, from a distance. The puppet *was* the person, in a real significant sense. Break the puppet, and the real person's bones would snap, too.

He hated the mutant part of himself. He thought he could scoop it out, like all that made him different could be changed with surgery. He'd fallen under the thrall of human supremacists. And willingly let himself be used by them.

Johnny Dee had manipulated things to send us to that bunker. He'd sealed us in. There were still bombs stored in that bunker, and he'd set them to detonate. He'd used his puppeteering power to turn us against each other.

One of the people Johnny Dee took control of was me. I'd pointed a gun at the head of my future-best-friend, Neena, and had to get the stuffing kicked out of me just to get him out of my body. I'd been aware of it as it happened. My body being snapped out of my control was the worst thing I'd ever felt.

It gave me a whole bunch of issues I would've liked to resolve with some cathartic violence, but I never had the chance. Johnny Dee was taken down a thousand miles away from me, in Washington DC, by the same bureaucrats who tried to pen us into the X-Mansion. They put him in prison. Outside of a couple glimpses of Johnny Dee when we were both at that refugee camp, I never saw him.[8]

Ever since, whenever I was stuck in tight spaces, I couldn't stop thinking about those bunker walls, about the doomsday weapons ticking away behind them. It made me feel like I was losing control of myself.

Heck, just coming anywhere associated with the X-Men had me thinking too much about it.

Unresolved issues are a mandatory part of this business. You deal with them as you can.

It seemed like a small eternity before Triage said, "Time to come out."

As soon as I could be, I was on my feet, donning my hat. I was glad there were no mirrors in the room, but I didn't need one to know that I was pale and sweaty.

The last thing I wanted to see coming out, though, was Triage looking just as pale as I felt. He and Tempus were hunched over a laptop. They didn't look at me.

The room felt three times as large as it had been as I walked over to them.

I needed a moment to make sure my voice would be even. "Hit me with it," I said.

"We're not seeing anything wrong with your muscles,"

---

8 Outlaw never quite got over the events of the *X-Men: Civil War* miniseries, outlined here. –Ed.

Tempus said, which relieved me more than I wanted to show. "It's always hard to tell what's normal with mutants, but there doesn't seem to be any kind of degeneration. It just looks like you've been using them hard."

"OK," I said. "So that's the good news. What are you hiding?"

"That I'm going to need to get back into my neurology texts," Triage said.

"Sweet Celestials," I said, taking off my hat. I needed to hide my face. Couldn't let them see me biting my lip.

This was how my dad had died. Early-onset Alzheimer's, complicated by congestive heart failure that meant less and less oxygen was reaching his brain. When he was still capable of understanding what was happening, he used to tell me that he could keep the neurology department of a university busy for years.

Watching him go had been the worst thing in my life. Just being here was sending me lurching from one bad memory to another.

Triage's mouth dropped open, as if he had only just realized how I had interpreted what he said. "I don't necessarily mean that there's a problem… just something unusual–"

"Textbooks aren't going to tell you anything, anyway," Tempus said. "This is mutant territory. Or at least metahuman stuff."

"Do you have any telepathic ability?" Triage asked.

"*What*?" I asked.

"It's all right if you do," Triage said. "You can tell us and it won't leave the room. Doctor-patient confidentiality. We understand that plenty of mutants want to, or need to, keep their abilities concealed."

It took me a moment to process what he was saying. "I've never had any 'telepathic abilities,'" I said slowly, as if I was speaking to an idiot. "Nor would I want any."

Tempus beckoned me over to their side of the laptop. "Take a look at what we're seeing."

I put my hat back on, and did as she asked. Not that it helped. All I saw on their screen was a false-color image of a brain. Mine, presumably. Different sections glowed in pixelated neon.

It all just looked like meat to me. Triage pointed to different neon sections as though it should mean something. "Most human brains only have a few states that they cycle between. For sleep, for activity, for meditation, et cetera. This pattern doesn't match any of those. There's a lot of additional activity around the sensory cortex and parietal lobes. Those are the places where you perceive and make sense of the world. All correlated with telepathy. If your brain is working like this a lot, it's no wonder you haven't had good sleep. I'm betting that, if we did a few more tests, we'd find neurotransmitter levels off the charts, and a whole bunch of other things that would keep you from sleeping, too."

They looked at me like they were expecting me to do the whole *English, please, doctor* bit. "You're talking about big chunks of the human brain," I said. "'Parietal lobe' covers a hell of a lot. What, specifically, was looking weird?"

Triage blinked. But he covered his surprise gracefully. "That's just the thing. It's not localized anywhere. It's just… all over, in that region. Increased blood flow, increased electrochemical activity. There are no abnormalities in its structure, just in its activity. How you're using it, so to speak."

"It could be that you're developing new abilities," Triage said. "You wouldn't be the first mutant to do that late in life."

"It's not late in my life," I muttered.

"Or this could indicate an ability you've had all along and never had the mental vocabulary, so to speak, to realize that you've had it. It would be like seeing a color that nobody else does. If you grew up seeing it, and nobody else talked about it or gave you a reason to, you'd get used to it pretty quickly. It would become background noise."

"Pretty sure it's hard to mistake reading somebody's mind for seeing a color," I said.

"It's just an example," he told me. "And telepathy doesn't always mean reading somebody's mind."

"It can be subtle," Tempus said. "Magik says it can be like plucking an emotion out of the air. Or getting an image, a smell or a taste, from somebody's memory without meaning to."

"I don't care what it is," I said. "It's ruining my life and I want it to stop. Can't you just make it go away?"

"If this is a mutant ability you're developing, I'd have real ethical problems with removing–"

"*I don't*," I interrupted. "It's not an 'ability' if it's keeping me from doing my job."

Triage looked like he was about to argue some more, but Tempus set a hand on his shoulder. "I'm starting to think it's time we called our instructors in on this," she said. "Even more, I'm thinking this isn't a good question for medical science."

He pondered that and, after a moment, nodded. I looked back and forth between them.

"What the hell does that mean?" I asked.

From science to sorcery, all in the space of a few hours. This life will give you whiplash in more ways than one. The doctors were sending me to see an honest-to-God wizard.

I'd never met Magik before. Heard a lot about her, though. I was a little surprised to find her in charge of a place like the New Charles Xavier Institute. She seemed like she'd have too much going on in her own life to become a teacher. But some of Neena's other friends had teaching gigs, too, and *they* seemed like they were doing a good job of balancing their professional lives with their protecting-all-mutantkind lives.

Magik's office looked deceptively normal. Fluorescent lights, filing cabinets, bookshelves. Professionally beige. It was in the details that things started to get weird. There were thin, charred circles burnt into the carpet. They were all about the same size, but in different places. Most were concentrated around the desk. One of the walls had a smeared chalk outline of something that looked like a summoning circle. On the wall behind me, several swords were mounted in brackets. A dark stain had worn into the edge of her desk. It could've been ketchup, or soy sauce, or blood. As if to prove that she wasn't entirely otherworldly, a hamster cage sat on one of the far bookshelves.

Magik herself sat behind the desk, chattering on a smartphone. Honestly, I didn't know why my outfit got so much attention when people like her were also walking around. Her midriff must not have gotten all that cold, is all I'm saying. She had hair longer than my own, and blue-gray eyes that gave me goosebumps to meet. It was easier to keep studying the bookshelves than meet her gaze.

The books on the shelves weren't anything like what I'd expected to find in a school. She had books about medieval and Renaissance swordfighting techniques. Books labeled *Lost Arcana of the Queens of the Mongol Khanate. Artifacts of the Atlantean-Lemurian Wars. Nine Known Times the World Ended (And How It Got Better). The Anatomy and Alchemical Uses of the Common Hamster.* And a whole bunch of others with blank spines, or whose spines were marked in lost languages or in glyphs.

I eyed the hamster cage on the cabinet uneasily. It was empty.

"So," Magik said, pocketing her smartphone with a dramatic flourish and steepling her fingers on her desk. "You're troubled by telepathy and want to get rid of it."

"How'd you know that?" I asked. I'd had my eye on Triage and Tempus throughout our walk here. They hadn't spoken with anybody.

Magik smiled.

Damn magicians. Everything's got to be a stage show, even when the magic is real. I folded my arms.

"I don't mean to be off-putting–" she started.

"Yes, you do," I interrupted.

"Don't make her mad," Triage whispered. He sounded even more uneasy than before, and I'd made him pretty darn uneasy.

"I'll take a look," Magik said. "Stand very still."

I did exactly the opposite. I backed up against the door,

with Tempus and Triage on either side of me. "I'm not having anybody read my mind," I told her.

"It's difficult for me to gauge your telepathic problems if I don't," she said.

"I don't care. Find another way."

"All right, then." I didn't like the way she smiled when she said that. Tempus and Triage, I noticed, were shifting away from me.

Magik stood up from behind her desk and walked over to me. She reached out, set her hand lightly on my shoulder, and walked a circle around me. I held my ground.

"You're going to want to hold very still, though," she said.

All at once, we were someplace else.

A sudden sharp, red-yellow light drove daggers into my eyes. It was more the heat than the light, though, that made me squeeze my eyes shut. Great big waves of heat washed over us, so hot that they made me shiver, like my nervous system had overloaded. There wasn't much pain, not yet, but it wouldn't be long in coming. The smell registered first. Sulfurous, choking smoke and ash combined with stink and sweat like we'd been clenched inside Satan's armpit.

My ears popped. In the second before I'd shut my eyes, I'd caught a glimpse of terrible black mountains, pressed tight against a sky shaded somewhere between blood and charcoal. It was hard to tell which parts of the ground were magma and which were rocks so hot that they glowed. Somewhere, high atop one of the sizzling escarpments, I thought I saw eyes.

I flinched, but Magik's touch on my shoulder had become a grip, keeping me from stumbling away. Good thing, too. Even with my eyes closed, I heard hissing behind me, like bacon on a fryer.

"My powers on Earth are limited," Magik explained. "If I was going to use more subtle, complex magic – to keep from 'reading your mind' – I needed to take you to a plane where I'm a little more comfortable."

"Yeah, I get it. You're a showoff."

"I really am."

Her other hand found my right temple and pressed lightly against it. Her touch tingled. I braced myself for... I don't know what, really. My mind being invaded. But all I felt was the uncomfortable kind of shiver I got when anyone held their hand to my skin for that long.

The heat around us was so intense it was difficult to interpret *as* heat. I thought of the first time I'd gotten into a hot tub as a kid, and the way my body had been so unprepared for something so hot that I'd started to get chills.

"*Oh,*" Magik said, as if annoyed. And then surprised: "Oh, my..."

"Care to enlighten me?" I asked, trying to keep my voice level.

"You've definitely been telepathically active," she said. "Or *activated*. A region of your brain is being used in ways that it never has been before. I think Triage was onto something. You may be developing a new ability."

"I don't want a new ability. I just want to be able to do my job. Make it stop."

"Maybe you didn't hear me when I said, 'it's a region of your brain.' It's not something you can turn off in any way short of a lobotomy. You may need to learn how to live with this."

"I don't need a talking to or platitudes," I said. "I need my life back."

Magik was silent for a moment. I wondered if what I said had gotten through, or if she'd become distracted by something else. I didn't want to open my eyes. Half of me wanted to shove away from her. The other half wanted to cling tight, in case she got it into her mind to strand me in Hell.

The tingling spread deeper into my temple. It started to hurt like needles. I hated that. Especially because, as the other two might have thought me too simple to know, I knew the human brain didn't *have* pain receptors.

And then it was over. In a *whoosh* of hot air mushrooming up from us, Magik and I were back in her office. My ears popped again. Triage and Tempus were coughing up all the ash-tainted air we'd brought with us.

"You want to give us a warning the next time you go dimension-hopping?" Tempus asked.

"No," Magik said, returning to her desk.

I brushed soot off my arm. And then I noticed it. There was a feeling of lightness in my head, right around where it had hurt. I felt – I don't know how else to put this – I felt unburdened. Like an ox finally unhitched from a plow. Lighter in a way that I couldn't explain, but in a way that was nonetheless a very material sensation.

"I put up a psionic barrier," Magik said, "around your active telepathic centers. You were reaching out. Trying to draw a connection with someplace else. It's no wonder you're tired all the time. A telepathic experience that active… would be like trying to fall asleep while you're pedaling on an exercise bike. Telepathy might not *look* very draining, not physically, but it takes a lot of energy."

I let a breath out. "So long as that's over–"

"The barrier isn't permanent," Magik said.

"You could've at least given me a minute before deflating my balloon," I said.

"I can't make a permanent psionic barrier that won't harm you in the long-term. But I can block the impulses for a little while. What you have right now should last… oh, I don't know, three to four days. I can't be precise when I'm dealing with a wild talent like yours."

"Does that mean I have to come back to you to have it renewed? That often?"

"Oh, I wouldn't renew it," she said. "If I do it too often, that might also harm your brain. Or stunt your development."

"You know, you could use some lessons in delivering bad news to patients."

She smiled. A smile that wasn't really a smile. "I'm not a doctor."

One other thing that made this office different than most others: the only chair was the one behind the desk, and it was already occupied. I had a mighty need to sit down. It was going to take me a long time to adjust to what I'd learned today. But I wasn't going to slouch on the floor. "So, you really do think I have telepathic talent."

"The telepathic segments of your brain are very active," Magik said. "What's more, they're trying to pull you in a specific direction."

I blinked. Triage and Tempus looked confused, too. I looked back to her. Magik said, "You have a strong psychic bond with a particular place, far from here. The telepathic parts of you are reaching out to it. That's why you are expending so much energy."

"So once this barrier of yours wears off... it's just going to keep happening."

"I suggested earlier that you might need to learn how to live with this," Magik said. "It looks like you might also have some unresolved issues that your new abilities are trying to address."

"Can you tell me where?" I asked, my throat dry.

Magik leaned back in her chair. She pressed her knuckles to her lips and studied me for too long a moment. I think she knew that I already had the answer. But she had the grace not to call me out this time.

"Tell me," she said, "what your dreams have been looking like."

SEVEN

Triage followed me all the way back out to Shoon'kwa's airship. It loomed over the Institute's landing strip, shadowed against the gray evening sky and looking like a particularly ornery beetle. Its stick-thin landing struts looked ridiculous underneath it.

"Are you sure you don't want me to go with you?" Triage asked, as I stepped up the boarding ramp. "We don't know what kind of side-effects a psionic block will have on you if you've never experienced one before. You shouldn't go without a doctor."

"Don't y'all have better things to do than follow me around?" I asked.

"This is the kind of work I live for," he said. "Honest. I want to help people."

The more I looked at him, the cuter he seemed. I hated to leave him like a lost puppy on the landing strip. But I really, *really* didn't want anyone coming along with me for this.

"Maybe next time," I said. "But I'll give you my number."[9]

---

9 For the adventures of Triage and Tempus, check out the Xavier's Institute prose novels starting with *Liberty & Justice for All* by Carrie Harris! –Ed.

I didn't look back as the boarding ramp closed behind me. I wanted to think of him as I'd left him. Bright red in the cheeks.

I had a mission. It was the last thing in the world I wanted to do, but once I made up my mind to do something unpleasant, I wanted to get it over fast. Ripping off that bandage was always going to be better than peeling it, or, worse, letting it fester.

"Drop me off in El Paso," I told Shoon'kwa. "I can get where I'm going from there."

She gave me a wary look. "You don't want me to take you directly?" I knew what she was thinking. Neena must have given her a talking to about letting me go off on my own.

"I appreciate it," I said. "And all the time you've taken for me so far. But I'm headed to the Texas boonies. A big airship like this is likely to draw more attention than either of us wants."

She pursed her lips, but didn't say anything as she ran through her preflight checklist. She was clearly weighing whether she trusted me more than Neena's spoken (or unspoken) instructions.

"I can handle this," I said, a lot more bravely than I felt. "I'll keep my phone on me. Let you know how I'm doing."

Shoon'kwa watched me for a moment. Then nodded. The airship's engines roared.

I didn't mean to fall asleep on the trip back. My head was buzzing with whatever Magik had done to me, and I felt like I had the energy to wrestle the world, but as soon as I saw that bunk in the back, time vanished.

When I woke up, I felt something I hadn't in weeks. I felt *refreshed*. Like I'd actually gotten a good night's sleep. The first in ages. When I was still on speaking terms with my relatives, and my older cousins with families told me how many times a baby could wake them up in the middle of the night, I imagined this was how they felt the first night they could get away with eight hours' sleep.

By the time I came out, night had scaled the sky. The cabin lights were out. Shoon'kwa sat where I'd left her, at her controls and still at full attention. Her seat hung just over the edge of the bubble windshield, so she looked like she was suspended over the dark, with only her reflection and the reflection of her instruments for company. The softly glowing displays gave her a deep orange tint. It was all very dramatic – an effect ruined by the bag of potato chips she was crunching her way through. An open energy drink can lay discarded in a deck-mounted recycling bin.

"Tell me you usually eat better than that," I said.

"I don't have time to cook," she answered.

Teenagers. "You're gonna regret all that when you're older."

She smiled thinly. "If I live to be old enough to regret that, I will consider it a win."

Knots of cloud whorled below us. Most were lit only in shades of reflected moonlight, but a few were painted in the orange of city lights. I had to step up to the edge of the bubble windshield, and look down, to see the street and building lights woven across the ground. From the fact that we were slowing, I guessed this was El Paso.

"Learning how to cook is one of the best things I ever did," I said. Dad helped teach me. To the extent I was ever reluctant to cook, it was because I knew I wouldn't measure up.

I was kind of glad I couldn't see more than the lights. I had mixed feelings about seeing any landscape that reminded me of home. I'd planned to use the travel time to mentally prepare for that, but had fallen asleep instead.

We'd left the Institute too fast to file a proper flight plan this time. I saw, from one of the few displays on Shoon'kwa's controls I'd learned to read, that the airship's radar-cloaking was on. Local air traffic control wouldn't be giving us any problems.

"You're welcome to come with, if you'd like," I said. I hoped I managed to keep my tone warm, and to hide how much I really, really wanted to do this alone.

"Domino called while you were passed out," she said. "We have a rush job. Our employer wants a bomber drone prototype stolen from an Air Force contractor. Gifted Mind Technologies in New Jersey. Employer says the contractor is using taxpayer money to build and design the thing, but is planning on selling it to Hydra. They want it destroyed tomorrow."

"I think my business is going to take a little longer than that."

"I figured," Shoon'kwa said. "So did Domino."

I had nothing to say to that. It hurt, though, to know Neena didn't want me along for this one.

"I don't like leaving my airship uncrewed in American territory," Shoon'kwa said. "Your government might steal it."

"It's all right. I understand." She wasn't going to step outside. "You're gonna want to get some rest before you head out, too." I folded my arms, took a deep breath of the cool, recirculated air. At least I was going to see Wheezer again. "Put me down at Eastwood Park. I can get where I'm headed from there."

When I was a kid, going into the city was billed as a major treat for Elias and me. Elias always enjoyed it. I never did. Going to the city was a pain in the ass. The trips usually came on the weekend and cut into my time playing outside. It meant hours in the car with nothing to do. It meant standing around while Dad did his shopping or haggling or whatever other business had brought him to El Paso. Getting to eat out wasn't enough compensation, especially when I preferred Dad's cooking, anyway.

Things got a little better in early high school, when I had my own car and could plan out my trips however I wanted. But that phase in my life didn't last very long.

I had to leave home. Too many people knew who, and what, I was. There was a whole big world out there that needed a righteous kick in the ass, and I was in the mood to give it one.

Elias had loved the city, though. One of the many things he and I never saw eye-to-eye on. He loved the people, and he loved the tall buildings (as tall as El Paso gets, anyway). He loved shoplifting small things, pieces of candy, like it was a game. He made sure I always saw him, just to prove to me that he could. He had bigtime Little Brother syndrome. He could never be stronger or faster than me. And so he had to show off in different ways, mostly by doing things that I wouldn't do – at least, not very often. It was important to him, when he was younger, that I was impressed by him. Later on, he went to the city to get up to capital-letters No Good, but I was gone by then. I'd gotten up to my own brand of No Good, so I shouldn't have judged, but… I still judged.

So I'd been to El Paso enough to know my way around. A lot had changed – always more than I expected – but the streets were the same, most of the major businesses were the same, and my phone was enough to guide me around anything that I couldn't remember. And I knew which rental agencies had the luxury cars.

Coming straight from Boston and Canada, the dry air was a shock. The cold bit at me, too. The predawn was the coldest part of the desert night, and I had to keep moving just to keep some feeling in my arms and legs. It was a nice distraction from my troubles.

I didn't mind the cold. If I did, I wouldn't have dressed the way I did.

I wasn't that far away from the jail where I'd bailed out Elias for the first time. It hadn't been the last.

Sirens and car alarms howled in the distance. Newspaper delivery drivers prowled the night, brake lights glowing. The clouds moved out from overhead. The air was crisp; even with all the city's lights, I could still see more stars than in most other cities.

I could've waited for the buses to start, but I wanted to walk. See what had changed. All the rental car dealerships weren't open until long after bus services began, anyway. I watched the first glimmers of sunlight touch the mountains west of the airport.

Two hours after the sun breached the eastern horizon, I was blazing out of the dealership in a bright red, current-year Ford Mustang. Convertible top down, sunshade down, new pair of sunglasses on. My car and I roared toward the sunrise.

I'm not gonna lie. The car felt good.

One of my rules of life, something that makes it so much better, is that whenever I'm having a terrible day, I'm that much more indulgent. Business with the gals had been good lately. I had the money for it. I *wouldn't* if I kept spending like this and they didn't take me back, but that wasn't worth thinking about right then. There was just the road, the gas pedal, and the speedometer. And, soon enough, the open desert.

The gas pedal got real well acquainted with the floor.

Don't get me wrong; I don't stay away from Texas because I hate it. There's a lot to love, and a lot in me that's Texan that I'll never give up no matter where I go.

But there are some places in Texas where the most dangerous thing to be is different. And there was no more severe kind of difference than being a mutant. When you're a mutant, people don't just hate you. They're afraid of you. And that means they won't just come for you. They'll come for your family, and do anything they think they have to, to get you out of their lives.

Where I grew up, you had to walk up and down hills for miles before you could even see my neighbors, let alone the crossroads, hotels, and gas stations that substituted for a town. Our school was in the next town over, and it was a forty-minute bus ride to get there.

But it was a life my dad loved and therefore, for a while, so did I. I learned about the world from decade-old textbooks, from staticky and unreliable satellite TV and Internet, from the comic books our one convenience store got in every once in a while, and from exploring and doing things for myself. And fighting. I learned lots of things from fighting.

You might think that putting so much distance between you and your neighbors would help you avoid them when they got judgmental about the whole mutant thing. You'd be wrong. What that really meant was fewer people to turn to for help when things went sour. It meant there was no safe place to run to. No good ways out. And no help.

When I was young, I knew that, in other places, mutants had banded together. It seemed like all that was happening on another planet. I had no way to get to them. (Probably a good thing, too; they would have just disappointed me earlier than they had.)

It's a weird thing to be me. I love Texas, love this land. I do more than cling to it. I broadcast it to everyone I meet, from the way I dress to the accent I've trained myself to keep.

But it was no coincidence that, the first time I could, I moved a long way away. I only came back to visit my family – well, Dad, really. And once he died, I didn't even have that.

No matter how long it had been since I'd been here, it would never stop seeming familiar. It was like eating a meal you haven't tasted since you were twelve. Even if you tried to forget, you couldn't. And I never really *wanted* to forget. I just didn't want to come back.

Every season is road construction season in this part of Texas. I got lucky this time, though. No stops. Outside of the usual morning weekday traffic coming into El Paso, the roads were open. I stopped paying attention to the speedometer. I drove by what felt right. Nothing was fast enough. I tucked my hat under my seat because I would have lost it otherwise. The wind played havoc with my hair, made me feel like cold fire was running across my scalp.

I left the freeway as soon as I could. I knew the state and county roads without having to try especially hard to remember.

It also meant it would take me longer to get back home. That was a feature, not a flaw.

People back home had suspected I was a mutant since I was a kid, when I had punched my fist through a tree trunk in front of half a dozen other kids. I wasn't as careful about hiding myself as I otherwise might have been. That wasn't the kind of person I wanted to be.

Dad, to his credit, recognized that early. He never tried to make me conceal who I was.

I can't even remember when we found out I was a mutant. From as young as I could remember, Dad was making sure that I was careful with my strength, both with how I displayed it and how I showed it. He was a smart cookie. His contacts with the outside world were just as limited as mine. Unreliable TV, convenience store newspapers that didn't always reach us, and chats with neighbors. And, every once in a while, when there was something he needed to look up for work or animal care, he went to the library a town over. Somehow, from all of that, he puzzled together that I was a mutant.

Not just a metahuman. Not just someone with special abilities. A mutant, specifically. Maybe he knew the X-gene ran in the family, even though I was the only one, that I knew of, that it had activated for. Dad and my brother both seemed ordinary.

It didn't matter. It didn't change the way he treated me one bit. He loved me just the same. I know mutants whose families rejected them, threw them out, or kept them in but treated them in insidiously awful, abusive ways. Or people like Neena, who never had parents in any sense of the word.

Even when I was young, I knew how lucky I was. And I treasured that. But Dad couldn't protect me forever.

It was the outside world, not anything I did in particular, that made my neighbors take their stand against me. Folk like my rancher neighbors could only hear so many second-hand news reports and propaganda about mutant plots to take over the world, plus the very *real* reports about the folks like the Brotherhood of Evil Mutants and the many ways in which mutants had been involved in near-world-ending cataclysms, before they decided that I was going to bring all these scary news stories to their doorsteps.

When I was seventeen, five cars came to our home one night after midnight. They pulled up with their headlights off. I heard them, though I was supposed to be asleep. Dad went out to meet them, like he was expecting company. They must've called him in advance.

They had no cause to come at night, not unless they were ashamed of what they were about to do. People in the country will sometimes say that the country's safer than the city, and I don't think that that's true even in the day. At night, though, the only reason people come out is for parties or for cold and ugly violence.

I listened from a cracked-open bedroom window. All my muscles were bundled up knots of tension, ready to leap out and fight. I nearly did. But they stayed near enough to the porchlight that I could see they weren't armed. They'd come for violence, all right, but it wasn't the clubbing or shooting kind. They told my dad that the whole town was ready to stop doing business with him. Neighbors. Grocers. Gas stations. Truckers. They were going to cut him off unless "something changed." They didn't have to say what that was.

There wasn't anything I could've done to convince them. I could have been the nicest, most heroic mutant that ever walked the Earth, rather than the teenage powder-keg that I was. I could have saved their sons, daughters, sisters, and brothers from burning buildings twenty different times. It wouldn't have made a difference.

They were scared, they were angry, and, in the face of everything else happening in the world, they felt powerless. They'd made up their minds to lash out.

Dad made me proud. In a voice as calm as if he was asking them what the weather was going to be like, he told them off. I learned plenty of new cuss words that night. Our guests didn't have anything to say to that. They just went back to their cars, glumly, as though their spouses had called them all home.

They'd come back. This was just the first step. The next one would be worse.

Dad didn't say anything about it the next morning. But I could tell he was shaken. He spilled his coffee. He'd left an open bottle of ibuprofen on the counter. Usually, when he got migraines, they didn't come until afternoon.

I waited a couple days before telling Dad I was thinking of moving to Dallas after graduating in spring. The wait had been for plausible deniability, so I could pretend I hadn't heard what I had. I think he knew anyway. He nodded, slowly, and cleared his throat. He took a long time figuring out how to answer. Then he told me that made sense, and that there were a lot more jobs in Dallas than here. That I could take my time working, and scout out different colleges when I was ready.

When I was young, Dad and I kind of assumed I'd stay on at the ranch. It had been a number of years since either of us had brought that up. I think he only left me half the ranch in his will because he didn't have the heart not to.

After I left, I visited home as often as work allowed, and damn the neighbors. Let them complain. But starting as a merc, putting my mutant talents to work for me, had made things a little trickier. You never know which of your enemies are going to hold a grudge, track you back home, and take things out on your family. But life as a mutant was always dangerous, mercenary or not, and the same went for having a mutant in the family.

I never told Dad what kind of work I'd found. He must have known, though, because he didn't ask. He didn't want me to lie to him. The feeling was mutual.

Even if I'd told him, he wouldn't have remembered for more than a few years. His memory was already starting to go, a bit.

It was sweet, slow suffering to watch him lose himself. I've always had a healthy fear of Alzheimer's and dementia after losing a granddad to them (and well before he actually died). If you're not afraid of them, you should be. Dad's life became one of constant disorientation. He became unmoored in time and space. I couldn't be home for it. I hated that I couldn't be, but it would just bring more trouble. And Dad would have hated being taken off the ranch, even more than he already hated not being able to work it.

The only upside, if you can call anything that came from this an upside, is that it helped Elias get his life back together. He took on the responsibility, and took it seriously. He gave up alcohol, gave up the "friends" who kept landing him in jail, and took care of the ranch. He only ever asked me for money once. He got it.

Elias lived with Dad and helped keep things together, even when Dad couldn't remember when he was anymore. Dad would wander from room to room looking for pets that had died twenty years ago. He was sure that his sister – who lived in Georgia at the time – lived in a house just over the next hill, and that he could visit her anytime he wanted, and he didn't understand why Elias stopped him from wandering that way. A lot of the time, he just watched TV. It was the only thing other than Elias that helped him get through the day.

The last time I went home was right after Dad had a stroke. He clung on for a few weeks, long enough for me to spend time with what was left of him.

After he died… well… I didn't think I'd have any reason to ever go back. And I'd promised myself I wouldn't have to.

I didn't want to dwell on grief. I didn't want to think of the life that I could've had if I hadn't been born who I was.

I had work to do. Other peoples' problems to solve.

Only a big part of me had obviously never left. I was connected to this place in ways I didn't understand, and didn't want. But that didn't change the fact of it.

As the day wore on into afternoon, heat piled onto heat. The wind kept it off me throughout the morning, but eventually the sun started shining right down on me, and I couldn't wear my hat to keep it off.

I sighed, steeled myself, and started taking all the right turns for once.

My phone sat on the passenger seat. I could have called Elias and let him know I was coming. When he saw my number, he probably wouldn't have picked up, though. He'd been happy enough to buy my share of Dad's property from me, but, when it came time for me to actually leave, he started dragging his feet on things, like he resented me going.

I never understood why. He knew how much work the ranch could be, even with hired help. I've thought a lot of unkind things about him, but one thing I never thought is that he wasn't up to the work. He's got a natural touch with engines and motors, too. Not only could he manage all the equipment he needed but, by the time I left, he was bringing in some nice side work doing truck repairs for the neighbors. Those that would come around, anyway. I was sure business had only gotten better since I'd left. I only heard from him every Thanksgiving, when he texted to ask if I was coming to our great-aunt's dinner this year.

The answer was always no. Great-Aunt Cindy didn't approve of me, and it had nothing to do with my being a mutant.

Things started getting more and more familiar in shades. I already knew all these roads. Now I was recognizing landscape features. The shape of the mountains crumpling the horizon. The sinuous creases running down their foothills.

About ten miles out from home, I slowed. I wasn't hiding myself. I looked enough like my younger self that anybody who knew me then would recognize me now. But I didn't want to draw attention, either. Last thing I wanted was trouble with the locals. I no longer thought of them as neighbors.

If they wanted a good fist fight, I'd give them one, but they'd probably just make life hell for Elias afterward.

I watched those mountains every day from the bus that

took me to school. I'd sat alone, in the back. The other kids had learned well enough to leave me alone.

I wondered if this was a little bit like how Dad had lived in his last days. His past and present blending together.

That scared me the most. Dementia ran in the family. Dad had it. Granddad had it. Pretty sure some great-grandmothers, too. And nobody, not even the folks at Xavier's Institute, had any idea how that kind of thing interacted with the X-gene. The X-gene could suppress it entirely. Or the disease could onset early instead, and with worse symptoms.

I hadn't been brave enough to tell this to Triage and Tempus. Or to think about it much myself, honestly. But my time alone in the car had left me too much time to do that. I would rather have kept living in denial.

If the disease was onsetting early, I might experience symptoms like Dad had, right before his diagnosis. Flashes of disorientation. Inexplicable lapses of memory. Trouble sleeping, or just unexplainable tiredness.

Different parts of my brain flickering on or off. Or a wild, undeveloped talent like telepathy manifesting as my neurons scrambled.

It belatedly occurred to me that, with the state I was in yesterday, it wouldn't have been safe for me to drive. Last thing I needed was a moment of disorientation on the highway, or lost time right before an intersection, or to look down and not know what the stick did.

That lightness of being after Magik's "treatment" hadn't left me. I felt better than I had in months. But she wasn't going to do it for me again. If I couldn't fix this… I didn't know whether I could trust myself to do anything else. This could have been one of the last times I'd let myself behind the wheel of a car, let alone work as a merc.

I'd lose myself.

Three or four days, Magik had said, and that was yesterday. Then her treatment would wear off. In the back of my head, the countdown was ticking.

By the time I reached the long road that led nowhere but home, I had dropped down to thirty miles per hour. That must've been a first for me. Every time I drove as a teenager, I floored it all the way down the drive. It was the only place I knew there'd be no cops. And a good opportunity to annoy the obnoxious neighbors.

The drive itself was half a mile long. To anyone else, it would've looked like a wasteland. It was full of fragments of my last life, memories twisted sideways. There were the desert willows my dad had planted when I was five. They'd been as tall as me when he got them. They'd kept pace for a while as I grew up. Today, they were far from the tallest trees I've ever seen – but, at the same time, impossibly huge. Like they didn't really belong there. There was the creek bed that, for fourteen out of the eighteen years I'd lived at home, had run every spring, but for the past several years had been dry as salt. Here was the pothole the size of the Hulk's fist, the one Dad had never quite gotten around to patching, and Elias still hadn't. It was even bigger.

The shape of the land was the same, even where the details were not. This area was a bad combination of rocky and hilly that had made it such a cheap buy for my great-grandparents. I didn't see home until I was nearly there. It was an old, reasonably well-maintained single-story ranch house with broad picture windows, a front porch, and a stone chimney Dad had been especially proud of. In spite of everything, the sight of it took my breath away.

Here was a mystery: somehow, in some way, my "telepathic ability" was connected to this place. That was all awfully vague.

I'd spent so long working at getting back here, and trying not to *think* about getting back here, that it suddenly occurred to me that I had no idea what to do next. I hoped my subconscious wasn't sending me out here to go on a journey of self-discovery or other horsecrap. Those things were never worth it.

The thing with being a merc – or, heck, with being a mutant most of the time – was that you were never going to resolve your issues. You might as well get used to it. You could try, but those issues would be back again, year after next. The best you could do was trick yourself into a false epiphany every now and again.

I was so caught up in ruminating that it took me longer than it should have to notice things were wrong.

All the plants on the porch were dead. Dad had meticulously watered the ferns and potted cacti when he was alive. Elias had kept up the habit. He wouldn't have dared disappoint the old man's ghost. Even the Christmas cacti were dead, and those things could go weeks without water. Come to think of it, the desert willows on the drive had looked a little scragglier than usual. My family had never believed in lawns, not out here, but we provided water for the native plants.

In the years since Dad died, Elias had built a standalone two-car garage. Both doors were open, but there was only a single vehicle inside: a 1980s Jaguar XJ-S my brother had been playing with off and on since before I'd left. The front two wheels were off, leaving the rims resting on concrete blocks. I knew for a fact that my brother had more cars than that, but none of them were here.

Then I saw something worse. The fence gate hung limply open. There was no sign of the horses, though, admittedly, there were plenty of hills they could still have been hiding behind. A deep pit opened in my stomach. That enclosure was where Wheezer had been.

I grabbed my hat and hopped out of the convertible, not bothering to open the door. Despite the missing cars, there were all kinds of tire tracks in the dirt. They were right where I'd seen that gang of townsfolk park the night they'd confronted Dad. Some of the tire tracks led around the side of the house and didn't come back. As if they were trying to hide from anyone approaching from the drive.

A crawling sensation on the back of my head turned to a sharp prickle.

Something small *clicked*, very distantly. If it hadn't been for the absolute stillness, I never would have heard it.

I started to move just in time.

The first shot took off my hat. Caught the rim and just blew it straight off me.

If I hadn't already been headed for the ground, I would have fallen anyway, just from the shock of it. My hat flew like a frisbee over the top of the car.

For the first time, I cursed my choice of car. The Mustang was a low rider. There wasn't enough space to take cover underneath. I scrambled on my hands and knees around the trunk. As I rounded the corner, another thunderous gunshot peeled off the hills. Spiderweb fissures split the windshield. Beads of glass sprinkled on my boots.

There's no cure for angst and dread like being shot at. If this hadn't been happening at my childhood home, I might've even felt better than I had this morning.

Whatever I was being shot at with was reasonably high caliber. A rifle, but not a sniper rifle. A military-grade sniper rifle shooting off my hat would've been like a punch to the temple. This had hurt, but mostly just from the shock.

When I was a kid, I scrambled all over this property, pretending to be caught in an invasion of black-hat-wearing bandits and bad guys. I didn't have to look to know where all the hills were, or what height they were, or which ditches were deep enough to hide in.

My hat lay dejected on its side, a hole torn in its fraying rim. I whispered an apology, grabbed it, and tossed it around the back of the car – just high enough to look like someone hunched was dashing out. Another gunshot rang off the horizon. The instant I heard it, I was moving, darting around the Mustang's hood, low as I could go while keeping a decent speed.

I made it behind the nearest hill before I heard the next shot. I didn't know where it landed, but it didn't land on me. I dove behind that hill and landed hard on my belly.

So. Those shots told me a couple things. My assailant should've *known* I wasn't wearing my hat. They either weren't all that bright, or were just plain nervous. They'd shot the first thing they'd seen moving.

I hadn't forgotten all the locals who'd come to intimidate my dad all those years ago. They hadn't been terribly bright then, either.

A flash of red burned across my vision. I hadn't been here in years. They had no reason to cause trouble. Not unless they wanted to chase Elias out, too. Maybe they'd already hurt or killed him.

I carried my Colt revolvers everywhere I could. One holstered on each side. The last time I'd taken them off had been to get in Triage and Tempus's scanner. I hadn't even unstrapped them when I was napping in Shoon'kwa's airship. I drew the righthand gun, and pressed my thumb to the hammer.

If people around here wanted to hate and fear mutants, then I was going to give them good reason.

EIGHT

With one hand holding my gun and the other hand braced on the ground, I stayed low, slipped around the side of the hill, and looked for a better vantage.

Outside the car, and with all my senses hyper-alert, I could more easily see things that were wrong. There were bootprints on the drive. Some of them followed the tire tracks, but others cut across them, heading right out. Several pairs of them overlapped in different places, and some of them were more wind-scuffed than others. Footsteps visibly of different ages went right by each other. Like whoever had made them were going out on regular patrols.

A quick peek around the side of the hill didn't find any shooters, but it also didn't get me shot at, either.

I was pretty sure where I had been shot at from. If the intruders went out on regular patrols, they probably also had a guard or two posted. Someone who'd seen me coming down the drive could have scrambled to a higher vantage to identify me and then take me out (or skip step one and go straight to two).

The best place to do that would have been the roof of the house. I hadn't seen anyone there when I'd peeked, though. The flat lines would have made it easy to spot anyone against the sky. The next best place for a shooter would have been the rocky outcropping to the front and left of the house. When I'd been younger, I'd climbed all over that rock. It had seemed like a mountain. And now that I was an adult, it was… still pretty damn big, to be honest. Plenty of hiding places.

This past day had been the first time in weeks I'd been able to think clearly, and now my brain was working in overdrive. This timing was too coincidental. Unless they'd camped out here for years and Elias had never mentioned them, I'd come back home at the same time that these people, whoever they were, were invading. Looks like I'd gotten my wish: whatever had drawn me back here *wasn't* a journey of self-discovery, after all.

I tried to remember if I hadn't been holding a monkey's paw when I'd wished that, but, nope. It was just free-floating irony. Self-discovery didn't seem as bad as it had a moment ago.

Someone inside the house was shouting. Another voice answered out back. The porch screen door clapped open, and two men dashed out. Neither were Elias. One – older, white, and salt-and-pepper-haired – held a rifle. He had the muscles of an old-timey railcar coal shoveler: overemphasized in the shoulders. The other was younger, East Asian, and unarmed. That was all I saw before I ducked back down.

This sent a trill of alarm up my back. I didn't recognize them. I'd been afraid these were my neighbors, come to punish Elias for some reason – maybe being related to a mutant, fear that he had a latent X-gene himself. *These* weren't my neighbors. I doubted they'd all moved in since I'd left, either. People out here tended to grow roots. This was good land to come to if you wanted to get stuck in a rut.

If any of them had hurt Elias, I'd crack their heads open with my fists. And if Elias had gotten *himself* into trouble, I'd do even worse to him.

The men who'd just come out were calling a name: "Milos." A reedy voice, probably Milos', shouted back. I heard "the hill" and "armed!" And then footsteps crunching on dirt. They were running down the drive, toward me.

I had extra ammo in the car. In this business, always travel prepared. That said, I hadn't quite been prepared enough – I hadn't grabbed the ammo belt when I'd hopped out. Too dangerous to go back for it now. Between my two revolvers, I had twelve shots on me. I'd have to make sure they'd count.

The pair running in my direction were just far enough away that I had time to get lost. I crawled through a short, dry ditch, and scrambled behind a low hill. I didn't have the time to cover my tracks. If my pursuers had eyes and two brain cells to spark together between them, they'd find my trail. But I didn't need to keep them off me forever. In fact, what I was planning would work better if they came after me and saved me the trouble.

I didn't even have to look to know which hills would hide me from which vantage points. I scrambled faster, and more quietly, than anyone except me or Elias would have believed. Elias and I, back when we could stand each other, played out here plenty.

I came up on the back of my assailant's outcropping in good time, with no sound of pursuit. I found the shooter right where I thought he'd be. He was a thin, reedy man laid flat up on the rock, his back to me. He had a dusty crop of brown hair that was part natural color, part actual dust. He had a rifle braced against the rock and was scanning across the hill I'd first disappeared behind.

I had a clean shot at him from here. I could have killed him at any time. That wouldn't have left me with anything but a corpse, though, and I needed answers.

Plus, there were times when death wasn't revenge enough. I needed him to *understand* how ticked off I was.

I might have been away for years, but this was still home. Kinda. I hadn't realized how protective of it I still was. And Elias, too.

Just to keep me from feeling too superior, I made a mistake on my way up. I thought I had the rockface memorized, but my boot hit an angle I wasn't expecting. I caught my balance easily, but the gunman heard the scuffing. He spun. His jaw dropped. A second later, he whirled his rifle around.

I rushed him and grabbed the rifle's barrel. He kept a grip on it, and I didn't have a good enough angle to wrench it away from him. I acted like I was trying to pull it toward me. When he shifted his posture to try and fight that, I yanked upward instead – and clubbed him in the chin with the butt of his own rifle. The sound of that was satisfying as hell.

His fingers loosened. The rifle slipped from him, and I tossed it away. It landed with a clatter. I couldn't stay up here, exposed, and so I kicked him hard in the side of his ribs. Still stunned, he rolled off his perch.

I grabbed his right arm and yanked it behind his back. "Next time you try shooting a person by surprise," I hissed, "aim for center mass. Not the head. Much less chance of things going wrong that way." I punctuated my advice with a punch. His head smacked into the rock.

By the time I heard the footsteps of his accomplices, I'd gotten him upright and held in front of me, with one of my revolvers planted against his temple. The other two men rounded the corner, saw us, and slowed. They still held their guns.

My captive spat blood onto the dirt. He must have bitten his tongue while we scuffled. I hoped it hurt. "You must be the mutie," he told me.

I was already holding his arm behind him so tightly that it was close to dislocating, but I gave it another little tweak upward. He gasped. Milos wasn't a very common name. Polish or Serbian, I thought. And his accent said Polish.

The others weren't aiming their guns right at us, but they didn't drop them, either. The man with the salt-and-pepper beard was shorter than the others, but older, well-muscled, and imposing. His younger partner glanced to him. It didn't take much to figure that he was in charge here. He wore old jeans and a dark blue shirt, and something completely incongruous – a priest's white collar, tucked around his neck so that just a white tab was visible. His skin was leathery, and he had a low cunning in his eyes that instantly made me wary. He looked irritated, not alarmed. Probably not a good sign.

"Milos," the man barked. "I expect you to make *some* mistakes, this being your first time out with us. This is too much." His voice was deep, discomfortingly gravely and resonant. He had a preacher's projection. I could hear him clearly from dozens of paces away, and he sounded like he was barely trying.

"She's a mutie, Wolfram," Milos protested. "Wasn't a fair fight."

I told my hostage, "You're awfully mouthy for a man whose shoulder I could break at any moment."

"You're a lookout," the bearded man, Wolfram, told Milos, as if I hadn't spoken. "Not a skirmisher. You don't engage on your own. You needed backup."

"I should've been able to handle it," Milos said, sullenly. "I'll do better."

I *really* didn't like how casual and confident the bearded man, Wolfram, seemed. I kept my gaze fixed on his eyes, watching them dart to the side, like they were watching someone sneaking up behind me.

"Why the hell are you all here?" I asked. "Where's Elias?"

The man who'd come with Wolfram said, quietly, "Isn't it time we finished this?" Hearing him speak gave me a chance to place his accent. Malaysian.

"It's all right, Milos," Wolfram said. "I forgive you."

Milos froze, like that was the worst thing he'd ever heard. Worse than anything I'd done to him.

I drew Milos' arm back a little farther just to remind someone I was here, and said, "I'm getting real tired of feeling invisible–"

Wolfram leveled his pistol right at Milos' gut.

I just had time to see that Wolfram held a Desert Eagle with a ridged barrel. Probably .50. Extremely powerful.

Powerful enough to pierce a body.

I didn't even see him pull the trigger. Just a flash of light, and a bolt of fiery pain ripping through my stomach. Milos jolted into me so hard that he knocked the air from my lungs.

The two of us tumbled backward together and fell off the

outcropping. I landed hard on my back, onto the packed dirt below. If the impact of the gunshot hadn't already driven the air from me, that would have done it. I pushed Milos off and rolled to the side, hands scrambling over my belly, checking for the entrance wound.

I've been shot before. Terrible experience. Would not recommend it. Obviously, I'd gotten better, at least physically. But I'll always remember the shock, and the way it hadn't even hurt at first. The feeling that stuck with me the most was that of hot blood spilling over my skin. It had been so warm it was almost comforting.

It took me several agonizing seconds to realize that I wasn't feeling the same thing this time. No blood. No gunshot wound. The impact had hurt plenty enough, like being shot while wearing a bulletproof vest. I'd have bruising up and down my ribs.

I'd gotten lucky. The bullet must have struck bone, deflected away from me. With my mutant endurance, I could have recovered from a gunshot (if it hadn't killed me outright), but getting shot would have left me down and vulnerable to a killing blow.

It turns out that, when I'd started to think of my opponents as dim bulbs, I'd started to get overconfident. Nothing will get you in trouble faster, in this business or any other, than overconfidence.

Above me, Wolfram's footsteps crunched across the rockface. Coming towards us. He was only a few steps away from having a great shot. He walked like he was out on a stroll.

Milos had landed at a bad angle. One of his legs had crumpled underneath him. He held his hands tight to his stomach, but blood flowed freely between his fingers. His face was screwed up, but he didn't have the breath to scream.

Even *I* felt bad for him. But I was out of time. I couldn't breathe, but I pushed to my feet and started running. My vision fringed black. If I hadn't been a mutant, I might not have had the strength to do it, and certainly not as fast as I had.

Another gunshot boomed off the horizon right before I dived behind the next rock. If it hit me, at least I didn't feel it. It took until I had a chance to check myself for gunshots that I knew for sure that Wolfram had missed.

My breath came back to me in heaving gasps. Color flooded back into my vision.

The shock had shaken my grip. My revolver had fallen loose. I drew the other one, cocked the hammer. I hadn't spent all that time on the practice range – firing at night, from distance postures, drawing after a sprint – for nothing.

The next time I heard the slightest sound, I zeroed in on it, snapped my arm out, and fired. I hadn't meant to hit, but to frighten and to cover for what I did next, which was to lean out from behind cover and try to draw a bead on anyone I'd just forced down.

All I saw was someone's boot – I think the Malaysian man's – disappearing behind a hill. He was a lot farther away than I'd thought he could have gotten. He must have started running the instant he could. I couldn't see any trace of the bearded man–

The rock face beside my cheek exploded. Red-hot pain punched into my face in five different places. Chips of rock, flecks of dirt, stabbed into me like pneumatic needles. All I saw was a flash of white.

I ducked back. A moment later all turned to haze, a deep red-pink color the same shade as the inside of my eyelids. The pain was everywhere. I couldn't tell which part of my face the fire was coming from, but the deepest sting came from my eyes.

Then that old familiar feeling – blood running down my skin – was back again. It was all over my face. My nose, my lips – under my eyes–

No. No, no, no, *no*. No.

I pushed backward, moving by memory, and fell into a shallow rut just deep enough to hide me. I crawled along it as fast as I could while the world spun in a pink haze around me.

I had to keep moving. Couldn't let the enemy catch up to me. Had to push my knowledge of the land as far as it would go, and make a few educated guesses, too.

It was not until half a minute had passed that I could spare a hand to wipe my face. I nearly wept with relief when I saw shapes and shadows moving when I pulled my hand away. At least one eye still worked. It took another few seconds of clearing the blood and grit off the other to verify that it did, too.

It hurt too much for everything to be all right and normal. Everything seemed covered by a film of haze and itching, burning pain. Probably scratched the cornea, maybe the iris if I was unlucky. That was going to hurt a lot worse soon enough. But at least he hadn't destroyed either eye.

Wolfram had come a hair's breadth of drilling me through the forehead. His aim had been stellar. And I had no idea where he was now.

Or why he'd come here, or what he wanted – or where my brother was, or anything, really.

I'd gotten a good distance from the house. I didn't have any extra holes in my lungs yet, so I'd managed to lose Wolfram for the moment. If he'd found and caught up with me while I was still wiping blood out of my eyes, I would have made an easy target. Downside was, I had no idea where *he* – or any of his accomplices, other than Milos – were.

Safest thing to do was stay put and keep my revolver ready. He was obviously a crack shot, and, with me half-blinded by the scratches on my eyes, he could outshoot even me. But a gunfight in this wasteland didn't come down to just sharp aiming. It was also about cunning, about using cover, and about knowing the terrain and taking advantage of it. Wolfram had proved himself no slouch in the first two, and his companion was still out there, too. I wasn't going to underestimate them again. I couldn't sit still and let them develop a plan.

I stayed crouched and low, ducking from hill to outcropping, and put more distance between me and my house. And then I circled around, toward the back – where all those tire tracks had gone.

To my surprise, there was only one car. My eyes were still stinging, watering, and it took a while to blink enough of the fog away to see what it was: an open-topped jeep, covered in the dust of a long trip.

There was also another person. With the haze in my eyes, I couldn't see much more than a dark shirt, and a form that didn't fit my brother's. He, or she, or they, were hustling away from the jeep and into the house. That made at least four invaders total, including fallen Milos.

There'd been more tire tracks out front than one jeep alone

accounted for. But, now that I reflected, the treads all had the same prints. The jeep had come and gone several times.

The question of why they'd come was just as much a mystery as why they'd stayed. Couldn't think of anything here that a group of criminals would want. If they just wanted a remote hideout, there were a bunch of other places out in the desert that wasn't a ranch with neighbors, business partners, clients, and debt collectors who would eventually come check up on them.

The only person of interest out here was my brother.

I'd been feeling pretty rotten about this before, but I was starting to get a *real* bad feeling about this now. I started to think about how many times I'd bailed my brother out of jail, or against my better instincts, sat as a character witness and lied for him in court. It had been over ten years since he'd gotten into *that* kind of trouble, though. Definitely not since Dad died.

I thought he'd gotten over acting like that. Maybe he'd just gotten better at hiding it.

But I put off thinking about that for a little bit longer. I was still being hunted. I was on my back foot and needed to get them on theirs, instead. The best way to get an enemy to make awful decisions is to get them thinking emotionally, not rationally (ask me how I know). If I was going to even the playing field, I needed to get them angry.

This was a low, stubby hill, crowned with jutting rocks like teeth. There were enough plants and outcroppings to hide my head from a cursory glance. And, best yet, though the sun wasn't near the horizon, it was still generally behind me. Better cover than I was liable to find anywhere else.

I drew a careful aim on the jeep's engine block. In this line of work, it pays to know the ins and outs of vehicles that see front-line military use.

My gun wasn't as powerful as Wolfram's .50 Desert Eagle, but it packed enough of a punch that the recoil would have been hell on anyone without mutant strength. It would have been more ammo-efficient to sabotage the jeep up close, but that would have put me out in the open. Besides, I needed them to hear this.

Bang.

Even with blood and crud and haze in my eyes, don't doubt my shooting. Something in the engine block hissed and gurgled. As if for good measure, the front left tire popped and deflated. I hadn't even meant for that to happen. The bullet must have fragmented.

Sure enough, I heard shouts from the direction of my house, and around it. The man I'd spotted just a minute ago darted outside. I couldn't see much more of him this time around, except that he had dark enough skin and hair to match his clothes. He was sharp enough to realize that I was drawing him out. With a shout, he disappeared back behind the door before I could draw a bead on him. He sounded young. Too young for this.

I hunkered down and waited.

It was like I'd called a meeting. They all came filing out of the house in a group, neat and orderly. Five of them, walking tight together. *Damn.* More than I'd counted on. I drew aim and almost fired, but something made me hesitate. They were walking too casually. Confidently.

One of them wasn't walking like the others. I wiped more

blood out of my eyes, squinted through the stubborn haze. That person at the center of the group was being forced along. The man behind him had an arm squeezed over his shoulder and a gun to his head.

I didn't need sharp vision to recognize my brother.

Elias didn't look good. He was thinner than I remembered. He used to have a reasonable gut on him. It was caved in now. Worse, though, was the blood on his forehead, and caked in his hair. It was hard to be sure through the haze, but only some of it looked new. Elias had been mistreated for quite a while.

Wolfram stood off to the side. The man in dark clothing held up the far side of the group. Between them was the Malaysian man. And the person pressing the gun to my brother's forehead–

My vision blurred. I tried to blink through it, to focus on that mop of brown hair. Clarity only came to me briefly, and with effort. But I saw enough.

The fifth person looked like the kind of guy who cut his own hair. It was an awful, unruly brown mop. The effect was too familiar. And so was the sullen, overgrown-teenager's face underneath it.

Johnny Dee.

He liked to hide what he was. He wore a bulky white shirt to cover the gaping mouth and tentacles underneath. There was always a sign, though, if you knew what to look for. My brother jerked forward, even at the risk of incurring the wrath of the man with the gun to his head. There was something brushing his back that scared him even more.

Johnny Dee scowled and jammed his gun tighter into Elias's head, but even that couldn't make Elias stop squirming.

"Little snake-spit," I hissed.

I hadn't laid eyes on Johnny Dee since the X-Men's M-Day refugee camp. I hadn't actually seen him in person when he'd tried to kill half the world's remaining mutant population, not to mention puppeteered my body and tried to make me shoot Neena. That was lucky for him. I would have staved his skull in. The other men, I noticed, kept their distance from him.

Johnny Dee's free hand clenched. I felt a strange tingling looking at it – and knew beyond a shade of a doubt that he held a little doll of me. The same type he used to puppet and kill people.

Only he *wasn't* controlling me. Magik's psionic shield was blocking him. But the barrier must not have been perfect, because I still sensed the tingling. Somehow, he was behind what had been happening. Had to be. But I didn't have time to think about it.

Johnny Dee looked straight ahead. Then, he raised his chin, turned, and looked straight to my perch. For a couple seconds, the air was so still I could hear all of them breathing.

"It says she's up there," Johnny Dee said, loud enough for me to hear.

Wolfram turned to me. I couldn't see his expression through the haze, but his voice left no doubt about the nasty grin he wore. "How about it, Outlaw?" he shouted. "I tried to shoot through your hostage. You want to see if you have better luck with mine?"

I could have blown his head off right there. As if sensing me think that, Johnny Dee cocked his gun's hammer.

"What do you want?" I called.

"You, Outlaw," he answered. "Out in the open. No weapons. We'll take the rest from there."

"Don't do it, Inez," Elias said. "They'll do worse than kill us."

I waited for Johnny Dee's bunch to hit or shoot him or something in retaliation for saying that, but they ignored him. Maybe they took what he said as too obvious. Something that I should have already known, anyway.

The Malaysian man kept quiet, but he carried himself confidently enough. I heard the name "Rayyan" muttered in his direction, and hazarded a guess that was him. Rayyan stood a step behind Wolfram, but I didn't doubt that he would step up and take charge of anything he saw fit to. When you've been a merc for long enough, you get a sense for the type. He said something to Wolfram. Might've been instructions, or advice, or just a one-liner – I couldn't tell.

The other man was a little easier to read. He was scared. He'd walked at the same speed as them, but he was constantly looking at the rest, as if calculating how much distance he could safely put between himself and the group. He seemed more worried about his companions than about *me*, though I was the one pointing a Colt at him. The haze made it difficult to see his facial features, but his stark blond hair was plain enough. His skin complexion was hard to place. Not Caucasian, not Asian. Almost golden.

A real diverse crew. I would say they were an equal opportunity gang of home invaders except, you know, no women. Funny how organized crime moves past some prejudices and not others.

The last prejudice people like these would get over was that against mutants. I wondered if Johnny Dee knew that. I couldn't forget the way Milos had spat the word *mutie* at me.

"Promise we won't shoot to kill," Wolfram said. Not the same thing as a promise to hold fire. "To be perfectly level with you, you're slightly more valuable to me alive."

"Yeah?" I called. "Why's that?"

Wolfram ignored my question. Too bad. I'd been trying to provoke him into giving away more information. "Either way's fine by me," he said. "I've been looking for an excuse to brain this twerp anyhow. You have thirty seconds to come down, or he dies."

If Elias died, Wolfram would go down next. He must have known it. He didn't seem to care. Seconds ticked down.

"Come on, Outlaw!" Johnny Dee called. "This is what you always dreamed of. A shootout against hardened desperadoes under a baking sun? Like right out of a Western! Isn't this the feeling you spent your whole life chasing?"

"Fifteen seconds," Wolfram said.

"I *know* you dream about it," Johnny Dee said. I didn't like the way he said that.

"Ten seconds."

My damn eyes kept burning and watering. That blast had scratched them good. I had to keep blinking them clear. The bunch of them turned to haze on me and back, like heat mirages under a waterfall.

In one of the moments of clarity, I drew as tight a bead as I could. The moment disappeared, but I held my aim steady.

"Do you trust me?" I called to Elias.

"Mostly," he answered.

Good enough.

One thing I'd learned over the past couple weeks was that there were limits as to how far I could trust myself.

But that didn't mean I was going to stop now. Wasn't in my nature.

I fired.

Johnny Dee cried out. In the same instant, Elias shoved away from him. That didn't necessarily mean I'd done what I intended to – sharpshoot Johnny Dee's gun right out of his hand – but I couldn't spare the time to verify.

I drew my best aim on the blur that was Wolfram and squeezed the trigger. And then again, firing at each of the men next to him.

I must have hit somebody because I heard a pained yelp of surprise. My ears were ringing too much from the gunfire for me to be able to tell from who.

That was where the good times ended. The rock right next to my face blasted apart – just split right in two in a shower of needle-sharp sprinkles. *Deja vu* made me flinch away, but no pain seared across my face this time. The unmistakable cannon shot boom of the Desert Eagle rolled across the horizon.

By the time I blinked my eyes clear enough to see again, Elias and Johnny Dee were scuffling. The two men around them were down, either because I'd hit them, or they'd dived for cover. Johnny Dee held one hand to the side of his head. Even through the blurring, I saw the bright red all over it. It looked like I'd hit his ear.

Elias *should* have gotten the better of him. He'd gotten into plenty enough fights as a kid (not as many as me). But he moved slow and shaky, like all of his muscles were cramped. I wouldn't have been surprised if he'd been bound for days. Johnny Dee raised a boot, kicked Elias hard in the chest. Elias stumbled.

A flash of sunlight reflected off something in Johnny Dee's good hand. Bastard had a knife.

"*No!*"

My nerves were too shot. I couldn't see anything more than smudges that blurred together. I drew my best aim, and fired.

I heard a grunt of pain and surprise from Wolfram, but I didn't even have the time to find it satisfying. Wrong target.

Johnny Dee plunged his knife into my brother's chest.

Then a punch like a freight train crashed into my shoulder. It knocked me to my side.

For an eternity of an instant, that shock was my whole world – all I could think, and all I could feel. My revolver dropped from fingers I couldn't feel anymore. My vision flashed white. Everything else shrank to the size of a pinhead. The shock was so great that I hadn't even heard Wolfram's Desert Eagle go off.

The shock didn't have to be lonely too much longer after it. The pain came flooding in soon enough. Everything shifted into sensory overload, a mélange of heat, agony, and a dreadful kind of clenching in my chest – the kind you get when your heart skips a beat, and gives you just enough pause to wonder if it will ever start again.

The pinhead shrank to nothing.

NINE

To my surprise, the world came back again.

I was on my side, having rolled just a little bit away from my perch. My top was drenched in blood. Blood had spattered on and darkened the dirt all around me. Hurt like hell to breathe – but I *could* breathe. That monster had shot me in the shoulder. His gun hit like a mortar shell.

The sun hadn't moved across the sky, but I was confident I'd fainted long enough that Wolfram and Johnny Dee's gang could have just walked up and shot me.

I heard their voices. They were shouting, hoarsely. They sounded farther away, though. For whatever reason, they'd left me alone. Maybe they thought I was dead. But that thought didn't sit right.

To my continued surprise, I had the strength to lever myself up and look around. No sign of the gang. Only a single blurred form, lying still in the dirt.

Elias.

I only had the strength to cover half of the distance between us. But, since it was my brother, I took an overdraft on the rest.

My mutant abilities weren't as flashy as eyeball laser beams, or super luck, or weather control, or flying all the damn time to show off that I could – but, when I really need it, it's my endurance and strength that gets me across the extra mile no one else can go.

Still, it took every little bit of it to make myself sit next to Elias, rather than just collapse. He was still alive and breathing. Relief made me sag. He looked more surprised by all the blood than he did at the pain. Belatedly, I also realized that he was startled to see me. My shirt and vest were soaked through with blood. They were more red than tan.

"Thought for sure they got you," he croaked.

"I had to leave a few pieces of me behind up there." I didn't say how desperately I wanted to make sure they hadn't got *him*. I tugged at the slash Johnny Dee had made in Elias's shirt, ripping it wider.

From this close, the haze wasn't as much of an issue. I gently peeled back his blood-soaked shirt to peek. His wound was bad – but it could have been worse. When Johnny Dee had shoved the blade into Elias's chest, the tip had glanced off his ribs. The blade had gone in at a steep downward angle. Better that than straight in, though it still could have ruptured his spleen or pancreas. The wound *looked* bad, though. Johnny Dee probably thought he'd killed Elias. And he and the others had run away too fast to make sure.

I thumbed the skin back to gauge the depth of the cut. Most mercs get used to the sight of blood before long – either that, or they quit, or die – but I'd been accustomed to it for a lot longer than I'd been on the job. Growing up around animals kept me from feeling sick about poking around in my brother's wound, even as I watched the cavity I'd opened refill with blood. A fresh stream of it squeezed out onto his shirt.

He'd lost a good amount of blood, but that probably wasn't doing as much to keep him down as the damage Wolfram and Johnny Dee's gang had done to him before now. I didn't have to look hard to find the deep red scabs and welts crisscrossing his wrists and ankles.

I didn't want to ask how long they'd kept him like that. I was angry enough.

Studying his injury kept my mind off my own. Contrary to what movies and TV will tell you, the shoulder is *not* a consequence-free place to get shot. I certainly wasn't going to be over it after a scene or two. My left shoulder was in agony. There could not have been more pain if it had actually been on fire. I could still move that arm, but it felt like it was at a remove, not all there – a ghost of the limb it used to be. My fingers were clumsy, like I'd just pulled them out of an ice bank. It wasn't going to be useful for shooting.

The back of my shirt was ragged, which at least meant the bullet had passed through. I'd never forget that punch, though – like being rammed by a semi-truck. The bullet had shed a great deal of energy on its way through. And all that energy had gone into shredding skin, flesh, and muscle.

My deadened fingers fumbled on Elias's shirt. I sure didn't have the dexterity to mess with the buttons. Elias half-heartedly protested as I ripped his shirt down the front. Even without fine muscle control in my fingers, my mutant strength was still with me. His buttons went flying. Next, I tore down his sleeves.

I lifted him just far enough to yank the remains of his shirt off his back. I wound the blood-drenched fabric around itself until it made a functional tourniquet, and then tied it tightly around his waist. To his credit, he only hollered in pain twice.

I paused, waiting for the gang to react to his shouts. I couldn't hear them anymore.

"What would Dad think if he could see us now?" Elias asked, when he could speak again. "At least we're getting along."

"I imagine what he'd say would depend on how we ended up here," I said, looking at him. I wasn't in the mood for subtlety.

He actually looked hurt – er, more than physically hurt, that was. "I could say the same to you. They came here asking all kinds of questions about you. Said they'd help me out financially, save the ranch, if I answered. When I tried to run them off, that's when they… well, you see what they did to me."

All the air came out of me. This wasn't his fault. Somehow, it was *mine*. I knew, *had* known, that their being here wasn't a coincidence. I hadn't wanted to think about it, and I'd had too much else to worry about. I had no choice now.

"I'm sorry," I said. "I didn't mean to imply–"

"Yeah, you did."

"–that this was your fault."

"Yeah. Well. I heard what you meant. No takesie-backsies."

"You little sh–" I started, and stopped myself in time. Yeah, *what if* Dad could see us now? So much for getting along.

I barked out a laugh. Elias grinned.

"I really ain't that bad anymore, Inez," Elias said. "You'll just have to take my word for it."

"So what'd they want, besides answers?" I asked.

"Bits of you," Elias said. "Old clothes. Hairbrush. Scrapbook. Old envelopes–"

"Anything that might have my DNA on it," I said, sourly.

Even with all the other pains wracking my body, the pit in my stomach stood out among them.

Magik hadn't been able to find the exact cause of my problems. She'd covered that up with a lot of vague and mystical-sounding words, like any good magician, but all she'd been able to suss out was the link between me and this place.

It had been easy to assume I'd been the cause of my own troubles. Easier still, given the brain scans that Triage and Tempus had done, to believe I was developing mutant telepathic abilities. And that I had a sentimental complex pointing me back home. Even I'd started thinking the same.

But Magik and I had taken the right puzzle pieces and fit them in the wrong order. The telepathic centers of my brain were active because I was receiving, not sending. *I* wasn't the source of my telepathic link with home. I'd been under attack. *From* here.

This house was a treasure trove of my DNA. Second best place in the world to go and get it. The best place in the world if you didn't want to take any risk of alerting me. I'd left a lot of things behind, and Dad had been too sentimental to throw them out. By invading here rather than my apartments, Wolfram and Johnny Dee could catch me completely off guard. And they had.

All those nights I'd felt like I'd gone sleepless. Or woken up in a place I couldn't remember. The lapses of concentration… the feeling that my brain was falling apart, that I'd never gotten more than two hours of sleep a night for months…

It had all stemmed from Johnny Dee.

He'd gone into my body. Maybe into my mind. Johnny Dee had been controlling me. He'd fed those bits of DNA into the maw on his chest, and it had made a doll of me. He'd seized control of me.

To do... what?

There was a lot I had yet to de-tangle. But I was closer than I'd been even thirty minutes ago. I knew enough to be pissed. A real deep, dark, red-tinged anger like I'd never felt. And I'd been plenty angry before.

Rage didn't make the pain go away. Or all the other, more deep-down hurts. Or the sense of violation. But it gave me the strength to shelve them for now.

"You hit two of them," Elias said. "Wolfram and Johnny Dee. They ran off to bandage their wounds. Said something about just needing to wait. I don't know if they'd thought they'd already gotten us."

"Nearly did," I said, hoping I wasn't jinxing us. With injuries like his, Elias wasn't safe yet. Not until he got to a hospital. One thing he'd said earlier caught up to me. "Did you say, 'save the ranch?'" I asked.

"Somehow they figured out I was in trouble," Elias said. "Must've looked up my record, figured I'd do anything to get out of the mortgages. Wolfram got real upset when I told him off." He spat red-tinged spit. "Careful of him, Inez. I think he's more dangerous than any of them."

"You were in trouble – and you didn't tell me?"

"I didn't want to beg you for money again," Elias said. "I figured you would think I wasn't telling the truth about why I needed it, anyway."

I was in plenty of physical pain; I didn't need any emotional pain to go with it. I sank my head down, touched my forehead to his. "Elias."

Distantly, I heard a car engine start.

"No," I breathed. I'd just destroyed their jeep. Elias's Jaguar was up on blocks. I hadn't seen anything else. I hadn't had my Mustang all that long, but I knew it well enough to recognize its motor. The keys were still in my pocket. They must've hotwired the damn thing.

I grunted with the strain of standing. I was about to whisper an apology to Elias, but he'd heard the engine, too. "Get them," he said.

I couldn't manage a run. The faster I moved, the more intense the pain in my shoulder got. But I could handle something between a stagger and a jog.

I rounded the house just in time to see the Mustang peel out across the drive. It didn't actually go *down* the drive, back toward the road. No, they drove it across the open yard, right over brush. The low-riding Mustang wasn't built for that.

They drove it right along the side of the fence that had once held our horses. The car was a red blur. I couldn't see who was driving it, or if they'd all gotten inside. My damn eyes hurt too much. The more I tried to focus, the more my scratched lenses stung and watered.

I drew aim with my revolver. But I could only hold it in one hand. My left hand was too weak and shaky with spikes of pain. They had already made the kind of distance that even I would only want to make with a two-handed shot. And, by my count, my revolver only had one bullet left.

I tracked them with the revolver's barrel, white-hot rage tempting me to fire anyway. But for once I listened to my better instincts.

I watched the Mustang melt into the blur of the horizon.

They still weren't headed for the main roads. All that lay in their direction were mountains and wasteland. The Mustang wouldn't make it very far.

They were up to something. They must have been heading that way for *some* reason. Damned if I knew what, though. There was nothing but wasteland in that direction. Hills, cliffs, and other rough terrain.

By the time I got back to Elias, he was levering himself up. He moved like a man forty years older than I knew he was. His tourniquet didn't look any redder, thankfully. He plainly wasn't going to stay put, so I didn't try to force him back down. I helped him to his feet, and to keep a shaky balance.

"You look like roadkill that was hit by a car with ice spikes," Elias told me.

"Thanks for the metaphor," I said. "Real literary."

"You look like you've been trampled on by a soccer team in cleats."

"OK, I get–"

"You look like you just walked out of an accident at the broken glass factory."

"I get it," I snapped. "My forehead's bloodied. The cuts are shallow."

"It's your eyes, too, Inez," he said. "They're all red."

All that pulverized rock shrapnel had made a hundred tiny lacerations all over my eyes. That was going to get worse before it got better. I knew, without looking in a mirror, that the kind of red he was talking about wasn't just "bloodshot." He meant solid red. Broken capillary red. The kind of red that made me look like a demon.

And my eyes kept watering, too. I wiped them clear, irritated by how that must look. Like a demon who cried a lot.

"We need to get you to a hospital," I said.

"I don't have insurance," he said.

"Why the hell not?" I snapped.

"Where am I supposed to get affordable insurance? An employer? You know how hard it is to get hired with a felony conviction."

"If the only problem was money, you could've asked me."

He shrugged. "I *had* money. But I had other bills to pay first."

"Yeah, and now I'm gonna have to pay that much more for you," I said. "Because I'm not letting you try on your own."

"I'll fight you," he said. Useless threat, and had been since we were kids. I'd always outmatched him. He'd still said it plenty then, when he'd wanted to get his way.

He and I had more in common than I liked to think. We both hated to be seen as weak. No, worse – we both hated to *think* of ourselves as weak. It was more the latter than the former that was bothering him.

"It may not feel like it," I said, "but sometimes the last thing people like you and I need is to be left alone." I bit my knuckle. Damn, but I wished Neena was here. Even Black Widow would be a sight for (literal) sore eyes. "I need to get in touch with my friends."

"Got your phone on you?" he asked.

My damn phone had been in the Mustang's passenger seat. And my extra ammunition was in the trunk.

"That's a problem," he said, when I explained. "First thing they did when they invaded was bust both my phones, then cut every line. Just in case I broke out of where they tied me up, I guess."

The last thing I wanted was to go solo. Once upon a time, I preferred to stick it out alone, but… that was how I got myself into the kind of trouble my brother was in now. And worse.

"The gang ever say where they were headed?" I asked. "Or why?"

"Just that they needed to wait something out."

Magik's psionic shield would last for another couple days. After that, I would be right back to where I had been: vulnerable to Johnny Dee.

I was sure that, somehow, they'd found that out. Their behavior didn't make sense any other way.

Elias said the gang had thought they'd finished me. Wolfram seemed competent enough to know not to take that for granted. If he'd wanted me dead, he would have come up and finished me off.

Slightly more valuable to me alive, he'd said. Something about me, specifically, was important to them.

Too many questions. And while I wanted answers, I wanted them a little less than I wanted revenge. Now that the adrenaline of the fight had worn off, a deep, dark rage was boiling inside me. Enough to keep the pain away, for now. Given a choice between getting answers and killing this bunch of pustulent boils – I'd shoot them down every time.

I never could sit through a villain's exposition. People going over their evil plans just made me itchy. I'd rather just cut to the violence.

The stolen Mustang left tracks that would be easy for me to follow – for now. Something dark was shading the fringe of the western horizon. I couldn't make out just what. It could have been the Mustang, but it could just as easily have been a rock outcropping. My sight was too blurred to tell. The wind around here could get pretty bad. I couldn't count on the tracks remaining contiguous into the next day. Especially if they got out and started moving on foot, as they'd have to if they kept heading in that direction.

I was a pretty capable tracker, but part of tracking is learning where the limits are, and how fast you'll need to move to keep up with your target. If I was going to find them, I was running out of time.

Another good thing to learn about tracking *humans* is to recognize when you're being led into a trap. And Wolfram and Johnny Dee's gang was headed in a direction that made no other kind of sense.

Elias may not have known all the details, but he didn't need to be a genius to suss out what I was planning. "You need to hurry up if you're gonna find a way to get after them."

"I'm not leaving you alone and hurt out here."

"I'll get to the neighbors."

"On foot? The Wayfields are miles away. You'll collapse first." And I didn't trust our neighbors. Their car had been among those that had pulled up to meet my dad that evening, before I'd left. OK – fine, I probably *could* have trusted the Wayfields enough to call an ambulance for a stabbed man, but some grudges die hard.

He scratched the back of his head. "Well… first thing Wolfram did after breaking my phones was dismantle my car, make sure I couldn't get away if I got out. But…"

"But you think you can fix it," I finished, preempting his bragging.

"What? Hell no. They were thorough. I'm not a miracle worker. But I was also working on a motorcycle in the back. Got it cheap, and it's real old. I had taken apart the engine. They must've thought the whole thing was junk, left it alone. But I bet I can put it together a lot faster than you'd believe. Two, three hours."

"A *motorcycle*? That'd be harder on your wound than just walking."

He gave me a coprophagic grin.[10] "Promise I'll ride so slow I'll get bored."

"Ugh. You want to give me an over-under on how many times you'd reopen your wound if you try this?"

"Hey, I'll be in better shape for my job than what you'll be in for yours."

I didn't want to say it, but he was right. Neither of us were going to do the right things for ourselves. And neither of us could stop the other. We had no recourse but to mutually disapprove of each other. Just like old times.

He was still smiling. I wasn't.

While Elias poked around with his motorcycle, I went out and recovered the revolver I'd dropped earlier. I plucked some bullets out of one rotary chamber and slipped them into the other, until they were closer to evenly split. That gave me seven shots between them.

---

10 We'll leave you to look that one up. –Ed.

And then I stopped by the place where Wolfram had shot Milos.

Milos was lying at his same bad angle, like a broken action figure. His leg remained folded underneath him. He hadn't moved a muscle, except to push an elbow against the dirt.

I realized what had saved me from being shot. Wolfram's bullet must have struck Milos' spine. The bullet had glanced off the bone, or embedded in it. If just tissue had been in its way, he definitely would have gotten me, too.

I wondered if this was how Neena felt, being lucky all the time. I sure didn't feel fortunate.

Milos was still alive. He breathed shallowly, staring dead-eyed into the sky.

Judging from the trickle of blood still coming from his stomach, like an artery was opening every time his chest rose, he wasn't going to last much longer. His wound smelled awful. Suffice it to say something had ruptured in his gut, and I didn't want to think about what. There was nothing I could do for him. He wouldn't survive a ride on Elias's motorcycle or, frankly, a ride on a fully stocked ambulance.

He blinked when my shadow fell over him, as if he hadn't seen me before now. I sat on the dirt next to him.

"Why were you and your buddies stealing my body?" I asked.

"Why should I tell you, mutie?"

"Come on. You really think those other guys are your friends? After they shot you?" I'd seen a lot of cold, cruel things in my time, but Wolfram's *I forgive you* was one of the worst yet.

He shook his head. There was a convulsive tremor to it. I couldn't tell if he was agreeing with me, or refusing to answer.

"I can help you," I lied. "But you've got to show me that you're somebody I'd want to help." After a quiet moment of listening to his uneven breath, I added, "It's never too late to switch sides, you know."

"You really think you're one of the good guys?" he asked.

He was shaking. Shivering, I realized. He was terrified. Funny thing was, he didn't seem scared of *me*. Or even of his death. He kept peeking over my shoulder.

This was a waste of time. And, frankly, a waste of emotional energy. Neither one of us wanted me to be here.

I stood and turned, and started heading in the other direction.

A grip like steel closed around my ankle, and yanked. I fell hard, landing on my knee. Next thing I knew, Milos was grabbing his way up my leg, reaching for my holster.

There was no *way* he could've moved with that speed. His palm brushed the grip of my revolver. I kicked him in the face. He hardly seemed to notice. He was like a zombie – single-minded, immune to pain, and with the strength of the damned.

I'd held back on my first kick because I hadn't wanted to kill him. On my second, I showed him a little more of what a "mutie" could do. My second kick cracked into his face. His head snapped back. His grip finally slackened. Blood spilled from his nose, onto his lips, but he didn't seem to notice. It wasn't natural. And, the moment I thought that, I knew what had happened.

The kick should have knocked Milos out, at the very least, but he only looked stunned. I scrambled backward. Milos levered himself up on his elbows and tried to stand. He faltered only when he realized – as if for the first time – that his legs weren't working.

The pause gave me enough time to draw the revolver he'd tried to grab, cock the hammer, and aim at his face.

"Johnny Dee," I said, coolly.

"You have no idea how frustrating you are, Inez Temple." Milos' voice was still his own, but his Polish accent was gone. "I could have killed you a dozen and a half times before all this. They held me back."

"You treat all your friends like Milos?" I asked. "Planning on stealing all their bodies?"

"Like he mattered," Johnny Dee said. "Miss your brother?"

It took me a long second to realize Johnny Dee thought he'd killed Elias. Thank all the stars in the sky that my brother wasn't there. He probably had enough of my brother's DNA on him, in the blood on his sleeves, that he could've taken over Elias at any time. If he'd known.

"You don't have to *keep* trying to get me mad at you," I growled.

"I enjoy it," he rasped. "I'm having fun." Milos' voice was flagging. Johnny Dee could keep pushing Milos' body without feeling Milos' pain, but he couldn't keep it alive when it was ready to expire.

"Why me? Why my family?"

"You know, you really bug the hell out of me. We were almost in position. We almost had everything set. And then through awful, dumb luck, you skip out on us at the end." Blood and saliva were dribbling from the corner of Milos' mouth. Johnny Dee didn't seem to notice. "You want to know why we chose you? It's because you're too much of a simpleton to realize what was going on." He grinned, horribly. "I bet you're *still* too much of a simpleton to have figured it out now, even with everything laid out in front of you."

I could have asked a hundred questions. I especially wanted to know who Wolfram was, and why he seemed to be calling the shots when Johnny Dee was the one with the powers.

Instead, I said, "I'm going to kill you, Johnny Dee."

"You've got maybe two days left before your protection fails. So don't chase after us. Spend the time saying goodbye to your friends and what's left of your family." Johnny Dee sneered, showing me Milos' bloody teeth. "And tell every mutant out there to do the same."

Then something *snapped*. Milos jerked, and went limp. His head slumped into the dirt.

I stood, slowly, keeping my revolver ready. I kept my distance for a bit, and then closed to nudge Milos with my foot. His neck flopped loosely from one side to the other – broken.

Snapped from a distance by his killer, Johnny Dee.

TEN

I stalked back to the garage in a blacker mood than I'd ever been in before. I couldn't chase away the feeling of Milos' iron grip on my ankle, or the sight of Johnny Dee grinning with Milos' blood-covered lips.

What I saw at the garage didn't improve my spirits. The doors were open and, aside from the one dismantled Jaguar, it was mostly empty. Dad had left Elias more cars than that. Elias must have sold them to keep ends meeting. He *did* have the motorcycle: a filthy, beaten old CB Super Hawk that looked like it hadn't been maintained since the 1960s. It looked more useful as a doorstop than a ride. No wonder the gang had left it alone. It was in five discrete pieces.

Elias had dragged all five out into the sunlight to get a better look at them. The idiot had strained himself doing so. His tourniquet was redder than before.

"How soon do you think you can do this?" I asked. "I need to get going before those clouds come in."

"Well, don't let my sorry posterior keep you waiting."

"I'm not gonna have any chance of catching up to them on foot. I'll need to drive you out to the Wayfields, and then go after–"

"Not very observant, are you?" Elias asked. I was about to snap at him when his gaze traveled to the horizon. I followed it.

It was like something out of a dream. The most beautiful dream. In fact, it *had* been the last good dream I'd had.

My bad arm hurt too much for me to forget about it, but my good arm flopped limp at my side. All at once, I forgot how to be grumpy.

"She must've heard your voice and come back to investigate," Elias said. "I haven't seen her in days. I didn't think I would again."

Wheezer darted across the horizon, weaving back and forth like she was uncertain if it was safe to get any closer. Her radiant mane floated in the wind like a heat mirage. She met my gaze out of the side of hers and then tossed her head, as if in just as much disbelief as I was.

Wheezer continued to loop back and forth. She recognized me, but didn't want to come in to see me. Whatever had happened had left her real skittish around people. She danced away from me whenever I called her. It broke my heart.

Elias and I both knew her well enough to name the keys to *her* heart, though. "I'll get her food," I said, at the same time Elias said, "You should get her food."

That entailed going inside, which I needed to anyway. I couldn't set out right away. Even under a deadline like mine, that would've been foolish.

The house seemed so small. When I was young, it had

been a castle. As an adult, it was like two mobile homes jammed together. I felt like I could cross the whole thing in ten strides. It must've seemed the same when I was seventeen and ready to leave. But it was my childhood I remembered most.

I hate growing old. I'd hardly managed to grow *up*, and still wasn't sure I'd managed that quite right.

The bathroom was a mess.[11] The PC was smashed, the phones were destroyed, and even Elias's several-generations-old PlayStation was broken into pieces. There were strangers' clothes laid out in Dad's bedroom. The kitchen had been ransacked for food.

Strangely, the dishes had been done. Someone had delicately stacked them on the drying rack. Huh. I'd have to wonder about that later. I *know* Elias hadn't been the one to do them. He never arranged them so neatly.

First bit of business: bandage and disinfect both the wounds on my shoulder, entrance *and* exit. The exit wound was nigh impossible to reach, and I couldn't bend my bad arm to get at it without gasping from the pain. But I wasn't going to drag Elias in to help, so I sucked it up. My face needed treatment, too. That entailed something I very much didn't want to do: look in the bathroom mirror.

Elias had been right: I looked like ground-up dog turd. Blood dried in drips and rivulets down my forehead. The whites of my eyes were as red as Gambit's irises. What Elias hadn't mentioned, though, was the dark stippling of dirt and rock splinters flecked all over my face. I looked like I'd been

---

11 Thank your lucky stars that Outlaw is eliding the sanitary horrors there. –Ed.

hit by the same kind of shotgun that always spun Daffy Duck around and charred his face, only it was a lot more gruesome in real life. I had to spend time tweezing those out of my skin.

With my mutant endurance, I healed a lot faster than most other people – but that came with its own hazards they wouldn't have thought about. I couldn't afford my accelerated healing scabbing and regrowing skin over all those flecks of debris. I'd let that happen once before, on my arm. Every time something touched it had been like scraping broken glass.

My shoulder wound, at least, would heal a lot faster than it would have for most people. But my eyes were another worry. I'd gotten flecks of dirt and grit in them and, as I'd found out with my arm, that would make them heal poorly. I'd already blinked out everything I could. The pieces still there were microscopic, too small to tweeze out. They'd embedded in my cornea.

There was nothing I could do about them but wait and see. Or not see. As the case may be.

Next: a rinse and change of clothes. My outfit was soaked through with blood. The last time I'd left home, it had been after Dad's funeral. I'd gone in such a blizzard of emotional turmoil that I hadn't packed. My spare clothes were in my old bedroom, piled into a mess. I hated to think of Johnny Dee coming in here, pawing for my loose hairs. I resolved not to think about that and was only partly successful. The important thing was that they were clean. I changed into a clean shirt, clean vest, clean jeans. Then a heavy brown jacket. Aside from the jacket, it wasn't all that different from what I'd worn in. The jacket was a desert necessity – in day to protect from the scorching sun, and at night to ward off the chill.

Next: weapons. A good merc will never turn down additional firepower.

Dad's old gun collection in his study was gone. No surprise there. Either Elias had sold everything, or the invaders had taken them. But the false floorboard beside Dad's bed was untouched. In it: a Beretta M9, the same kind he used to carry in his service days, plus a plastic case with fifty rounds.

I still remember the hoarseness in Dad's voice when he'd told me about that floorboard. I'd been seventeen. Like most country Texans, I'd shot a lot of guns before then, but this was the first time he'd let me have access to one without locking it away afterward. He went over how to load it in the same grave voice he'd used to tell Elias and I that Grandma had died. I listened just as somberly, and even pretended I didn't already know where the gun was.

He'd shared all this with me about a week before our neighbors pulled up in our drive after sundown. I'm not sure Dad ever told Elias about this gun.

When Dad's mind started to fail, Elias and I debated taking his guns away from him. But he remained as gentle as I'd ever known him. Even when his memories went, his judgment stayed. And when *that* went… well, the rest of his body failed too quickly for it to be an issue.

My belt was starting to sag with holsters. But I wasn't done yet. The invaders hadn't made it out as far as the tool shed, where Dad kept his coyote rifle. A misnomer, really. It was a Ruger .223 ranch rifle, easily capable of taking down a person. I strapped it over my shoulder. (My *good* shoulder, that was. Even that weight made my wound throb.) Then I broke the lock on the cabinet that held its ammunition.

There was a good hunting knife in the cabinet above the TV, complete with sheath. I tested the blade: unused, and still sharp. Then there was a vintage 1950s flip pocketknife in one of the tool drawers. It was much smaller than the hunting knife, but easier to conceal and still plenty dangerous.

Finally: a hat. Dad and I wore the same kind. His hats were still stacked inside his closet.

Two high-caliber revolvers and a military-grade sidearm on my belt, a rifle strapped on my back, a vest full of ammunition, a hunting knife hanging from my belt, another knife in my pocket, and dark, bloody red eyes – I looked *almost* as dangerous as I felt.

All this weight would have slowed most other people. But I was a mutant. I felt *lighter*.

And a little closer to being myself again.

I noticed that Elias hadn't cleaned the carpet since Dad had died. I must've been feeling better, because I found the energy to disapprove.

My eyes started burning and watering the moment I got outside. My vision was still bad, and sunlight made it worse. Haze blossomed across the horizon, and made the whole sky seem on fire. But I could still see enough to spot Wheezer. And her eyes were definitely good enough to spot the bananas I held.

All the crimes humans had committed against her were forgotten, for now. She trotted up as eager and sprightly as a three year-old foal. A funny thing about her was that, even at her sickest, she would never eat bananas peeled. The full peel had to be on, or nothing.

"Yeah, you're just as food-motivated as Deadpool, aren't

you?" I scratched behind her ears to her complete indifference. "*Good girl.*"

Getting her saddled was a little harder. She wasn't used to it. She was also a little too old to be a riding horse now, but I knew she could handle this one trip. As much as it pained me to lose more time, I took breaks to pat her nose and reassure her. She looked a trifle underfed, but not much. She'd done well for herself out on her own. She breathed out hard when I mounted the saddle, but, otherwise, it was just like old times.

Good. I didn't want to think of her getting old any more than I wanted to think about *me* getting old.

I had one last bit of business with my brother before I took off.

He hadn't fainted yet. Somehow his motorcycle was in more pieces than before, and he was cussing at it. This was normal. Basically how he did all repairs. I halted Wheezer several horse-lengths away.

"Pop quiz," I said. "First thing after you get yourself treated, who are you contacting?"

"Your friends," he grumbled.

"Their *names*?" I'd drilled this into him just a few minutes ago.

He sighed. "Domino, Diamondback, Atlas Bear, White Fox, and Black Widow," he said as if I'd forced the names out of him, like they were ridiculous, which – well, fair enough. He came from a world of family names with long histories, and I'd long ago traded those in for a world of super hero callsigns and codenames.

I'd given him a sheet of scribbled instructions of at least three different ways to contact Shoon'kwa's airship. I couldn't count on his message reaching them in time for them to help me, but if he could manage it … well, their arrival would change my odds in half the time it took to snap. A good merc learns to make their own *deus ex machina.*

Good to verify this, but that wasn't the business I had with him. "Elias," I asked. "Why didn't those men just kill you?"

He made like he was preoccupied with his motorcycle's engine block. "Hmm?"

"It's not that I wish they had," I said. "But, thinking about it from their perspective, I don't see any reason why they wouldn't have. They're cold-blooded enough that they don't think twice about murder."

He kept fussing with the engine, though he did it silently this time.

"I had to tell them something to keep them from killing me," he said, at last.

"And what was that?"

He pushed the engine aside and looked up at me. "You think I was working with them? That I would lie to you about that? Is that what this is about?"

"*What* did you tell them?"

"I told them who you were working with," he said. "The things you said about them. Domino, Deadpool, Agent X – those kinds of people." He turned back to his disassembled cycle, obviously trying to sound unaffected.

I just about stepped away right there. Didn't trust myself to speak. The sheer panic at the thought of my team being in danger was like a blow to the belly.

When he spoke again, his voice cracked. "And when they stopped being able to do… whatever they were doing to you, the only way I could keep them from killing me on the spot was by telling them I would make a good hostage, and that you would try to protect me."

I let my breath out, long and slow. When I spoke again, I kept my voice level. "I'm not upset you told them that. You did what you had to. I *am* upset that you waited until now to tell me."

He must've been so damn scared. And he was trying his best to hide it.

He shrugged, subdued. "Yeah. Well. I didn't want you thinking I was weak, and all."

"I'm so sorry," I said. I don't think I'd meant anything I'd told him more sincerely. "One of the weird parts of my life must have brought this down on us."

"I know you had to leave home," he said.

This was probably the closest thing to reconciliation that either of us could get at the moment. "Anything else you can tell me about them?" I asked.

"Be careful of Wolfram. He was taking the lead. He gave orders to the others, even the mutant with the – thing on his chest. He told me he used to be a priest, or played being one. He would preach to big crowds of people at tent revivals, get them fired up, take them to the middle of nowhere promising a second baptism, then rob them. Just take their bus and leave." Elias shuddered. "He told me that if he wanted to kill me, he wouldn't just shoot me. He'd take me out into the desert, tie me up, and let nature take its course."

My rage stoked hotter. "Who are the others?"

"I didn't see them that much. Wolfram kept me in the closet. They were quiet when he brought me out to interrogate me.

This is just a gut feeling from the way the others looked at him, but I don't think they were all working for him. Johnny Dee and Milos, sure–"

"Milos is dead," I said.

"Good," he said, and then resumed, "–but I don't know about the others. They kept their distance." That tracked. Rayyan, whoever he was, was some kind of outsider.

"I'll make them pay."

"Take care of yourself out there," he added. "But don't make them pay. Make them hurt."

As reluctant as Wheezer had been to let me saddle her, she was eager as a racehorse to set off on the Mustang's trail.

Whoever was driving the Mustang had no idea how to handle it. The poor thing wasn't an off-road vehicle to begin with, but there were still better and worse ways to treat it. As I followed the tire tracks, I found flecks of red paint on low-lying rocks, and even a piece of fender on a dry creek bed. They'd tried to take the creek at a high speed. After that, though, the driver seemed to have straightened out, and been more careful. I hated to imagine what the car looked like now.

"What do you think, girl?" I asked Wheezer. "Insurance gonna cover this, or stick me with the bill?"

Wheezer snorted.

"Yeah, you're right." The rental insurance contract protected against theft so long as "all reasonable precautions" had been taken... which meant *of course* they were going to try to screw me. Never trust an insurance company lawyer with a nebulous phrase to weaponize.

No, I hadn't rolled the convertible top up before I left. I was too busy getting shot at. Yes, I took the keys with me. No, I can't prove that – I left them behind to fit more ammo in my pockets.

Yes, you specifically said mutant powers voided insurance obligations, but this was a gunfight, not a super hero smashup!

No, I didn't divulge that I was a mercenary, but you see that little line there that says, "Self-employed…"

No, I don't personally know the Hulk. I understand you're not big fans, but I don't see what that has to do with–

Mapping out a nice, heated blood feud with an insurance agent kept me going. I would have liked to say that riding Wheezer was just like old times, but it hurt too much to pretend. Wheezer had never been a gentle ride, and she'd gotten more headstrong as she'd gotten older. Every jostle speared a spike of pain through my shoulder. Elias would never have made it far traveling on her. Every bounce would have reopened his chest wound.

The Mustang had cruised into what was now becoming a red-tinged sunset, which meant Wheezer and I were in dangerous territory. Traveling into the light would have been dangerous enough with good vision. The scratches on my eyes turned everything into a red-gold blur. Wolfram and Johnny Dee's gang could have parked a couple hundred feet ahead, and I'd never have seen them. They would have absolutely no trouble seeing me.

I would've preferred to wait until night, use the darkness as cover, but these goons had gotten a big enough head start already. What I did instead was weave back and forth across their trail, using hills as cover, and peering down parts of the landscape that weren't as hazy as an insurance contract's acts-of-metahumans clause.

Not long after that big glob of sunset melted into the horizon, I found the Mustang.

It was sitting out in the middle of nothing. Both its doors hung open. The seats were empty. It took me a while to circle it, verify no one was waiting to ambush me. I hopped off Wheezer for a closer look.

First thing I noticed was that the hood was loose. Not propped, but not closed quite right either. I thought maybe they might have overheated it until I peeked inside. Everything was fine except the spark plugs were gone. This was sabotage. They'd left the car out here deliberately, and disabled it before they'd left.

My phone was still on the passenger seat, where I'd discarded it. It was smashed. They'd even ripped out the SIM card. Then they'd tossed it back onto the seat, a cheeky little joke for me to find.

Other than Wheezer and me, nothing was moving. Not even a bit of wind.

I checked the trunk. No spare ammunition there. They'd taken my ammo belts, though I doubt any of them carried the right weapon to fire what they contained.

I didn't have to look hard to find the footprints leading away from the Mustang. Four pairs. Like Imperial stormtroopers, they hadn't bothered to hide their numbers.

They expected me to find their trail. Wanted me to follow.

With the way those dolls of his worked, controlling my body as well as my mind, Johnny Dee could have snapped my neck any time he'd had me under his control. He wouldn't have forgotten or forgiven his last meeting with me, and the feeling was mutual.

Somehow, he'd gotten out of his supposedly secure prison.[12] Then, before I'd had a chance to realize anything was wrong, he'd gotten me under his control. That I was alive now meant two things. First, he hadn't finished whatever he'd kept stealing my body to do. Second, he hadn't expected Magik to create a shield to block his control, even temporarily.

He was not going to repeat that last mistake. If my shield ever faltered, if he got control of me again, he was going to break my neck. Or shatter my skull. Or twist my spine into a Mobius strip. Or any one of a thousand other terrible deaths before he gave me up again. He was a death sentence, hovering over my head.

The gang's footprints trekked out of the surly wastes, and up toward the craggy ridges to the west. Headed up into the mountains. The Mustang wouldn't have gotten them very far in that direction. Heck, *Wheezer* wasn't going to get me far up those slopes.

"I hate to do this," I said, patting the side of her nose, "but you've done all right without people. Not gonna be the last time I see you. Promise."

She would never stay by the car, of course, and it would have been cruel to tie her up. In case I didn't come back, she needed to be free to find water and forage. Even when she'd been chased away from the ranch, she'd hung around. I was maybe more certain than I should have been that I would be able to find her again. I pulled her tack off and left it in a heap on the rocks. I couldn't very well take it with me.

---

12 With powers like Johnny Dee's, no prizes for guessing how *that* happened. –Ed.

She still followed me for a little while – damn it, my heart can only take so much breaking in one day – but as the terrain started getting rough, she stopped.

It never got so rocky that the gang's trail disappeared, but I was hiking mostly uphill now. Exposed limestone towered to every side of me but the path back. The sun dipped farther below the rock faces with each step, and at first it was a relief. The red limning the horizon was enough to see by without overloading my scratched-up eyes. Then, as the darkness deepened, the fog set in.

The rest of my injuries were getting better. My bruises were shadows of their old selves. The cuts on my face had long since scabbed over, and skin had started to come back in. But my eyes were different. The haze hadn't gone away. I didn't even know if it had diminished. The darkness kept me from telling. Like I'd feared, too much tiny debris was stuck in my eyes for them to heal well. I was going to be hampered until I got them cleaned out.

Half-eroded calciform towers made strange curlicues across the sky. They seemed to move whenever I looked at them. I couldn't gauge distances. The towers could have been rock formations or, for all I could tell, high waves on stormy seas. The ground dipped and rose under my feet before I saw it. This was the first time I'd felt seasick inland.

There's usually no more beautiful night sky than the dry Texas desert. It had been one of the few things I'd unambiguously been looking forward to coming home and seeing. With no big sources of light pollution for miles around, you didn't just see stars. You saw a *river*, a cascade of light flowing from one horizon to the next, a million million stars…

The haze took that sky from me. All I saw when I looked up was a pale gray cloud, the color of ash. An astral boneyard, luminous but dead.

I suppose even the unfiltered starscape wouldn't have been the same. I've never been off-planet, but I've had enough brushes with the celestial[13] to know about all the galactic empires out there, the planet-eaters, and the battles between gods and aliens and progenitors.

A lot of what I saw when I looked at the stars now was chaos and danger and things I didn't want to think about. So many of the stars were dead and devoured, and only their light was still reaching us.

The funny thing about growing old is that you never run out of ways to do it. Some part of me had thought that, by coming back here, I'd see the skies I'd used to see when I was a kid rather than the same one I saw everywhere else.

It was a lot easier on my spirits to stay focused on footprints ahead of me, and the men I was tracking down to kill.

The haze and darkness obscured some details, but so far this wasn't a subtle game. One of the pairs of tracks was dragging, their heels scuffing along in the dirt, and sometimes stumbling. Tired already. They hadn't had time to pack for the trip. They'd left their spare clothes back at the ranch. They'd spent enough days in the desert to know how cold it got at night – damn cold – but that didn't mean they were prepared for it. *I* could handle it. Even if endurance hadn't been one of my factory-default mutant features, I'd come with heavy clothes.

---

13 Like in *Hotshots #4!* –Ed.

I had to rely on my other senses. I stepped along carefully, testing each foot before placing it. The desert night was as silent and deathly as the stars above. I heard each breath as I drew and released it, and was confident I could hear anybody within fifty feet do the same.

I'm not sure if it was some combination of those senses or instinct that first told me something was wrong.

After several seconds of stifled breathing and watery blinking, more of the land around me resolved. The gang's footsteps wandered up a shallow slope and between two rounded rock walls.

The terrain had become steadily rockier. I'd come close to losing the gang's trail a couple times as they'd passed over bare stone. In fact, *that* was what had stopped me in my tracks. The slope leading into the valley had plenty of rocky surfaces. They'd chosen a sandy path to go up instead, where their tracks were easier to see.

Definitely a trap.

In spite of myself – heck, in spite of everything – I grinned.

I turned away from their trail. Instead, I trod lightly over to one of the rock walls, and felt along for a path that seemed climbable or walkable. It only took a few false starts before I was silently pulling my way up. I moved so slowly that someone like Neena would have gone out of her mind if she were here. She never took things slow. The first kind of fight she'd trained herself to get through had been a brawl. But the first time I'd held a gun, it had been on a hunt.

I had to move like a snail to keep my breathing low and stifled, while keeping my ears open for the slightest indrawn breath. I climbed one-handed. Any time I put pressure on my bad arm, I came close to gasping in pain. Too much of that, and I wouldn't be able to resist.

But I got where I was going. I was patient. I had no doubt my quarry was, too.

I lost track of time. Had my vision been better, I could have traced the stars across the sky, and told you how many minutes or hours I'd spent carefully pulling myself over the chalky rock wall. I may not have been moving very fast, but my mind was racing.

There were so many things to focus on and consider with each step: the rock under my feet, the feel of the grit through my soles, how likely each footstep was to make noise, the shapes of the shadows around me, all the places where a person might have been hiding, and how visible my silhouette against the stars appeared from different vantage points.

If there was anyone waiting in the shallow valley below, looking up at the right moment, they could have seen me outlined against the sky. I kept those moments to a minimum, and I doubted there was anybody down there anyway. The trap only made sense if they'd planned on luring me down that path and then taking advantage of the higher ground.

All the aches in my body hated taking things slow even more than they'd hated riding Wheezer. The truth was, though, that I felt better than I had in ages – since before I'd started having my exhaustion and concentration problems. I was at the peak of my game. I was doing what I'd trained all my life to do. And I was about to make someone very, very sorry they had chosen me to mess with.

Very gradually, I became aware that I was hearing more breathing than my own.

There was someone just ahead. They were crouched against the lip of the canyon wall. No – laying prone. There was a long, lanky shadow hunched on the ground, shivering. A long, slender rifle barrel rested on the rock.

The sniper's breath was stilted, halting. Whoever they were, they were freezing their butt off and trying not to draw in too much air because of it. Their clothes rustled as they trembled.

If I'd followed the obvious tracks, the shooter would have seen me stumbling into the valley. Easiest shot in the world.

Except for the shot I could have made right then.

I set my palm on my left-hand revolver. Reconsidered. If I took this man out, the shot would let all his partners know where I was.

Frankly, there's no point in having a cake if you can't eat it, too. Sneaking up on someone and silently killing them was a lot more difficult than they make it seem in movies. But it was far from impossible. I'd done it before. It would have been nice to prove – to them, to myself, to the stars above – that I could do it again.

But being a merc had trained me to always have a backup plan. I kept my hand on my revolver as I crept forward. I measured each step carefully, and placed my weight softly. Eventually, I was standing right above him. Despite the cold, I was slick with sweat. He could have jerked his elbow and hit my ankle, but he was too focused on the canyon.

From this close, I recognized this man's blond hair. This was the one who'd looked so pitifully timid next to his partners, with the golden complexion. His breath steamed in front of him.

I flexed my fingers, held my own breath, and sized up the angles.

Then, in one movement, I clamped my hand over his mouth and jaw, and, with all the mutant strength I could muster, jerked his head hard into a direction his neck couldn't support. The snap came quick, easy, and satisfying.

I breathed out.

Pain exploded from the base of my skull. I careened forward with a gasp of surprise and colors kaleidoscoping across my vision.

I hardly had time to realize what had happened – *someone had clubbed me* – when another set of hands grabbed the scruff of my jacket and yanked me back. My assailant had been waiting for me. They'd gotten as close to me as I'd gotten to the sniper lying beneath me. I'd never heard them.

"First rule of a good con," Wolfram hissed in my ear. "Always let the mark think they're the smart one."

ELEVEN

I didn't know how Wolfram had gotten this over on me, and I didn't have time to think about it. His taking the energy to speak was the first mistake I'd seen him make. It was a small one, but it gave me just enough time to twist left, before the next blow.

His fist struck my shoulder rather than my head. My bad shoulder.

For a moment, I lost track of where I was. I was adrift on a sea of starry haze and mind-shattering agony. It hurt so much I couldn't tell which way was up, and for a lurching, nauseating moment, the dead-but-luminous sky was underneath me.

I really *was* falling. By reflex, I'd pushed myself in what had seemed like the only safe direction: away from Wolfram. Over the cliff.

It was a short fall. Only a second or so. I landed hard on my safe side. Good thing, too – even with mutant endurance, if I'd hit my wounded shoulder, I probably would have fainted. As it was, I got scraped up pretty bad. When my forehead cracked into the ground, for a moment I thought I could see clearly again – but, no, the stars dancing in front of me were just the after-effects of the blow. They were as sharply defined as the rest of the world was blurry.

But I was still Inez Temple, and it was going to take more than that to drop me.

My momentum kept me rolling when I hit the dirt. On the second roll, I braced my knee to stop myself, and pushed half-upright. One of my ammo pouches had caught on something and torn, and I was going to have some rifle-stock-shaped bruises on my back, but everything else had held. The first weapon my hands found was Dad's self-defense Beretta.

I'm a quick draw, but I have limits. I was still dizzy from the fall, and could only draw one-handed. It took me a second too long to aim.

A tall silhouette stood atop the cliff. Not Wolfram. It was too thin. I boggled as I recognized the sound of the blond man's wheezing breath. The breath he shouldn't have been able to draw at all.

With strange and drooping grace, like a melting candle, my target slipped from the wall. He didn't so much jump as *flow*.

I backpedaled. I had no choice but to put myself in the same spot that would have made me an easy target earlier. There was nowhere else to go.

A grunt in the dark betrayed where he'd landed. I made a guess as to his position, and lashed out with my foot. I kicked him square in the chest. I'd been aiming for his face, expecting it to be low, but he hadn't even crouched when he'd struck ground. He stepped back, but that was all. I didn't hear an expulsion of air that would have meant I'd winded him.

"Who are you?" I asked, backing away.

My first thought had been that Johnny Dee had possessed this man. But that couldn't be true. Johnny Dee couldn't raise the dead, couldn't do – whatever this man had done to himself to get here. And when he spoke, he didn't have Johnny Dee's cadence, either.

"I was really, really hoping you wouldn't come after us." He sounded broken, upset.

I would have sworn he was at least three arms' lengths away from me, but his fist crashed into my face.

The punch was nothing compared to what the fall had already done to me. It just made the dancing stars spin a little faster. I took a step back more from shock than pain.

If I hadn't seen him get back up after I was sure – *beyond* sure – that I had snapped his neck, I would have thought that, between my bad vision and the dark, I'd underestimated the distance between us. But I'd tangled with a lot of metahumans in my time. I knew for sure I was facing one now.

So when he took a step forward, even though the distance between us didn't seem like brawling range yet, I was ready. I bent backward, rolled my head so that his next blow glanced off my chin – and then I snapped my hand up and grabbed his wrist. I yanked him toward me.

He stumbled, but only for half a second. Then his wrist *shifted*. With a dozen painful-sounding *cracks* and *pops*, the bones flexed and bent in directions that should have broken them, and maybe did.

With nauseating fluidity, his tendons rippled under my fingers, and melted away, reforming in what had once been his palm. His fingers bent backwards and curled around my wrist.

With his newly reversed hand, he grabbed mine, and tugged me off-balance.

Now, I have a pretty strong stomach, but I'd be lying if I said I wasn't horrified. My guts lurched. What he'd just done felt as painful as everything that had happened to *me* today, combined. The biggest *snap* had come from a clean, spontaneous fracture across his knuckles as his fingers had bent backwards. Now those same metacarpals felt as solid as my own. He hadn't made a peep, not even a grunt. He was reconfiguring himself, his whole body. I'd only felt his bones do it, but I wouldn't have been surprised if the rest of him could, too.

Given this gang's interest in *me*, I put nine out of ten odds on this man being a mutant, too.

He hit me again, surprisingly lightly. The punch landed in the middle of my nose. I was already backpedaling from revulsion, but the blow wouldn't have made me move on its own. The sweat on my hand let me slip free. Rather than press his advantage, he took a step back.

From this angle, my opponent made a clearer silhouette. His leg shifted back, much farther than it should have. But it didn't stretch, not exactly. He was no Mister Fantastic. His leg seemed to flow *up* his thigh – I winced at the sound of grinding femur – and his ankle and heel disjointed almost to a straight line. That plus his height gave him a step twice as far as I could have made.

Thing was, he wasn't particularly fast or strong. He probably relied on revulsion and surprise to carry him in combat. Those had worked on me – to a point.

I danced closer to him, sidestepped the punch I knew was coming, spun on my heel, and landed a whirling kick in his gut.

He might have had a healing factor, but it didn't seem to be as fast as someone like Wolverine's. I bet it needed conscious control to manage. If I moved fast, I might overwhelm it. I was rewarded with a pained *whuff* of air, and the feel of flesh underneath my heel.

"No, please–" he started to say, with a strangely choked cry.

I wound up for a punch, but then his fist cracked into my chin. This punch was much, much harder than the last. My momentum faltered.

In astonishingly rapid succession, he landed hits on my forehead, the bridge of my nose, and my good shoulder. I braced that shoulder toward him to protect my weak side, and tried to hold my ground.

The weak punches were all gone. He'd been holding back on me. These were full-powered MMA moves. If I'd been in peak shape, I could have fought punch for punch. My left shoulder and left arm were singing a symphony of agony just from what I'd done so far.

The best I could do was the unexpected. I slammed forward, ramming my good shoulder just underneath his sternum. It knocked the wind out of him. I stepped back. He moved again to swing at me, but raw medical fact took over. He didn't have the energy to keep going. He backed off to catch his breath.

Something dangling from his belt, rounded and metal, caught the starlight. It made the sound of a chain *clinking*. Handcuffs, I realized. These men intended to capture me.

I would have preferred that they just kill me.

I didn't want to show how badly I needed air, too, but I couldn't help gulping for it. "You have a name, so I'll have something to put on your tombstone?" I asked.

"He's just told us his name is Josh," he said. "Haven't been able to get anything else out of him."

My breath caught. That voice had come from him, but, at the same time, sounded nothing like he had just a moment ago.

He came at me again: fast, hateful, and cruel. Punch to the jaw. Another blow at a physically impossible angle to my temple. He tried to grab my right arm, spin me around to get at my wounded side, but I slipped away just in time. That didn't get me any respite, though. In my haste, I'd jerked my chin too high, and the next strike landed square in my neck.

I'd written off Johnny Dee too early. He hadn't been controlling this man at the start of this, but he sure was now.

I choked, and nearly fell to my knees. The blond man hadn't just become a vicious fighter, but a stiff one. He held his arms too straight, and didn't make use of his uncanny skeleton as often as he might have. But he fought like exhaustion and muscle tolerance didn't matter to him. And they *wouldn't* have mattered to Johnny Dee. Just like Johnny Dee hadn't had to feel Milos' agony as he'd died.

No, please, my opponent had said. He hadn't been baiting me. He hadn't even been talking to me.

He didn't want to be doing this. He was a hostage.

I wasn't a coward, but I was sensible. So I did the only sensible thing: I ran.

I didn't get as far as I'd hoped. I made it a hundred yards up the slope, where one of the rock walls fell away and opened into a deep, dark pit of a crevice. Then the fact that I couldn't breathe well caught up with me. (Honestly, it should have felled me much earlier, but, well, mutant. It's hard to tell the difference between super-endurance and super-stubbornness. Cussedness is a super-power.) But my pace finally flagged, just a little. It was enough for Johnny Dee's vessel to catch up with me.

He crashed into me, latching onto my back. A flurry of three or four elbows jabbed into my sides. I didn't want to think too hard about how his body was contorting to make *that* possible. We tipped to the ground in a tangle of limbs. I tried to lever myself up, but for once Johnny Dee did something clever with his victim's abilities. His leg snapped in so many places that it seemed to turn to jelly, wrapped around mine, and then resolidified as a tangled chain of bone.

"Of course, we're also thinking about naming him the Freak," my attacker rasped. Johnny Dee's words. "It's what most of us call him anyway."

"You think your friends call you anything different?" I asked.

"I *am* different," he snarled. I couldn't miss the sudden defensiveness.

My bad arm was caught painfully underneath me. He grabbed my other wrist, and tried to keep me pinned long enough to take one of his hands off. I tried to buck him off, but I didn't have a good angle, and the pain from my shoulder was sapping my strength.

"You know we found him working with the Reavers," Johnny Dee said, as if he was making casual conversation. I knew about the Reavers. One of many organized anti-mutant groups. "He hates muties just as much as I do. Kinda makes us one of a kind, don't you think?"

I didn't have the breath to answer. Then I heard the clink of those handcuffs. A bolt of terror coursed through me. I *wasn't* going to become Johnny Dee's prisoner. I tried again to throw him off me, but succeeded only in dislodging his grip. The spiked bone corkscrew stayed tight around my leg.

My free hand scrabbled over to open air. We had landed close to the open ledge. I couldn't see how far down it went.

I didn't know my attacker. He was a mask Johnny Dee wore. But I'd seen glimpses of the person underneath. I couldn't forget the way those dishes back home had been washed and stacked. Someone had been trying to carve out their own little corner there, find a little bit of peace. Someone who really hadn't wanted to be there. The first punches he'd thrown at me tonight had been soft as kisses, like he'd been performing for an audience watching us from above… or trying to warn me off.

I didn't know *that* man very well. But if he felt anything like I did at this moment, he would rather die than let Johnny Dee keep having his way with him.

It was all I had to go on.

"Sorry," I told him, "but not sorry."

I grabbed the vertical face of the cliff, and, with my last burst of energy and for the second time that night, I pushed myself toward the void. Johnny Dee, his puppet still clambered onto my back, didn't seem to realize what was happening until the darkness swallowed us both.

The second fall of the night turned out to be a lot longer than the first.

TWELVE

I hadn't been in great shape when I'd joined Neena's posse – physically, spiritually, or morally. She'd found me in some godforsaken Oklahoma-bordering hellhole, the kind of small town where people mistake drinking for culture. When I'd been younger, I'd thought that was everything I'd ever wanted from the outside world.

I'd blown into town as a bodyguard-for-hire for a man who, as it turned out, hadn't intended to pay me afterward. Neena – funny coincidence! – was there to kill him. After Neena showed me proof of his ill intent, we put both of our heads together to resolve this impasse and, *why, what do you know,* the numbers worked out better for the both of us if I betrayed my employer. I started working with her.[14]

I understand now that she was trying to take me under her wing. She wasn't *that* much older than me, but she had ten times the mercing experience. I would have resented her tutelage if I'd figured out what she was doing but, for someone who cusses and kills as much as she does, she can be surprisingly tactful.

---

14 You can read more about Outlaw, Domino, and Diamondback's first meeting, and showdown with the despicable Professor Salvage, in *Domino Annual #1!* –Ed.

Before then, I'd always felt the best mercs were cold and hardhearted. That was who I'd tried to be. That was, at first blush, who I'd thought Neena was. But she'd taught me a few more things besides being more discerning about who I hired on with. Even in a profession like ours, conscience is essential. *Without* conscience, you're something less than a merc. You're a monster. Or just a henchman with delusions of grandeur.

Never hire a heartless merc unless you're in the market for either of those. In which case, there are more efficient ways to get them.

I'd blacked out. Suffered a flashback. Never a good sign. Honestly, I'd taken so much head trauma in this business, I was surprised my brain hadn't liquefied and poured out my ears.

I'd had enough sense to toss him over me, to try to arrange things so that I'd fall on him. He wouldn't have been much of a cushion, but he would have been better than nothing. His bones could obviously take punishment mine couldn't.

I didn't have the time to complete my last-minute maneuver. We crashed to the ground.

I woke with a mouth full of dust and grit mixed with blood. I spat the grit out, but fresh blood came right back in. When I opened my eyes, I saw only black. Bad sign. Then I craned my head back, and the nacreous haze of stars blurred into being. That was a better sign. Then a thunderous headache followed my moving. Bad sign again.

Voices called out of the dark. At least one – "Hey, Freak! Get back here!" – was some distance far above us.

A pain-dulled horror settled over me. I was still mashed against my opponent.

His breathing was ragged, but he was very much alive. I heard a steady *click-click-click* like knitting needles as his bones fused themselves back together.

At the beginning of my career, I would've thought myself weak for sticking around with my attacker. But I wouldn't have left him. At least, I don't want to think I was ever the kind of person who would have left him. It took me quite a while of working as a merc to figure out that it took *more* strength to stay than to go. All my instincts, every bolt of fear in my body, wanted me to get the hell out of there.

But they were calling for him. If Johnny Dee was still in control of him, they wouldn't need to do that.

The other reason why you never hire a heartless merc is that they rarely test their courage. Cowards, the lot of them. You *have* to have a conscience to stand your ground when every other part of you is screaming to run.

I couldn't leave the fear behind, though – no more than I could the pain in my head. Another thing that I learned pretty quick when I started working with Neena is that a joke can cover up a lot of emotion I'd rather not show.

"So I'd call that a tie," I told him.

He was awake. "You're atop me," he pointed out. "Pretty sure the ref calls it for you."

I grinned, and some of the fear vanished. The rest of me hurt too much to laugh, though.

"Feeling all right?" I hazarded. What had Johnny Dee called him? Josh?

"Never better," he said. But there was a slur in his voice.

I was pretty sure I heard Johnny Dee's voice calling with all the others. In a way, though, hearing him was a good thing. It didn't seem likely that he could both search and telepathically control his puppet at once.

Johnny Dee didn't need to see his victims to control them. He saw through their eyes, heard through their ears – did everything but feel their pain. I had no doubt Johnny Dee would be controlling Josh right now if he could. Something was stopping him.

"Very sleepy," Josh said. "Would like you to get off me now." He didn't sound all that old. Late teens, maybe. Next to me, he was a kid. A tall kid, but a kid.

"Did you hit your head, big guy?"

"Mmhmm," he said, dreamily. "On the way down. Bounced off the side of the cliff."

I doubted I'd actually broken his neck earlier. He had known that I was coming and must have remolded himself so that I hadn't hit anything vital. Falling off the cliff hadn't given him time. If I had to bet, based on everything I'd seen so far, his healing factor likely needed conscious control. And energy, too. The concussion had robbed him of both.

The right side of my scalp felt warm. In the desert night chill, that probably meant blood. He seemed to have gotten it worse, though. The battered and shaken clockwork of my cognition was rattling back into order.

"Whoa, there," I told him. "Stay awake. I need you here." When the only answer he gave was a muzzy mumble, I pinched his ear. Hard.

"Owww," he whined.

I wanted to tell him to keep his voice down, but any quieter, and he might drift away. "Come on. *Stay.*" Trying to keep his mind on the situation, I asked, "Is that mangy-haired creep trying to control you right now?"

"Ohhh yeah. What's up with him, anyway? What's his– what's his problem?" He was fading away again, and so I pinched. His voice sharpened. "He's trying to control me now. Can't."

"Head injuries block him. Good to know." I remembered the scans of my brain Triage and Tempus had shown me. The centers of telepathic ability were physical structures like anything else in the brain. They could be jarred or damaged.

"He was bounced out pretty hard," Josh said. "Usually... last thing he does before leaving me is erase my memories of what he did. Didn't have time to... time... to... the time to have time..." He chuckled, finding something funny enough to hurt himself laughing. Then he winced.

I didn't have a moment to shudder at the idea that, whenever Johnny Dee had taken over my body, I'd been aware of it and not able to do anything about it. "Hurt much?" I asked.

"Just my ear," he slurred. "I'm good."

"The hell you are." Not two minutes before we'd fallen off that cliff, he'd sounded beyond scared. The only reason he wasn't now was because his judgment had been knocked as senseless as the rest of him. "Is what Johnny Dee said true? Did you used to be with the Reavers?"

"Could we not... talk about that right now?"

For the first time since Wolfram had clubbed me, I had a bare second to think. Wolfram had been armed the last time I'd seen him. I doubt he'd lost his guns or run out of ammo. He could have shot me. From where he must've been standing, he would've had a good shot. I would have been silhouetted against the sky.

He'd settled for cracking me over the head. Why? It certainly hadn't been out of concern for my welfare.

He'd wanted me for something. And I didn't have to be healthy for it. "What do Wolfram and Johnny Dee want?" I asked.

"Be evil." I rolled my eyes, but he couldn't see it. "Take over part– port– prominent mutants. Big names. Names people know, who assoth– associate with mutantkind. Commit crimes." He shrugged. "And make money."

"Was that what they were doing with me? Just… commit crimes."

"No. Doing something special to you."

"Check down there!" called a commanding voice, high above us. Malaysian accent. Rayyan. I couldn't tell if he'd heard us or just gotten lucky. Either way, time was short.

The world spun as I stood. It tried to throw me off into the galaxy of pain whirling around me. I stayed upright.

I put my good arm under Josh's shoulder. I may have been battered and dizzy, but I still had my strength. I could've carried him. Heck, I could have juggled three of him. But when I stooped to lift him, he pushed me away, and strong enough to let me know he was serious.

"He's getting closer to stealing me again. I can feel him sinking his teeth into me." I couldn't see him smile, but I could hear it in his voice. "Good news, I guess, as it means I'm recovering. My healing ability's coming back. Can't really control it sometimes."

"In other circumstances, that'd be a real neat power."

"You don't know the half of it."

I couldn't see much of him in the dark. But if I *could* have seen, I bet I would have seen his cuts and scrapes start to close, and bruises ooze back under his skin.

Josh didn't deserve any of what was happening to him. If Johnny Dee got his tentacles back into him, I didn't know that I could save him. Another blow to the head might knock him out, but at the price of a life-threatening concussion.

I felt terrible, and not just from the fall. I didn't know what I could do for him. I was inadequate. If Neena were here, she could have thought of something.

A bare handful of minutes ago, I'd snapped his neck. Now the thought of abandoning him to these vicious, lowdown, jumped-up goons felt like the most shameful thing I could have done.

But he was right. I had to go. I couldn't fight Johnny Dee using a living puppet as both combatant and hostage.

I couldn't think of anything else to do. I really must have been getting old. I'd never failed at anything as hard as I'd failed tonight.

"Stay strong," I said. I brushed my hand across his forehead, hoping it wouldn't be the last kind touch he'd ever feel.

'Course, he had to ruin the moment by saying, "Yes, Mom." His voice was just slurred enough that I couldn't tell if he was hallucinating or being sarcastic.

Still, the irritation distracted me from the many pains, physical and otherwise, of running. For a while, anyway.

When my body gave up on running, I staggered-walked a good distance – long enough for the sky to turn the wan gray color of the grave. Then my injuries caught up with me.

Well – that wasn't quite true. They'd always been with me. They made my head spin so much that I couldn't move in a straight line. They jabbed spurs into my bones every time I took a step. But it wasn't until that predawn, however many hours since I'd left Josh, that the rest of my body kindly tapped me on the shoulder to let me know I couldn't go on.

It wasn't a feeling I got all that often. Last time had been… well, I don't think it *had* ever happened before. I'd always been too cussed to quit.

I wondered if that was one of the signs of growing old – losing your cussedness. That would have been one super-power down. The most important one.

I'd stumbled from tragedy to disaster with nothing to show for it. Three months ago, I was fine. A week ago, I thought I was fine. Yesterday, I thought I was on my way to healing. Every time I'd set to climb myself out of a pit, I'd stumbled into a deeper, darker one. I'd landed knee-deep in a nest of snakes. I'd left a mutant hostage to murderers and monsters.

My body was kind enough to give me time to find shelter, but its ultimatum stood.

I had no idea how far I'd traveled, or in what direction. I was surrounded by strange land formations, half-eroded and punched through with uncannily smooth holes. They towered around me. The rest was flat desert. It was a contradiction of a landscape, lunar in theme if not in realism, like a matte-painted background from a 50s sci-fi movie. I had no doubt the rock was beautifully layered in red, orange, and yellow, telling tall tales of thousands of years, but all the predawn showed me was black and gray.

I crawled a little bit up one of the taller of the spires, over the rim of an eons-old depression. It was more a bowl than a cave, but it was all I could manage. Its taller side was facing east, which was enough.

I would have loved to catch some of the dawn's rays, although not for long. If I fell asleep under the desert sun, I could wake up burnt so bad I had blisters. The air would warm soon enough anyway. I bundled my tattered and dust-smeared coat over me, and huddled at the bottom.

If I'd been concussed, and I certainly hurt like I had been, the most dangerous thing for me to do was fall asleep. I should have been fighting against that as hard as I could, just like I'd made Josh stay awake.

But I didn't have that kind of fight in me anymore. I fell asleep immediately.

One thing you should know about merc life: the moment you think things are at their worst, something even more awful comes along, just to prove you wrong. There's nothing this lifestyle likes doing more than kicking you while you're down.

Icy tendrils pushed into the back of my sleep. I tossed and twisted. Even in my deadened, dreamless slumber, I knew the feeling.

Johnny Dee's clammy mental grasp, squeezing tight around the back of my brain.

THIRTEEN

I jolted awake. The feeling of Johnny Dee's tentacles slipped away like worms sliding between my fingers. It was one of the most nauseating things I'd felt, and I would have thrown up right then if I'd had anything to eat in the past several hours.

I'm no stranger to a good hangover. This was like that times ten. Midmorning sky pried through my eyelids even with my arm cast over my face. My throat was as parched as the rock I lay on. And my headache was an unholy synthesis of dehydration, concussion and the stress of prolonged terror.

None of it had been as bad as those tentacles. They'd felt as real and slimy as the ones sprouting from Johnny Dee's chest. I waited for the puppet strings to tighten around my limbs.

Nothing happened. For the time being, I was still myself.

But I sure hadn't imagined that feeling.

I woke up with my eyes irritated and wet, like they'd been watering all night. No surprise, given how scratched-up they'd gotten. But, to my relief, what I *could* see was clearer. Some of the grit still in my eyes must have shaken loose, and my eyes had healed around them. It wasn't all gone, but it was better.

In daylight, and with a little less fuzz in my eyes, the landscape no longer looked like an alien planet. Color flooded everywhere. Brown, burgundy, pale tan, and yellow-white limestone. Something about the rock towers tickled the back of my mind. I didn't have the spare capacity to chase that thought, though.

I squinted into the open sky. I hoped Elias was safe. I hoped, just as fervently, that he had gotten a message through – and that, sometime soon, I'd see Shoon'kwa's airship up there.

For now, I was alone.

It belatedly occurred to me that I'd betrayed Wheezer. I was heading away from the direction I'd left her. Too late to change course now.

I had no idea how long I had left to myself. Magik had said her shield would last three to four days, but Johnny Dee had talked about it like it would come down tomorrow. Magik *was* one of the best in her field … but she hadn't known her barrier would need to defend me against concentrated attack. I had to assume Johnny Dee was right.

I'd rested enough. No matter how much my body needed more sleep than the three to four hours it had gotten, it wasn't going to crash on me as hard as it had last night.

I still had some cussedness left after all.

Time to take stock. To my immense relief, both of my water canteens were still with me. They had leather skins but steel backing. One of them had gotten banged up pretty bad (against my thigh, *ow*), but neither of them had breached. I couldn't help myself – as soon as I tasted water, I guzzled the contents of one of the canteens in under a minute. Afterward, I felt like maybe a third of a human being again.

My protein bars had been crushed into protein dust, but *protein* was the important word. So long as I didn't think about it, the nausea of Johnny Dee's touch didn't come back. I squeezed the wrappers out over my mouth like a ketchup packet. Up to half of a human being.

Then – weapons. My hunting knife had gotten dented in one of those falls. The tip had bent over ninety degrees inward, leaving it about as useful as a can opener. But the pocketknife was fine. More worrying was all the ammunition that had spilled last night. All I had left for Dad's Beretta was what was loaded in it. I found two loose bullets for the rifle floating around in my other pocket. My revolvers were fine, miraculously.

What shouldn't have stung as much as it did was that I'd lost Dad's hat. I hardly went anywhere without a hat, and I *needed* it out here. But it was gone. Dad would have said, kindly, that there was no use crying over something lost. And he would've been right. But I still didn't feel like myself without it.

My bandages were dry, at least. The wound hadn't bled again. That was the end of the good news. My arm was now so stiff it felt like somebody had stolen it overnight and bolted a plank of wood onto my shoulder. It hurt worse than Thanos's ego after that time Squirrel Girl beat him. Worse than Black Widow's catsuit-chafe. Worse than that time I'd heard Tony Stark's self-sealing armor had come down too close to his chest and pinched his nipple.[15]

That was something else that kept me from feeling like myself. I didn't have anybody to share witty analogies with.

---

15 We can neither confirm nor deny that this happened. –Ed.

I triple-checked my revolvers, made sure nothing had jostled loose in the chambers, and clicked their cylinders into place. I was a hunter again.

A hunter chasing hunters. In my concussed stupor last night, I'd apparently retained enough sense to scramble over rocks, and to scuff my trail passing over sand... though I could remember doing either of those things.

But I had not been retracing my steps for long before I found other bootprints passing over mine.

There were four pairs of them. They included Josh's... once again Johnny Dee's hostage and puppet.

A dim memory resurfaced. At one point last night, I'd left some obvious tracks as a feint. I'd gone into a dry creek bed leading toward a rocky gulch, and then scuffed out my backtracking. It had worked. The gang's footprints led right toward the creek bed.

They'd followed the creek bed for a while and then left, still heading toward the gulch. By the time they'd reached this point, they must have realized they'd lost my trail, but they neither stopped nor slowed. They just kept marching.

Maybe they'd given up following me. They might have figured out that, if they made their tracks obvious enough, I'd be following *them*.

They didn't have to chase me. If they couldn't find me, all they had to do was wait me out. Magik's telepathic shield would die, and then Johnny Dee would have me.

The desert morning was absolutely still. Yesterday, crawling along the top of that cliff, I'd imagined I could have heard anyone's breath from fifty yards off. Today, unvarnished by the surety of my own superiority, I knew what the quiet meant.

Anyone lying in wait would be able to hear *me* from even farther away. My heartbeat was a drumbeat in my ears.

Worse, though, was a static that started to fill my ears. It was dreadful and pounding, like a headache if it were turned into a sound. Sometimes it was a car radio stuck between stations – I kept hearing fragments of voices caught between screeches and howls and harsh staccato pops.

It didn't take me long to figure out the static wasn't natural.

Johnny Dee's voice said, "–have her."

I couldn't help it. I froze in place. It was like the icicles sinking into my spine were real, and jamming my nerves.

I recognized Josh's voice: "–can't be worth it to you guys–"

Then there was a static pop harsher than all the others, as heavy as a physical blow. Wolfram. "Stay *quiet*, you little sh–"

"I know where she is now," Johnny Dee.

Silence. A long silence, full of muted static.

Then: "Hi, Outlaw."

"Johnny Dee," I said.

He confirmed what I was afraid of, that he could hear me, when he said, "I'm… thrilled you remember me. Last time, we weren't face-to-face all that long."

"Yeah, well. Just luck. As mutant-hating psychopaths go, you were pretty forgettable." A little black lie. I never could have forgotten anyone who'd violated me like Johnny Dee had. My grudges were as immortal as the eons of fossils under my feet.

But I wanted to piss him off. See if I could prompt some unforced errors. It wasn't like he would do anything worse to me than he was already planning.

"What's your deal, anyway?" I asked him, echoing Josh. "I

can make a guess. You hate yourself as much as the rest of us hate you, but you've convinced yourself the problem is that you're mutant, not that you're just a garden variety scumsucker."

He didn't snap at the bait, but even through the telepathic static, I heard the anger mounting. "You really ought to be nice to me."

"Gonna wish me into the cornfield if I don't, you overgrown, overpowered brat? You can't control me right now, or you already would be."

I'd always felt a good offense made up for a weak defense. For a few seconds, he was quiet enough that I thought it had worked.

Then he said, "I can feel how scared you are, Outlaw."

I blew air through my nose, but didn't bother arguing it. If he really could sense my emotions, then denial would make me look worse. "What've you been up to, Johnny Dee? Your powers didn't used to work like this." I'd always thought of him as more of a puppeteer than a proper telepath.

The moment I asked the question, though, I started second-guessing. Johnny Dee could puppet people from a distance, which meant he had to see through their eyes, and hear what they heard. Some kind of telepathy *had* to be involved.

When I'd first realized that it was *his* pull that had pointed me home, not my own fatal nostalgia, I thought I'd had it all figured out: our telepathy was one-way, from him to me. He tried to puppet me, to give me commands, and I just received them.

But I hadn't been thinking about that carefully enough. I had to be *sending* something back if he were receiving sight and sound from me. At the New Charles Xavier Institute,

Triage had looked at the scan of my brain confidently, like he'd seen this a dozen times before. He worked with telepaths; he knew what a fully-functioning telepath's brain looked like. He'd thought I was developing telepathic abilities because *he'd* seen no reason why I couldn't both send and receive.

Two-way meant there was room for backwash. Feedback. Piggyback signals.

Carefully, very carefully, I wormed my way toward him. I wanted to see what *he* saw. Hear what he heard.

"I like to hold some things back, for surprises," he was saying.

"I've got some surprises, too. I'm looking forward to showing you."

"You know how this is going to end, Outlaw. You could be making things so much easier on yourself. We might hurt you a little less."

"You're right. I *have* been thinking a lot about how this is going to end."

I tried to slam the metaphorical phone on the hook by imagining increasingly bloody and inventive ways to kill Johnny Dee.

He didn't speak for a long while after that, but I could sense his presence. It was dull static crackling in the back of my brain.

God, but I hated telepathy. At least with smartphones, I could get the satisfaction of ending a call by smashing the damn thing against a rock. This was as awkward as a call that never ended. A real *you hang up first, no you hang up first*.

The static in my head amplified, but not enough to obscure his words. "Bit by bit, your shield is falling… bit by bit."

Thus began an intermittent series of the most agonizing conference calls in my life.

"Do you know you're everything I can't stand about mutants?" Johnny Dee asked.

This was just an example of the scintillating conversations Johnny Dee treated me to as I tracked his gang.

He kept me from thinking clearly about how I was going to keep myself from walking into a trap *this* time. No doubt that was what he wanted.

"You try so hard to blend in with normal humans," he said. "You're so sure that you're *just like them* underneath it all. You keep trying to fit in, and it never ever works. You can hardly survive out with the dregs."

"Talking about me or you?" I muttered.

The sands of the west Texas desert were never so loose that they fit what most folks imagined when they thought "desert." What they had in mind was really more Saharan. There were no dunes here. This sand only got more tightly packed and brown as I went on. An anomalous rain must have spritzed through like a dog shaking off after a bath.

I tried to put Johnny Dee out of my mind and focus on where I was going. The land had teeth. I knew what it was about these rock towers that had tickled my memory earlier. One of the many mistakes people make about me is to think I don't like to learn, or that I know nothing. Dad had taken Elias and me out here plenty of times – not this area in particular, but the region. Dad had been a real naturalist. He lived out here because he loved the land as intellectually as he did emotionally. I took after him in my heart, if not my career path. Just because classrooms and I didn't get along, that didn't mean I couldn't understand and appreciate.

These jutting towers were remnants of prehistoric volcanism. Millions of years ago, this whole region had been underwater. Molten rock had squeezed up through cracks and crevices in the softer seabed. Then everything around them had weathered away. The igneous columns were all that was left.

The towers were so old that they were pretty weathered themselves. They were like old tree trunks, knotted with holes. Piles of calved-off rock played the role of roots. They were a damn sight impressive up close.

And they offered plenty of cover for just about anybody to hide behind.

The gang's bootprints were headed toward the gulch, but they could have doubled back around. I kept a careful eye on the towers as I passed and stepped carefully around their bases, letting one of my revolvers lead the way. My nerves were taut as an overdrawn bow. Sweat stung my eyes, which didn't need help stinging, thank you very much.

"Getting warmer," Johnny Dee told me.

It had been a long time since I'd been out this way. This part of my world hadn't changed since the last time I'd looked at it, but, like the stars, it had... shifted. Or something inside me had changed. I didn't see the same things I used to. There was danger here, now. Ambushes.

"Colder," Johnny Dee said.

I'd lost count of the number of times my patience had snapped. "Will you shut the hell up?"

"Coldest," he said. "Damn, Outlaw. You might as well give up now."

Slowly, I let my gun drop. He was just messing with me, but, at the same time, I had to assume he saw everything I did. That may not have *always* been true, what with the way his voice sometimes faded out, but I had to proceed like he did.

It was hard to hunt under these circumstances… but not impossible. Once I was confident I was close, I'd have to leave their trail, keep my eyes on the ground. Not show Johnny Dee any landmarks he could use to pinpoint my location.

"Why'd you come to your old man's house without backup, anyway?" he asked. And then: "You weren't expecting to meet us there, were you?" As if he could sense that he was getting to me, he said, "I keep overestimating you, Outlaw. Expecting you to put two and two together. Or have any idea what you're doing. But you just keep bumbling into trouble."

"Somehow, I'm still not as deep in it as you," I said. "Your bosses hate you, you know. You should've heard what Milos had to say about 'muties' before he died."

"They're not my bosses." He sounded bitter. Good.

"They sure aren't your partners. They're using you, Johnny Dee. I don't know what for, but I bet you've seen enough that you could piece it together. Unless you're living in denial."

Silence followed. He was having to talk aloud for me to hear him, I realized. He didn't want to say too much in front of his partners.

Maybe he'd said too much already.

All the while, as he taunted me, I focused on trying to make out more from his side of the link. Shadows flitted across my vision.

At first, I tried to ignore his voice, thinking it was drowning out everything else. But I couldn't force it out. In the end, strangely, it was *focusing* on that voice that helped most. His voice gave me an anchor – something I could grab and hold onto, keep the rest of him from getting too far away. When I focused on his voice, the rest of his senses started to follow.

Shadows swam beneath my eyelids like afterimages from a camera flash. Every time I blinked, the same afterimages formed. Gradually, they resolved into a landscape –high, rocky walls, a shaded dirt floor, and the pit of an old campfire. And the shapes of men.

I was so caught up in this that I almost missed one of the more incredible things I ever found.

I followed the gang's bootprints into the rocky gulch. It was a big gash in the ground, following the course of an ancient waterway that no longer existed. The closer I got, the bigger the gulch seemed. A combination of my bad eyesight and close-to-the-ground perspective had kept me from gauging the size of it.

As the day became hotter, a breeze had drifted in. It was the kind that was just strong enough to move tumbleweeds. Not enough to cool my forehead, but enough to kick up a curtain of dust. As it lifted, I halted in my tracks, certain I was hallucinating.

I was looking down on a stone city.

FOURTEEN

I rubbed my eyes, looked again. The city was still there. But the perspective was off. For a moment, I thought I was looking at it from very far above. I swayed dizzily before I realized what I was seeing. The buildings were a lot smaller than I was accustomed to.

Some of them were carved right out of the cliff face, and others were made from quarried rock. Long, dusty years had painted them the same knobbly texture as the limestone around them. Some were missing roofs or walls. It was ancient, and gorgeous.

I couldn't find my breath. I had severely underestimated the size of this depression. From a distance, it had looked like a faceless gulch. But "gulch" wasn't the right word. It was actually part of a deeper, more complex system, the true extent of which the horizon still hid from me.

For a moment I forgot all my aches and pains. I stood there, dust swirling around my ankles, in awe. Then I saw all the shadows and blind corners. Lots of hiding places.

An escarpment path led downward. The bootprints tracked

down it. I had to follow them into what I now realized was a canyon. Sidetracking would have taken hours that I didn't have.

With one hand on a revolver and the other held out to steady myself, I started downward.

The stone dwellings weren't on the canyon floor. They perched in the middle, on a shelf overlooking the rest of the canyon. A nice and defensible position. Anyone attacking whoever had lived here could only have entered from a handful of directions, each of which involved a precarious climb. This was the easiest-looking path, and I still had to fight for balance.

A high and sturdy rock wall, hardly touched by time, guarded the path. It had a single carved entrance. Gun ready, checking each corner as I passed, I found nothing but shadows.

Before colonization, this area had been inhabited by a whole bunch of different indigenous people. A lot of Mogollon and Pueblo peoples built cliff dwellings like this. I didn't remember any being discovered around here, but, hell, I didn't stay up-to-date on archaeological digs. Just because I liked to learn, that didn't mean I was an encyclopedia.

Some of the shock of the beauty was wearing away. This whole place had a stink of invasion. It would've been hard for anyone to eke out a living up here. No space for pasture or crops, and poor hunting above. This was a redoubt. A place where people came to shelter during a storm, or where invaders might retreat to while waiting for reinforcements against hostile locals.

Someone had set up plastic placards inside most of the structures. I picked one up. It declared that this "archaeological site was left preserved for future investigation" and promised retribution by some state code or other if the site was disturbed.

I set it carefully back in place. Hey, I can be respectful.

In the next dwelling over, an identical placard lay upside-down in the corner. Someone must have picked it up to read, as I had, and then tossed it away.

Dad would have loved to see this place. He'd taken Elias and me all the way out to see Mesa Verde once. And while this place was nowhere near as big as those castles, it still would have left him floored, and spending hours filling up the memory on his camera.

"Who was he?" Johnny Dee asked, so suddenly that I whirled around with my gun already in hand.

Nobody. Johnny Dee's mocking chuckle echoed through our telepathic link.

"You must've loved him quite a bit if you're feeling that way about him," he said.

I didn't like what this implied. It was more than my senses that he'd gotten into. He was poking through my *thoughts*. He'd traced them far enough down their rabbit holes to realize I'd been thinking of a specific person, a man.

My heart had skipped several beats. I felt like I needed to sit down, and for once it didn't have anything to do with the physical abuse I'd suffered. Of all the things I needed, this was the last. I stayed on my feet, just to prove to me – and to him – that I could.

"Your daddy died ugly, didn't he?" he asked.

I couldn't help it. At the mention of Dad, a hundred little flashbacks of the way he'd died played out in the back of my mind. Dad stumbling to remember my name. Getting lost in his own field, and admitting later that he'd gone out to work because he hadn't wanted to feel useless.

But there were new memories tangled up in those. Things had become entwined. Talking to Neena in that hotel room. Confessing to her. The way my friends – and everyone else – had looked at me in Tony Stark's debriefing room. How I'd felt when Triage and Tempus had pulled me over to look at that brain scan.

"You're right to be afraid of getting old," Johnny Dee said. "A mutant like you is just good for fighting. Who's gonna want you around when you can't even do that?"

"I've never been the type of gal to have a retirement plan." For as long as I'd known what I was, I didn't figure that I would be able to settle down somewhere.

"Give up while you still have some dignity left, Outlaw. Don't make us search for you like you're a lost toddler. Or like you're your old man."

He was tired of talking. He wasn't saying this because he wanted to. The cruelty was all his – but our mental link was showing me some of *his* fears, too. Wolfram's eyes were hot lead weights. Johnny Dee squirmed under them. Wolfram must have ordered him to keep up contact with me.

I thought about mentioning it, but that would have given away the game. I didn't think Johnny Dee *knew* I could see the ghosts of what he did.

"Let me share with you a little bit about things, as I see them," he said. "You're trying so hard to be part of a world that would never have you. I don't know how you haven't figured out that there's no more hateful, anti-mutie people on Earth than salt-of-the-earth rural folk. Especially out here. Hell, they make *me* look tolerant, and I think the world would be better off without us."

"You know, that's the first time I've heard you talk about mutants as an *us*. Your friends been reminding you how different you are?"

He wouldn't let me change the subject, so I figured I was right. "I've caught your memories about your neighbors. You think people like that would ever have you? That they'd ever let you make nice and live next to them, knowing what you are?"

"I happen to believe people can get better, if they want to." Even Magneto, former leader of the Brotherhood of Evil Mutants – one of the mutants who'd made regular folks so frightened of us – had switched sides. "It's why I don't hold out much hope for you."

"They've never been the people you want them to be, Outlaw," he said. "Your style, the way you dress, the way you talk, your whole shtick about the Old West… the 'Old West' never existed. It's just a TV fantasy. The people who actually moved out here, the settlers and the outcasts, were even more hateful and violent than your neighbors. They would have killed you even faster. Just like they slaughtered the people who were living out here before them."

I tapped the tip of my boot against the side of one of the rock structures, just to feel it. It was plain to me now that Johnny Dee wasn't here. Neither was his gang. I was alone with the stone and the shadows.

I didn't want to have this argument with him. In large part, he wasn't wrong.

"At least I have my ideals," I said, my throat dry. Foolish or not, they were part of me. I'd even tried to talk myself out of them, more than once, but hadn't been able to do it. That was how strong they'd stuck.

They felt pretty foolish here, standing among the bones of a displaced civilization. The only comfort was that it probably hadn't been my ancestors who'd forced this village's inhabitants away. These walls had been set up to defend against attackers without gunpowder, which suggested they predated white settlement by centuries. Not that that changed the broader story.

"I'd feel bad for you if we weren't trying to kill each other, Outlaw."

I was still mostly sure he had to speak aloud to talk to me. I couldn't hear him outside this telepathic link. Either he wasn't here, or my real ears were getting their signals crossed with his telepathy. His voice sounded like he was right next to me.

Johnny Dee fell silent. I got the distinct impression, though it was hard to pin from what, that he was focused on something other than me.

I breathed out. I was going to have to watch my thoughts carefully. The last thing I needed was him figuring out that Elias was still alive. But not thinking of Elias was like not thinking of a pink Hulk. Couldn't be done. I'd done a good job of keeping Johnny Dee distracted then, but I'd need to figure out a way to keep him out of my head for good. Or make him *want* to stay out for good.

This pause gave me a chance to focus on *him*. So far, he hadn't seemed to notice me doing it.

"I'm bored of this," he complained.

Somewhere, Wolfram growled, "Tough."

"This isn't getting us anywhere. We need to go to ground, wait for her shield to fall, and then just kill her–"

"No."

The afterimages were damned elusive. They vanished whenever I tried to look at them. My real sight overwhelmed what I was getting from him. Everything was hollow, unreal, and seemed to drift from me. If this was how Johnny Dee controlled his victims, it was a miracle he'd accomplished anything at all with them. Of course, he *had* had a lifetime of practice... but I suspected I was just receiving a shadow of what he did. He had more natural telepathic ability than me.

"She's dangerous," Johnny Dee said. Then, more insistently: "She's *annoying*."

"I don't throw away assets because they're annoying," Wolfram said. "If I did, I would have chucked you to the curb long ago."

Johnny Dee fell silent. A sullen kind of silent.

That was when I realized I could feel emotions over our link, too. Johnny Dee hated Wolfram. And he knew the feeling was mutual.

The only reason they'd be working together was some greater cause... money, maybe. Anti-mutant rabblerousing. Or some plan I hadn't gotten a whiff of yet. I had to find out.

Johnny Dee turned his attention back to me. I had to pretend I hadn't just seen and heard all that. "You've been thinking so much – and not at *all* defensively, oh no – about how you have hidden depths, cowgirl." His voice sounded stronger when he meant to speak to me. "You really think you know who I am?"

"Yeah," I said, after only a moment's consideration. "I really do. So how about it, Johnny Dee? What are *you* doing this for?"

"Myself."

I blew air out my nose. "Come on. You're in too deep for that."

"I mean it. Mutantkind has been nothing but hell for me, all my life. I'd be better off without you and, honestly, so would the world. M-Day almost made mutants extinct, but there are still too many of us left. People know all about us. They know enough to hate us. And especially now that they sense weakness, they'll never leave the rest of us alone."

I'd felt more and more tired the longer I spoke with Johnny Dee, but nothing matched the exhaustion that swept over me now. "Do you mean to say that you don't want there to be mutants… *because* people will judge you for being one?"

"People are right to be afraid of mutants, Outlaw. That's the thing. How many times have different mutants come close to destroying the Earth, or enslaving humanity, or both? Prison left me with nothing but time to think about this. I'm more sure about it than ever. People aren't wrong to mistreat us, Outlaw. They treat us poorly because *we deserve it*. Mutants are a menace."

I'd never heard a mutant so calmly echo anti-mutant sentiment at me like it was the most natural thing in the world. If I hadn't needed to keep my guard up, I would have sat against one of these rock walls.

These were the same kind of things that bigots like the Reavers or the Sapien League said about us. Only Johnny Dee was talking about himself, too, when he castigated mutants. Even at the same time that he held himself above us.

Johnny Dee said Josh had been in the Reavers, once. I wondered if that was how Josh and Johnny Dee had gotten together. Mutants who hate mutants. I'd have to find that out, if I ever got the chance.

"If the rest of you weren't around," Johnny Dee said, "nobody would *need* to treat me like they do."

"You'd still be Johnny Dee," I said. My voice tasted like ash. "Can't escape that."

"Yeah, but I'm fighting for a future that can happen. You want a past that never existed. The world in westerns and country music and just… just really tacky things. I can't even begin to express to you how tacky you are."

"Hey, blow off," I told him, earnestly. At least I could get righteously angry about that rather than depressed-angry. Heck's sake, everybody's a critic.

I could make out more of Johnny Dee's surroundings. Colors came to me in flashes when I blinked. There was a cliff wall to one side, and an open drop to another. He was definitely sitting by a blackened firepit. Flakes of ash sat on the charred logs, light as snow. I'd never seen any smoke. But – of course Johnny Dee knew when I'd been sleeping, and also knew when it would have been safe to light a fire.

Wolfram sat hunched on the opposite side of the fire like an angry bobcat warding his territory. Blood marred his torn shirt sleeve. I'd hit him in the gunfight back at the ranch but, unfortunately, not severely. Rayyan looked significantly worse than the last time I'd seen him. Downright wretched, even. His neat hair disheveled, his clothes sand-coated and filthy.

He stared dead-eyed at the ground. Wilderness survival didn't agree with him – unlike Wolfram, who only looked a *little* more haggard than I'd seen him last. No sign of bedrolls or food waste. They hadn't taken much with them. No wonder Rayyan looked so spent.

Josh sat off to the side. For the first time, I got a good look at him. Blond hair, sharp chin, and still filthy from our fight.

"It was always the plan that we wouldn't keep her around forever," Johnny Dee complained to Wolfram. "Why not just off her now?" Not that he would have volunteered to kill me. Something had happened with Milos, something at the very edge of my memory. But Magik's psionic shield gave him a good excuse.

"I don't throw away a good hostage before their time," Wolfram said.

All of the others, even Josh, looked at him.

He glanced back and forth between them. "What?"

"Leaving aside what happened to Milos," the Malaysian man said, and gently, as though speaking to an especially dangerous child, "you all told me Outlaw is a nobody. A merc. Hardly famous. That's why you chose her." I have to admit, that hurt.

"Yeah, but she has friends," Wolfram said. "And it's the friends who'll pay the most."

It took every ounce of self-control I had to not twitch a muscle, or do anything that would give away to Johnny Dee that I was listening.

I knew their plan. The knowledge came not in a flash, but like a stray memory – like something I had known for so long I couldn't even remember the moment I'd learned it.

There was a place along the canyon floor that they could cover from sniper perches. By timing their ambush right, waiting until I'd gotten out in the open, they could force me to shelter behind a fallen rock, and pin me there. Then they could send in Josh. A hostage I wouldn't hurt, to take *me* hostage.

I tried to nab some clue about their bigger plans, but Johnny Dee's mind was jumping in too many different directions. I couldn't just pull out what I wanted.

His fingers stung and tingled, like he'd just gotten an electrical shock. An unwelcome memory pulsed through me: Johnny Dee crouched over his doll of Milos, twisting its neck between his fingers. A short, sharp shock of telepathic feedback had nearly thrown him back. It made him toss the doll away.

The moment of Milos' death had sent a neural shock back into Johnny Dee. It hadn't used to be like that. Johnny Dee had once killed his victims with impunity. He'd spent a lot of time in prison developing his telepathic talents, though – strengthening the bonds between him and his targets, learning to see and feel more through them. Those talents were a spigot he couldn't turn off.

His heart had raced for hours after killing Milos, and his fingers still hurt. They were symptoms of some kind of neurological shock he was trying his best to hide from the others.

Josh sat farther from the old fire than the others, like he knew he wasn't welcome there. I had a hard time making out his face, but he looked miserable. His cheeks were bruised blue and purple. My anger burned hotter. Hopefully the

"And what kind of world are you after?"

"One without mutants," he said. "Wasn't all *that* long ago that there weren't any."

"You're wrong. There's never been a world without mutants. We've always been there."

His voice turned hard as flint. "That's a lie. Mutant propaganda. There are no mutants in history books. Not in prehistory, not in ancient Rome or China. None. We're the products of a degenerate nuclear age."

He wasn't reading the right kind of histories. "Doesn't matter if they wrote us into books or not," I said. I had the fire to match Johnny Dee's flint. More fire than, until that moment, I'd known I'd still possessed. "We were *there*. Living with mutants is part of what it means to be human. And vice-versa."

"Never has been. And, soon enough, never going to be again. Your time is almost up. Your telepathic shield is almost down."

I felt Jonny Dee's fingers all over me, while they played with that doll – giant-sized, clammy with sweat, rough-skinned and careless.

But there was more. My foot was tapping the ground. Nervous energy. Johnny Dee's was doing the same, I noticed. Same rhythm, too. I'd started first. He was taking after *me*.

An idea started to percolate.

"We'll be seeing you, mutie cowgirl," he said. "Real soon."

I'd been waiting for a long time to show my hand. And to say this. No better time. I'd probably only have one shot.

Johnny Dee sat in easy reach of Dad's old sewing kit. For a moment, I was tempted. But never more than tempted. I knew what the right choice was.

"You can kiss my chapped mutie cowgirl ass," I told him.

I drew back Johnny Dee's foot, and, with a swift, hard kick, booted the case of Josh's blood samples over the cliff edge.

I reached toward the sewing kit, but it was already too late. Johnny Dee's muscles locked. Josh was the first to bolt upright. The others followed suit half a second after.

Wolfram's face was a mask of outrage, fixed on Johnny Dee. "What in Hell's name are you doing?"

Josh didn't wait to ask questions. He bolted.

I couldn't do anything more for him. Johnny Dee froze me out. He'd figured out I was there. I couldn't control his body through the link – not really. What I had done was send an impulse, and he hadn't been on guard against it. Now he was. I couldn't do it again.

Wolfram drew on Josh, but half a second too late. Josh had broken his spine into a C-shape and was running low to the ground like a cheetah, his hands almost touching dirt. Wolfram's aim was too high.

Then the doll of me slipped from Johnny Dee's fingers. The telepathic bond broke. I lurched back into my body.

Coming back to myself felt good and awful at the same time – like the relief you get after throwing up, or the hollowness from a migraine finally surrendering to pain-killers.

As far as ending long-distance conversations went, it was a trifle bit more satisfying than slamming a phone on its receiver.

I didn't have time to appreciate it. A gunshot echoed through the canyon. Unmistakably the heavy *boom* of Wolfram's pistol.

I hadn't seen the landscape around Johnny Dee clearly. Everything had all been blotches and ghostly afterimages. It had been all I could to do make out faces among those purple shadows. I didn't know if there had been cover for Josh to run to. I hoped so, but hope was all I could do.

I listened for another shot. None followed.

FIFTEEN

I'd lost the gang's tracks while I'd checked the corners and shadows of the cliff side village but picked them up again easy enough. They'd left a wide path, heading out on a downward slope. They hadn't bothered to hide themselves. They'd *wanted* me to know where they headed: down, down, down, to the lower levels of the canyon, with all its shadows, caves, and crevices.

They'd been confident. I broke into a run. I had to move fast, while they were startled and discombobulated. I chased the sound of the gunshot. The canyon didn't leave me many other directions to go.

Fast as I went, I couldn't go fast enough.

I was only minutes out from the cliffside village, on a descending escarpment a couple dozen feet off the canyon floor, when the rock wall behind me exploded in a cloud of dust and shards. I felt a needle-spray of limestone chips strike before I heard the crack of the rifle shot.

I jumped.

My legs stung when they struck the sand, but that and the adrenaline was just enough to let me know I was alive. Almost felt good.

I landed behind a broken-off chunk of a boulder. A deep scour in the earth behind it showed where it had fallen and scraped a trail, and pretty recently – "recently" here meaning the past century or so. I nestled into the divot it had carved out.

This wasn't their planned ambush site, not as Johnny Dee had pictured it. They'd had plenty of time to scout the area beforehand, though. And maybe Johnny Dee had figured out their first plan was compromised. I couldn't risk poking my head above cover just to look around. There'd been too many places where somebody could have shot at me from. The rim of the canyon, the caves in the wall, even the calved rock strewn about the bottom. But just before I jumped, I thought I'd seen motion around the shadows of the next bend in the canyon's path.

The shot I'd heard a few minutes ago had sounded farther away. My attacker must have run toward me as fast as I'd gone at them.

I shrugged off my rifle's shoulder strap and then my jacket. Then I waved the jacket over my head, above cover. A gunshot swiftly followed. I'd used this trick once before, but that had been on Milos, and the others hadn't seen it. Someone's nerves were high-strung – or they had eyesight just as bad as mine.

I didn't think high-strung or poor eyesight described Wolfram. Johnny Dee didn't fight with guns. That left Rayyan.

"Made you shoot," I shouted, gleefully.

OK, adrenaline might have been making me a little giddy.

That second shot had come from a different place than the

first. I thought I had a pretty good mental map of the battlefield now.

Wolfram had been pretty competent so far, but he made the mistake of talking. "Outlaw!" he called. "Throw out your weapons, and I'll let you talk–"

Wolfram had a weakness for talking when he shouldn't have. His voice helped me figure out where he was. That meant Rayyan was probably in the other position.

And I had one more advantage – I knew that, at least as of a few minutes ago, Wolfram hadn't committed to killing me. He also had a steady aim, which meant that I had to worry most about Rayyan. *He* was freaking out, and the most unpredictable.

I rose above the rock, whipped my rifle around, and fired in his direction.

My eyes were still bad enough to turn everything into a glassy motion blur, but my instincts were sharp. If you spend enough time sharpshooting, you learn to trust your instincts as much as your eyes. And my hearing picked up the slack where my eyes failed.

A miss. A cloud of dust erupted where I'd shot. I couldn't tell if I'd hit cliff wall or the ground. The important thing was that I forced that shooter to take cover.

It would have taken time to rechamber my rifle, and I only had a few loose bullets to spare for it, anyway. I tossed it aside. And then I leapt from cover and ran like Hela herself was snapping at my heels.

Another rifle shot split the air. Nothing touched me. No way to tell if the shot missed deliberately or by genuine accident. If Wolfram hadn't yet given up on taking me alive, he would soon.

Marvel Heroines

I ran pell-mell across the canyon. There'd been just enough time for someone practiced at this to slam another bullet into a rifle's chamber. I half-ducked, half-twisted. The sand behind me exploded in a gray cloud. A rifle shot echoed between the cliff walls. If Wolfram wasn't aiming to kill, he was certainly willing to risk it.

But I had almost made it across the canyon. My surroundings solidified from a blur. The person I'd shot at, probably Rayyan, had fired at me from the cover of a rocky cleft. The cleft wasn't deep enough to be a cave. It had no ceiling. It was a jagged crack that extended all the way up the canyon wall. Its walls and steep shadows had kept me from seeing him right away.

A metallic, scraping, clunking noise gave my attacker away: he was frantically trying to reload his rifle, and not managing very well.

I rounded the edge of the cleft and found Rayyan exactly as I'd thought he'd been: crouched over his weapon, pumping the chamber ready. He looked up, saw me, and swore. I could *taste* his fear-sweat.

Felt real good to have someone be afraid of me for a change.

I darted around the rock wall an instant before another of Wolfram's shots blasted a chunk off it. *That* shot had been aimed to kill me. Rayyan was crouched behind the cleft. He rose and aimed his rifle at me, but too late. I snatched the barrel and yanked it away from him. Then I smashed the stock into his face.

He fell backward, too stunned to cry out. He still had some fight in him, though – the fight of the desperate. I stepped beside him, angling to hook him around the neck and drag him farther into cover, but he elbowed me under my ribs and did an admirable job of making it hurt. I stuck my foot behind his ankle and shoved him into it.

The easier thing would have been to wrestle him to the ground, and count on us being too tangled up for Wolfram to shoot. But Wolfram had already shown me how little he valued his companions. So I did my opponent a favor: after tripping him, I grabbed him by the scruff of his collar before he toppled, and dragged him into the crevice.

That gave him the chance to kick my shins like a child having a tantrum. Ouch, ouch, and *youch*. One kick was hard enough to make me break out words dad wouldn't have been proud of me for using.

The kicking lasted until I got him back far enough that I could stop hauling and plant a revolver against his head. He stopped instantly.

"Sorry about the shins!" he said. "That wasn't personal."

"'S OK." My voice was slurred by the after-effects of his elbow meeting my nose. "You were just doing your job."

Several awkward seconds passed. Not very professional of me. I'd been so focused on reaching him that I'd forgotten what I'd planned to do next. He seemed content to just hang out with my gun to his head.

"Well?" I asked.

"Well – what?"

"Are you going to apologize for the rest of it, too?"

"Oh. Nah." He sniffed some blood back into his nose. "None of that was really my idea."

"You were just happy to go along with it." I'd been happy to go along with the comedy routine for a while, but time was pressing, and that answer had ticked me off. I pushed my revolver's barrel into him hard enough to tilt his head to one side.

"Hey, I'm just trying to get as far from Wolfram as I can. Guy's leapt so far off the rails that we're in the stratosphere. If he had any idea what I was going to report to my bosses, he'd kill me. You want me to switch sides? I'll switch sides. Just *protect me* from him."

"What the hell is going on here?"

"I'm just a scouting agent. I'm from the Blackguard Network."

"I think I've heard of you guys. Bigtime international crime syndicate?"

"More of a bigtime crime franchiser. Anyone who wants to use it, and get our tech and secret bank network, can set up their own branch. But they have to prove themselves first. That's why I'm here – to scout Wolfram's operation, see if it's good enough to join."

He *really* shouldn't have been telling me this. He was more scared than he was letting on. From rumors and backchannel chatter, I already knew about half of what he had told me, which was enough verification that I figured I could trust the rest.

I reduced the pressure on his temple minutely. "What's he planning? What about Johnny Dee?"

"Forget Johnny Dee. He's just a tool. Wolfram wants to use Johnny Dee to 'recruit' people, powerful people, to do his break-ins and other crimes. If they get caught or killed, well, who cares? They were just the puppets. Can't be traced back to him."

"And I was just the first mutant you chose to target." It

was taking real effort on my part to keep from cracking his skull.

Rayyan didn't seem to notice the effort I was making to restrain myself. "It seemed like a reasonable enough plan in outline," he said, like he was making casual conversation. "Creative. Not so high stakes to begin with, but lots of room for expansion. I'll admit, though, that the Blackguard Network doesn't have much experience with mutants. We didn't expect you'd be able to get help so soon, or that you'd be able to block telepathy. Wolfram wants you back under his control, bad. He should have cut his losses and run. If I can just get out of here alive, that's what I'll report back. Wolfram's too unstable. His plan's not viable. We shouldn't work with him."

"What kind of crimes were y'all maybe thinking about?"

"That's at the franchisee's discretion. I don't know, honest. Wolfram mentioned wanting to use mutants for things like bank robberies, but, gosh, doesn't that seem a little gauche to you? A little old hat?"

"It *is* a little Evil Scheming 101," I admitted. It didn't quite match with what Johnny Dee had said, either – but I suspected he and Wolfram didn't plan to be working together for long. Double-crosses always came sooner rather than later with these types.

"He has a good sense for opportunity. He did a good job getting that mutie from the Reavers and putting him to work – and was starting to do a good job with you, I suppose. He might have eventually come up with something more creative, but, to be honest, I was leaning against giving him a deal even before he started threatening the rest of us. Now I'm thinking the Blackguard Network should do more than refuse him, but should start targeting him as an enemy. Help me get out of here, and I'll help you ruin all his plans."

With the words "that mutie," any whiff of sympathy I might have had for Rayyan vanished, like a fart into a tornado. "Oh, please," I said. "You think they'd just let you go? Mind-controlling the henchman as he reports back is on the Evil Scheming 101 exams."

"No way. We're not idiots. They know to watch me when I come back. Johnny Dee needs to maintain concentration to control people. Sooner or later, he'll slip. And I've made sure Johnny Dee didn't get any scrap of my DNA."

"I bet that's what Milos thought, too. Didn't stop Johnny Dee from using Milos to chat me up, and then killing him." Johnny Dee would have had endless opportunities to collect DNA. He wouldn't need much, not if he could control me with an old hairbrush. I bet even Wolfram thought he was safe.

A pause from Rayyan. Then: "*What*?"

Something in his tone had changed. He sounded afraid in a way he hadn't before. He covered it quickly by clearing his throat, but seemed to know he'd given away too much.

He'd been acting, I realized abruptly. Playing scared. What I'd just seen had been real fear coming through. Something was up. He'd only told me so much about the Blackguard Network because he expected I wouldn't survive the next few minutes.

I figured that some of his fear had been real, like fumbling with the rifle, but this was the first time I'd heard him *shocked*. He'd been putting together a plan on the fly, improvising delays.

"Where's Johnny Dee now?" I asked, pressing my gun tighter. "Surprised he hasn't taken you over yet."

"No way. He can't. He's busy."

"Busy doing what?"

Even Rayyan seemed to realize he'd said too much. He didn't answer.

My revolver's hammer went *click* right next to his ear.

I dropped my voice, went all soft and husky and dangerous. "What does it matter if you tell me? Especially if I'm gonna kill you if you don't?"

"He's pil–"

I couldn't hear the rest because something blurred moved across the other canyon face, and I was already shooting at it.

My revolver went off right next to Rayyan's ear. He flinched away. He must've been waiting for me to take my gun away from him. In that same, swift motion, he stomped on my foot and cracked the back of his skull into my nose.

I didn't know what I'd fired at. Shooting had been a reflex. I didn't think it had been a person. It moved fast, whatever it was – shadow of a bird, maybe, or even Wolfram using my own thrown-item trick. But I didn't have time to be embarrassed about that. Whatever it was had given Rayyan his opportunity.

In an instant, he'd stopped playing dumb. He grabbed my bad arm, wrenched it, and then drove his elbow into the place where Wolfram had shot me yesterday.

I had started to heal, but I wasn't all the way there. My nerves definitely weren't ready for another blow. My vision went black and red, speckled with motes of stardust. The pulse of agony cleared just in time for me to see Wolfram step around the corner I'd seen the shadow fly over. He leveled his pistol at Rayyan and me.

My fingers twitched nervelessly, grasping empty air. The pain had been so much I'd dropped my revolver without feeling it. I still had my other weapons, the second revolver and Dad's Beretta, but didn't have time to draw either.

I still held Rayyan in front of me. He slugged my chin, but I barely felt it. All told, he hadn't had such a bad plan. But he was still an idiot. First, this had exposed him to Wolfram, a man who'd already demonstrated he had no qualms about shooting through one person to hit another. Second, and more importantly, he was trying to wrestle a mutant.

Not just any mutant. Me.

I picked him up by the back of his neck and just *threw* him at Wolfram.

I caught a glimpse of Rayyan's eyes bulging with surprise before he tumbled heels-over-head. Then Wolfram's eyes doing the same before Rayyan crashed into him.

Rayyan hit with enough force that Wolfram's feet briefly left the ground. I was pretty sure that my non-gunshot-deafened ear had heard something *pop* in Rayyan's chest, probably a rib. The sheer g-forces of the throw would have been as bad as the crash.

The impact jarred Wolfram's trigger finger. His gun discharged but the shot went wide. He and Rayyan crashed to the ground in a tangle of splayed limbs and shouting.

Somehow Wolfram had kept a grip on his gun. He was struggling to aim it at me again.

I was out of breath from the pain. That snot Rayyan had picked the right part of me to attack. But I wasn't so winded I couldn't quickdraw.

All my hours at the shooting range, practicing drawing from

the hip, fantasizing about showdowns at high noon – all of it focused in on this moment. Hell, it may have even been high noon.

I shot the pistol right out of Wolfram's hand. I did it by shooting *through* his hand.

His arm flew back in a spray of red. That Desert Eagle of his went farther, clattering across the rocky canyon floor. It clinked to a stop a dozen feet away.

Wolfram's face was a screwed-up mask of pain, and I'd be a liar if I said I didn't find that satisfying.

Rayyan tried to push himself off Wolfram. Adrenaline got him that far. But he hadn't gone farther than five feet before lack of oxygen got to him. The force of the throw alone had knocked his breath out of him, and that had been before the sudden crash at the end. Even so, he tried to claw away from me until I leveled my remaining revolver at him and Wolfram. Aside from choking for air, he froze instantly.

Johnny Dee had said I was too fond of westerns, but he was wrong – about the *too* part. This was my favorite part of the genre. The sudden reversal of fortunes. The moment when everything changes with the clap of a gunshot. Even Wolfram stopped breathing when I aimed my revolver's barrel between his eyes.

I kept my pistol raised, smirked, and advanced.

"I have some questions," I told him. "How long you live is going to be determined not just by *if* you answer, but by how well I like your answers."

Wolfram glared at me. He needed a moment to catch his breath, but, when he did, his voice was surprisingly level. "Ask."

"Is Josh safe?"

"Not for lack of trying to kill him on my part. I couldn't shoot the twerp fast enough when he ran."

Bold of him to take that tone about Josh while I had him at the end of my revolver's barrel. He *had* given me an answer I'd liked, though: Josh was still alive. I stayed my trigger finger, this time.

"Next question: when you had Johnny Dee take me over, what kind of crimes did you have me commit?"

Wolfram's eyes rolled over to Rayyan. "You told her what the plan was, huh?"

Rayyan still had some choking and gasping to do before he could speak. "I didn't figure it would matter."

"You are a guest in my party," Wolfram said. "You were here to observe. Not make decisions."

"If you hadn't taken your time coming to help me, I would have had to."

For an instant, there was nothing but murder in Wolfram's eyes. It lasted just long enough for Rayyan to see it, and then it was gone again.

"If that's the way you want it," Wolfram said. Then, ponderously: "I'll have to find it in my heart to forgive you someday."

Rayyan snapped his gaze to Wolfram. He looked just as sheet-white terrified as he had when I'd told him Johnny Dee had puppeteered Milos.

I was running out of patience with these clowns. I had one more of them to hunt. "Where's Johnny Dee?" I asked.

"I don't know where he is now," Wolfram said.

My revolver's hammer *clicked*.

Wolfram smiled at it. Just a flicker of a smile, with no mirth in it. "I figure I do know what he's up to, though. And that's double-crossing me."

"How do you figure?"

He flicked his eyes up a little, like he was looking at something behind me. Last thing in the world I was going to do was fall for that old trick.

It wasn't until I heard the whine – steady, insistent, and growing, like metal screaming against metal – that I realized something really was back there.

I spun. I wasn't too late, but only because there wasn't any such thing as *late* here. I could have turned at any point, and it wouldn't have given me any more options.

I had just enough time to see the curtain of metal and white fog barreling toward us.

Remember how I said that good mercs will always look for opportunities to make their own *deus ex machinas*? Sometimes that goes really, really wrong. It only takes a little twist of the plot to turn a *deus* into a *diabolus*. A devil sweeping in from off-stage, coming to sucker punch me.

I never saw this coming. Maybe I should have. The fact remains: I didn't.

The machine barreling toward us, skinning the side of the canyon wall, belching white thruster gases and moving too fast to stop, was Shoon'kwa's airship.

SIXTEEN

I'd hoped to see that beautiful Wakandan airship every hour I'd been stuck out here, but this was all wrong. I knew that from the sound of the engines alone. They only made that high-pitched, housefly-like whine when they were stressed. Shoon'kwa was too good a pilot to be doing that. The airship was coming in too fast and too low. As I watched, one of its wings clipped the cliff wall, sending a cascade of dust, splintered rock, and torn metal raining downward. The thunder-crack of the impact shifted the ground under my feet.

The canyon was too narrow. Half a second after the airship clipped the first wall, one of its many slender, bladed wings smashed into an outcropping jutting from the opposite side wall. The wing snapped in a shower of torn metal and sparks, and then a gout of flame as one of its fuel feed lines caught fire. An explosion rippled across the hull. The whole ship shuddered. Pieces of the wing pattered to the ground, showering smoke contrails like leaves from a willow tree.

The impact jerked the ship's nose higher. Whoever was piloting the airship had aimed it right toward us – all three of us – but that last little bit of lift knocked it oh-so-slightly off-course. If anything happened after that, I didn't see.

I covered my head and ran – not away from the airship, but *toward* it, trying to get underneath before it crashed into us.

What little time I had left to do this meant it didn't make much of a difference.

A shadow fell over me. The noise was immense, so overpowering that it wasn't really sound anymore, but a feeling: a terrible weight in my ears and a rattle in my chest. A split second of intense heat, like the gates of limbo had opened above me. It was followed, strangely, by a gust of intense, bitter cold air. So cold it hurt like fire.

Later, I figured out that a ruptured thruster feed line must have passed a few feet above me, and all those decompressed, expansion-cooled gases were spilling onto me.

Something hard and heavy smacked me in the back of the head. It sent me sprawling. My last revolver flew from my hand. Then the fist of a raging God battered me into the canyon floor.

For a while, all was noise and darkness.

When I came back to myself, rocks and other bits of smoldering metal were still falling from the sky. In fact, I think it was one of those that brought me back around – a baseball-sized conk to the noggin, a little joke from the same angry God that had swatted me down.

I smelled burning somewhere, and I hoped it wasn't my hair. Of all the things I should have worried about, my battered brain was suddenly concerned about having to wear a wig.[16] My skin felt dry as snakeskin. I'd been cooked and flash-frozen in the space of a few seconds.

By some miracle, I hadn't been hit on the head as hard as last time. That terrific headache was back, though, and I was so dizzy I didn't think I could get up. I felt like I was clinging to a tilt-a-whirl that had been sucked up in a tornado.

The sheer dread coursing through my system forced me to look up regardless.

I found exactly what I'd expected to, and it was every bit as awful as I'd feared.

Shoon'kwa's airship lay like a squashed tarantula against the next bend in the canyon – all splayed and broken limbs and wings. Its nose had smashed up against the rock and lifted in a way that the rest of the airship's sagging body couldn't support. The whole frame of the airship had crumpled around it as its momentum had tried to turn its spine into an accordion.

I knew it was a machine and didn't feel, but it hurt to look at it, the same way that a slow-motion replay of a wide receiver's ankle breaking hurt to watch. That body just wasn't meant to look like that.

Thick, oily smoke boiled out of the engine exhausts. The engine was still making that whining noise, barely perceptible over the ringing in my ears, but it faded away even as I listened. The bubbled cockpit window had shattered. Smoke poured out of that, too.

My friends were in there. In trouble. Seeing that made the

---

16 Which Outlaw has had to do, more than once! The merc lifestyle isn't easy on long hair. –Ed.

pain go away. Or at least helped me ignore it.

At the very least Shoon'kwa had to be in that cockpit. She never let anyone else pilot. I didn't know who else could have been with her. The whole posse, maybe, if they had gotten Elias's message.

A vast plume of dust and smoke occluded the sun. The sky had been cloudless before; now everything was gray as ash. I forced myself to my knees. The world spun, but not so hard that it knocked me down again. As I staggered ahead, and for the first time since the airship had crashed, I had a second to think.

Wolfram had never answered me when I'd asked him what crimes he'd had me out committing. Regular, boring old crimes like bank robberies didn't make sense. They lacked imagination. Wolfram was too cruel for that. It took imagination to be cruel like he was. That part of Rayyan's story didn't make sense. He'd been covering something. There'd been no excessive reports of break-ins or anything where I'd traveled.

Of course.

Johnny Dee and Wolfram had been having me steal, all right. But DNA samples. Other mutants' DNA.

And my friends'.

He's piloting, Rayyan had been about to say about Johnny Dee, before Wolfram had interrupted us.

A burning white rage drove me to my feet. Dizziness knocked me right to my knees again, but the rage fought back and the rage was winning. I pulled to a stoop, and then wavered to my feet... one step in front of the other, in front of the other...

When someone grabbed underneath my arm and tried to pull me back, I nearly smashed their skull. Only the gentleness of their grip kept me from doing it.

It was Josh. His fingers shifted queasily as they repositioned for a better grip. He was pulling me, carefully but firmly, away from the wreck. Ordinarily, I could have overpowered him without hardly trying. Dizzy as I was, I struggled just to stay upright.

Maybe it was the after-effects of the concussion, but I felt like I had quite a reasonable and erudite argument if only he'd listen:

"Nngh," I said.

He wasn't moved.

There was too much ringing in my ears for me to hear his rebuttal, but I was sure it wouldn't stand up to scrutiny.

In case he hadn't heard me, I restated my case: "Nrrgh! Leggo!"

He gave rational debate a second try after I tugged him to a standstill: "–can't go in there! It's on fire!"

"It's got fire suppression systems!" And they ought to have been coming online any second now. Any second–

He shook his head, but didn't try to pull me back again. I'd gotten enough of my balance back that he wouldn't have been able to, anyway. Instead, he supported my good shoulder as we staggered toward the wreck.

It took me a moment too long to realize that I was feeling better. Breathing more easily. The pain in my head was fading.

A strange warmth passed between Josh's hand and mine. When I glanced down, I caught a flicker-flash of energy crackling between us. I slowed.

He didn't just have a regeneration power. "You're a healer," I said, abruptly.

"I don't like to talk about it," he said.

He didn't have the power to reshape just his own body. He could do it to other people, too, just by touch. Not bad for an untrained talent. He had a real potential to be powerful.

For right now, though, his talents were limited. Color fled his face. He sagged, and the energy flowing between us halted. He'd been pushing himself a lot these past few days, and I doubted Wolfram's gang had let him eat or sleep well. I still wasn't in great shape. My ears rang, my eyes remained scratched and blurry, and I was covered in cuts and bruises. But I could think and speak coherently.

"Where'd you come from?" I asked him.

"From hiding," he said, with a tone of voice that suggested it would have been nuts to expect him to have been anywhere else. "Hard to miss something like this happening. Came here and found you."

"Just me? Where's–"

My senses were so well attuned to the *click* of a revolver's hammer that I heard it above the dying whine of Shoon'kwa's engines. I instinctively spun, placing myself between the sound and Josh.

It was Rayyan. He haltingly levered himself up from behind a fragment of twisted hull plating. His clothes were blackened and his hair was singed, but, unfortunately, he didn't seem to have been hurt worse. He'd found one of my lost revolvers. He had the tremulous glee of a bad poker player – too excited to hide the fact that he'd been dealt a good hand.

I didn't have time for this. My friends were in that airship, and probably hurt. But Rayyan had a bead on me, and there was no cover nearby.

"It looks like the Blackguard Network can at least come out of this with a couple hostages," he said. "Wonder who'll pay more, Outlaw? Your friends? Or mutant eliminationists?"

A weight on the back of my belt told me that, somehow, I'd managed to keep one last gun – Dad's old Beretta M9. But it was in a bad position to draw. Both my hands were visible, and Rayyan had a solid bead on both Josh and me.

"OK," Rayyan said, "let me tell you how this is going to go."

The center of his chest exploded in a fine red mist. The blast tore a neat hole through the center of his shirt.

Rayyan's eyes bulged. The thunderous report of the Desert Eagle echoed up and down the canyon, and set my ears ringing again.

He stumbled, his knees already failing, and turned. "I didn't think you could shoot that well with your off-hand," he said, somewhere between awe and incredulity.

"Neither did I," Wolfram growled.

Wolfram had propped himself against a boulder about fifteen yards back. His gun leaned against it, resting in his left hand.

Rayyan raised his hand as if to shoot back. Then the fact that no more oxygen was reaching his brain finally caught up with him. His heart had been pulverized. He'd been a dead man standing, running down his clock, since Wolfram's shot had landed. He collapsed.

"I should've known better than to try to link up with him,"

Wolfram said, in the same even-keeled tone he might have used to say he hadn't liked a particular brand of detergent. "Don't need anybody. Should've stayed independent."

He looked worse off than Rayyan had. It wasn't just his clothes that were charred. Some of his hair had burnt away. The scalp underneath was a web of angry red welts. And, of course, his right hand was streaming blood where I'd shot it. His clerical collar was charred, and so was the skin on his neck. I'd say that he looked as bad as I felt, but for once that would have been overselling my various miseries. Not even *I* felt that bad.

He'd braced his new gun hand against the boulder to steady it. He kept his aim on Josh and me.

As much as I couldn't stop thinking about the weight of that last gun on my belt, I kept my hands visible. Maybe if Josh hadn't been here, I would have tried my luck. Because his life was at stake, too, I had to be all responsible.

"Outlaw," Wolfram said. "I don't know that I've forgiven you yet."

"Is that good or bad?" I drawled. "I lost track."

He smirked.

That comforting weight on my belt vanished. The cool barrel of my Dad's Beretta pressed into the side of my head. A hand gripped my shoulder – not to hold me, but to let me know that whoever it was could feel any hint of my starting to move.

The hand on my shoulder was gloved, and what I could see of the sleeve was all black. I caught a glimpse of auburn hair.

Black Widow.

"How do you want to do this?" Black Widow asked Wolfram,

in a voice that was hers and also wasn't. "Shoot them here and now? Or do you still think they'll be 'of use?'" From this angle, I couldn't tell if she was banged up. There was no sign of the rest of the team.

"Bold of you to assume we're still on the same side, Johnny Dee," Wolfram said.

"That crash was more complicated than you think," Black Widow said. "They were fighting back."

"You know you can't make it on your own against the survivors," Wolfram said. "That's why you're trying to make nice with me now. Pretend you hadn't meant to kill me."

Black Widow's voice dropped dangerously. "If I wanted to betray you, I could do a lot worse to you."

"You picked your time. Now you're too cowardly to follow through."

"Hey. I never needed you. I could have gone it alone." Even speaking through Black Widow couldn't hide the tremor in Johnny Dee's voice. That was how I knew, immediately, that Wolfram was right. Johnny Dee had tried to kill *everybody* here. And now events were getting away from him, and he was second-guessing. Backing off.

Johnny Dee had an incredible power, and a lot of hate to back it up. But no guts. No follow-through.

Wolfram phrased it more succinctly: "You don't have the guts."

I risked a slight glance aside. Perhaps wisely, Johnny Dee hadn't tried to hold onto Josh. Given Josh's mutant talent, he wouldn't have had anything reliable to grab. But Josh had halted in his tracks a few steps away. He'd gone rigid from fear.

I was being held hostage for Josh's good behavior. Damn it.

I really don't do the damsel thing very well.

"I'm starting to get it," Johnny Dee said, through Black Widow. "I know why you're always so damn reluctant to kill people you should've disposed of long ago. You wanted to have extra levers against me."

"You can only control one person at a time," Wolfram said. Strangely enough, I got the idea that he wasn't talking to Johnny Dee. He wanted *me* to know this. Maybe Josh, too.

"Don't tell me things I already–" Black Widow stopped. I wondered if Johnny Dee hadn't figured out the same thing.

Out of the corner of my eye, I saw Josh inch closer. I braced for him to do something stupid. At least I knew Johnny Dee couldn't be controlling anyone else on my team right now. I just had to hope they were still alive.

Johnny Dee found Black Widow's voice again. "The more prisoners and hostages you took, the less power I had overall. So, if something happened to *you*, I wouldn't be able to control the whole operation."

"I planned to use you," Wolfram said. "I'd have been a fool to trust you."

"This would have gone so much smoother if you had," Black Widow snarled. "I'd be in control of everything now."

"You never could've handled it. You're a loser, Johnny Dee. Always have been, always will be."

Wolfram's aim shifted minutely. It was very slight, but all my battle instincts screamed that he was aiming at Black Widow. I couldn't let him shoot her any more than I could let him shoot Josh.

Damn. Surrounded by hostages. And I *was* one. Worst possible situation. No time to plan it out – I just had to act.

Luck chose just that instant to intervene. Behind Wolfram, metal clapped against metal. One of the airship's dorsal hatches had opened. I caught a glimpse of a slender figure struggling out. It had black hair with a cheeky silver streak.

Neena.

SEVENTEEN

Wolfram's attention wavered. Johnny Dee glanced toward the airship, and the noise Neena had made shoving the hatch open.

And I slammed the back of my head into Black Widow's face.

Johnny Dee didn't feel his puppets' pain. I had to aim to cause actual damage. And head injury.

My head slipped free of the Beretta's barrel. Johnny Dee reacted fast. Black Widow pulled the gun backward, and the barrel brushed the tip of my forehead. Moving faster than I could think, I grabbed Black Widow's hand and wrenched it away. I guided the Beretta's aim as near to Wolfram as I could manage.

Black Widow's finger depressed the trigger. The shot went off so close to my ear that I didn't hear it, just the agony of ringing afterward. A splash of blood blew out of Wolfram's shoulder.

Black Widow fought to point the Beretta back at me. With a whispered apology, I straightened her arm, and then slammed the heel of my palm into the back of her elbow. With a *crack* I hated to feel, her arm folded back in a way it had never meant to.

I *really* do not do the damsel thing well.

Johnny Dee may not have been able to feel his puppets' pain, but he also couldn't make their bodies work through that kind of shock. The Beretta dropped to the ground.

Then things went wrong. Well, more wrong.

All that work and luck and skill to shoot Wolfram, and he barely flinched. That's one thing about gun fights that westerns don't often show you: people don't often drop instantly when they're shot. A bullet isn't an off-switch. Even Rayyan had had a few seconds of coherent action and Wolfram had shot him right through the heart. Any pain and shock hadn't caught up with Wolfram yet. His weapon hand remained steady, propped against the boulder.

I drove my foot behind Black Widow's ankle, tried to trip her and drive both of us to the ground, but she braced herself and held firm. Josh slammed into us from the side, trying to shove us down.

My breath caught. I couldn't move in time. I was too startled. Too slow. And, in the back of my head, there was a voice that said my reflexes weren't what they used to be.

The *boom* of Wolfram's Desert Eagle echoed through the canyon an instant before Josh's body convulsively jerked.

The three of us crashed to the ground. Josh landed hard atop me, limp.

I pushed to my feet. I had no time to feel. Not while Johnny Dee was still in control of my friend's body. I hadn't even taken a breath before I rolled over, set my palm atop Black Widow's head, and slammed it into the dirt.

Difficult thing to do, give somebody a concussion without accidentally cracking their head open. I hadn't exactly practiced. I was repressing a million out-of-control emotions all at once. But, somehow, I think I managed it. Black Widow's whole body jerked, but she didn't go limp. And then, suddenly, she yelped in surprise and pain.

I didn't figure Johnny Dee could have faked pain that convincingly. Black Widow was herself again.

The firecracker report of another distant weapon echoed between the canyon walls. Wolfram shuddered. Then he exhaled, as if in relief.

The Desert Eagle slipped from his fingers. He fell facedown onto the rock.

Neena stood atop the airship, a one-handed grip on her pistol.

The distance between her and Wolfram should have been too far for a hand weapon, but I bet she hadn't even needed to aim. That was how her luck powers worked. If she consciously put herself in situations where she needed a thousand to one shot to win, she got it. Every time. I'm not jealous.[17]

I repositioned Josh, propping his feet on a rock and setting his hands on his stomach. He took great gulps of air. His forehead shone with sweat. He stared at the sky without really seeming to see it. He was in shock. His ratty, filthy shirt was deep red with fresh blood.

He may have had a healing factor, but that didn't mean he was indestructible. He wasn't Wolverine; his body had to have limits. He'd been struck in the stomach. A quick feel around his

---

17 She's jealous. – *Ed.*

back didn't find any exit wound. I hated to think about what had happened to his gut if that high-caliber bullet had shed all its energy inside him.

"Idiot," I told him.

He must have been more aware than he looked. "You're welcome," he muttered. Even sounded a little miffed.

Black Widow cradled her arm. She lay on her back and made no move to get up. She was herself, but not entirely back. I'd had to be pretty rough on her. The human brain wasn't made to take that kind of punishment. I just hoped she had the cognitive capacity to figure out what was happening. Just the thing I needed was to fight a punch-drunk super-spy.

She understood enough when I placed her hands on Josh's gunshot wound, and told her to keep it compressed. She nodded and did as I asked. For whatever good it did. Blood immediately welled up between her fingers.

"What they said was true, you know," Josh said. "About me being in anti-mutant groups. I was in the Reavers, before I found out what I was."

I couldn't help the reflexive tightening of my jaw. "I don't need to know this," I said, and then: "Why are you telling me this?"

"So you don't feel too bad if this doesn't work."

Josh closed his eyes. The muscles on his brow went tight. A flicker of energy rippled up his arms, and over his chest.

He had to be marshaling his healing factor. Making one last grasp to cling to life.

The blood flowing underneath Black Widow's palm slowed. Then it stopped. His breathing slowed, and steadied.

He grabbed Black Widow's arm. Her *broken* arm. She

flinched, but, with her concussion, she didn't have the reflexes to move away fast enough.

There was an awful grinding noise – bone on bone, the same thing I'd heard when Josh had altered his own body. When Black Widow pulled back, her arm no longer bent at the wrong place. She wiggled her fingers.

Josh had been pale with shock and blood loss before, but somehow he went even whiter. His hand lolled back. His fingers went limp. He'd fainted with the effort.

I hoped he'd saved some of that healing energy for himself, but couldn't count on it. He seemed stable for the moment. We needed to get him to a hospital. Most mercs have *some* amount of medical training – it's a job necessity – but no one in Neena's posse was a doctor. There had to be a phone or functioning communications system left on that ship.

At least Black Widow was still woozy. He'd known better than to try to heal her concussion. But that thought came with a cold feeling in my gut.

I don't have second sight, danger sense, Spidey-sense, the Force, or anything else that super hero-types call a bad feeling in their gut. I just had the bad feeling. And a prickling on the back of my neck. My heart juddered against my ribs.

I turned. Neena was still standing atop the wreck, gun in hand. She was looking around as if dazed – or getting her bearings.

"Drop your weapon!" I called. "Kick it as far away from you as you can!"

Neena looked behind her and around her. Then she set her hand on her chest as if to ask, "Who, me?" Still no sign of Shoon'kwa, Rachel, or White Fox.

I would have had plenty of time and opportunity, while under Johnny Dee's influence, to get DNA samples of all my friends. That postage receipt I'd found, drenched in rain, the last time I'd lost myself – whose DNA fragments had I mailed that time? God forbid Johnny Dee had gotten anything from Tony Stark while I'd been near him, or any of the mercs and heroes our business regularly brought us into contact with.

"Peaches," I called, "if you never trust me in your life again, I need you to trust me now."

Neena raised her gun hand.

I didn't know how much more of this I could take. I was having trouble catching my breath. Now that I'd stood still for more than a few seconds, all my pains were catching up with me. It felt like my energy was leaking out through the gunshot wound in my shoulder. In fact, I was pretty sure it had opened up again.

I was more than tired. I was worn through. I was old. I didn't have it in my heart to fight Neena if Johnny Dee had gotten a hold of her. Fact was, if she aimed that pistol at me, I didn't know what I would do. Probably not even move.

Neena swung her arm and released the pistol. It flew far away. I breathed out.

"Bet you're wondering how I ended up in this situation?" Neena yelled. She held up her hand as if another thought had occurred to her, leaned against a raised engine nozzle, and, calmly and businesslike, threw up. That crash landing must have been as rough as it looked. When she was done spitting, she added, "Me, too." She started clambering down the side of the wreck.

A pale hand reached from the hatch behind her, seized her ankle, and yanked.

Neena's luck power is prickly. The way she explained it to me is that she has to *actively* be trying to do something for it to kick in. She could be caught unawares, and her luck would never save her. Similarly, she can't sit back and wait for something lucky to happen. She has to be out there, putting herself in danger, *doing* things, for luck to find her.

And so nothing saved her as she crashed bodily onto the airship's hull, knocking the wind out of her. She rolled down the sloped side of the wreck, toward a thirty-foot fall to the jagged remains of a wing below. It wasn't until she spread her arms that her luck found her. Her fingers snagged the rim of a thruster exhaust nozzle. She dangled from the edge, gasping for air.

White Fox climbed out of the hatch, her face a mask of rage that looked utterly alien on her. She climbed toward Neena and tried to stomp on her fingers.

It turned out I had some energy left, after all. I left Black Widow holding Josh's guts in place and started running. I didn't remember making the decision to go. But, by then, Neena was herself again. She dropped from the ledge and, without even looking, landed in the one spot of clear ground underneath her.

By the time I reached the airship, Rachel had started to crawl out of the hatch. Her dazzling violet hair was unmistakable. It fluttered like a flag in the rising smoke. "What in the nine circles of Hell is happening?" she demanded. Neither Neena nor I had the breath to answer.

White Fox stepped away from the edge, and answered her

with a hard kick to her stomach. Rachel's rattled, indignant voice *whoofed* out of her.

White Fox didn't need weapons. She was a *kumiho*, last of a mystical species of nine-tailed fox. She had retractable claws that came with the form. But she wasn't using them. She wasn't fighting like herself in general. Johnny Dee was a cruel, vicious fighter, and he had White Fox's strength to draw on. But he lacked her finesse and had no grasp of her subtler powers. No claws, no hypnotic voice, no long-distance jumping.

Johnny Dee probably couldn't sense what the people he puppeteered had on their person before he took them over. I was glad he hadn't picked Rachel. Her belt was studded with the diamond-shaped explosives that had been her trademark since her days with the Serpent Society.

I jumped onto one of the airship's tail fins, ran up its curve, and tugged myself onto the airship. Neena had found her breath again. She was just a few steps behind. There was no time for reunions or questions. Just a shared glance that asked *What NOW?*

White Fox battered Rachel against the side of the open hatch. Rachel was shielding her face with her hands, but her guard had started to droop. Once that happened, White Fox would be able to land a killing blow.

I rushed White Fox. She must've heard me coming. In a blur of motion, she whirled. Pain speared through my cheek as her fist connected. White Fox was trying to turn aside my momentum, but I didn't let her. I crashed my good shoulder squarely into the center of her chest.

She wasn't a mutant, but, as a *kumiho*, she had strength equivalent to mine and braced herself against the hull plating.

In the contest of my strength against hers, it was the plating that gave out first. The metal pushed up behind her heels, crumpled, and then snapped loose. It flew out from underneath her. Then we crashed onto the wreck. I drove my elbow into her stomach.

White Fox gasped in pain. I figured that meant it was her. Johnny Dee wasn't that good an actor. I took my weight off White Fox at once.

Neena's fist slammed between my shoulder blades.

The shock reverberated through my bones, into my lungs. I staggered forward, breathless. The muscles in my throat convulsed. For several seconds, I couldn't draw in air.

One thing that's hard to understand about these kinds of fights until you've been in one is that they're not so much about inflicting pain as sapping energy. Pain can be tolerated, especially when you fight on the level of a super hero. But no one, not even the invincible Wolverine-types, can fight if their heart just can't get oxygen to their muscles.

I was at an immediate disadvantage against Neena. And that was before *her* advantages kicked in. I spun, raised my arms in guard position. Neena's mouth twisted in a snarl. Her luck was still working for her. Her punch "just happened" to slip through the one gap in my guard large enough for her to do so. My world turned to stars and sparks.

My counterpunch missed by fractions of an inch as Neena spun away. My fist had come so close I could feel the warmth of her skin. She stuck her leg behind mine, apparently without meaning to – actually, *definitely* without meaning to – and tripped me as I took a step she couldn't have predicted. Lucky lady.

I slammed onto the airship's hull, landing on my back. I couldn't force myself up, and I couldn't beat her in a straight-up fight, even with Johnny Dee at her controls. All I could do was keep my hands up to shield my face.

White Fox caught her unawares. Her heel landed in the small of Neena's back. Neena lost her balance, staggered to her knees.

White Fox rolled to her feet. Neena was already bouncing up. White Fox swung a second kick toward her. Neena reached down as if she knew exactly where the kick was going to land, and caught White Fox's foot under her arm.

But something had changed. The snarl was gone. Her stance had loosened. Neena released White Fox's foot without doing anything to punish her for letting herself be caught.

Johnny Dee had left Neena. I didn't understand why. She could have kept smashing us. The only thing she'd accomplished was get all three of us in the same space–

Well, damn. OK.

I rolled to my side, just in time to see Rachel finish pulling herself out of the hatch. Every trace of pain in her expression had vanished, replaced by naked rage. Johnny Dee must have seen the diamond-shaped explosives on her belt. She grabbed for them.

I couldn't move in time. My chest burned for lack of air.

Neena stepped in front of us as Rachel threw. She swiped her arm at just the right time and just the right angle to deflect a spread of three grenades, and without any of their razor-fine points digging into her. They careened past us, and exploded over her shoulder a second later.

My hearing must've been in bad shape. I hardly heard the

detonations. The heat, though, felt like standing next to an open incinerator door. Neena's hair ruffled in the searing breeze.

Damn. I wished I could look that cool. I was just kind of boggling at everything, trying to suck in air. "Love ya, girl," I said, when I had the breath for it.

Rachel's eyes widened. She took a step back, and reached for the other side of her belt. If Johnny Dee had any brains – and I was starting to realize that he did – she would be throwing more grenades in a wider spread this time.

Gunshots popped across the horizon. I recognized the reports. They were from Dad's old Beretta M9.

Black Widow had torn Josh's shirt into a bandage, wrapping it tightly around his stomach. She'd grabbed my fallen gun, and propped it on a rock to steady her aim.

With that concussion, she couldn't be thinking clearly. She certainly couldn't shoot straight. All her shots were going wide, pinging off the hull to Rachel's right.

No – not *just* hull.

Sparks ricocheted off the hump of one of the airship's dorsal main engines. The hull there had bent and warped, exposed the airship's exquisitely engineered guts, its dark spiderweb filaments of sensors and circuitry. And, among them, a fuel reservoir. That was what Black Widow was aiming for. A spark bounced off its surface. The next shot–

The boom was loud even to my ears. The shockwave knocked Rachel and Neena flat to the hull. Rachel's knees cracked against metal, but she hardly seemed to feel it. Johnny Dee was still in control. She was once again reaching for her explosives.

But Black Widow's clever shooting had given me enough time to catch my breath and shove myself to my feet. I booted Rachel's head down, and then cuffed the heel of my hand into the back of her skull. Her forehead cracked against the hull. She went limp.

I was feeling bad about many things just then, but also, absurdly, for mussing up that perfect hair of hers.

"Head injuries," I blurted, now that I had breath and a second. "It's the only way to keep Johnny Dee from controlling you."

Somewhere in the distance, I was aware of Black Widow, dizzily trekking her way toward the airship. She left a confused, wobbling trail in the sand behind her.

"Johnny Dee?" Neena asked, although with less of a question mark and more of an interrobang.

"Johnny Dee," I confirmed.

"*Johnny Dee*," she said, and this time her voice was more of a growl.

"Why do you keep saying his full name?" White Fox asked. "Is that an American South thing?" Then, a moment later: "Also, who?"

The top of the hatch banged against the hull. Shoon'kwa pulled herself up. Her golden arm guards glinted in the sun. Her braids were as artfully cared for as ever, but one side of her face was a red-violet splotch of bruising. She snarled.

She could have gotten injured in the crash, but I knew what had happened. *She* was the one Johnny Dee had puppeteered to crash the airship. The others, not knowing what was happening, had tried, too late, to force her out of the pilot's seat. She'd fought back. They'd had to do the same.

It made my heart hurt to see that my friends had done this to each other. I was going to make Johnny Dee's heart hurt worse.

But, for the moment, I didn't have the means. I was unarmed. And Shoon'kwa held a Wakandan ring blade tight in her grip. She stalked toward us.

The ring blade's edge gleamed with sunlight. It shone into my eyes and kept me from seeing which angle she'd meant to attack.

Neena's hand wrapped around my neck. She held me between Shoon'kwa and herself like a shield. I'd made a fundamental mistake. The rage on Shoon'kwa's face was her own. Johnny Dee had hopped back into *Neena's* body.

Neena grappled to get her palm on my chin, trying for a stance to break my neck. I tried planting my foot atop Neena's to trip her. She nimbly sidestepped, probably without realizing it. She turned toward White Fox. White Fox had thrown a punch at her, but, as soon as Neena saw her, the warped hull plating under White Fox's feet shifted, and the punch went wide.

But Neena was outnumbered. She couldn't keep an eye on us all the time. Johnny Dee didn't have the real Neena's practice dividing her attention. As soon as Neena's focus was off me, her hand slipped off the sweat on my chin. I whirled her around, and Shoon'kwa swung the flat of her blade toward Neena's head. Shoon'kwa only clipped Neena, but the blow must have been strong enough to shake Johnny Dee loose. Neena released me immediately. She took a step back, hands raised.

A second later, and Johnny Dee's rage was on White Fox's

face again. She came at Neena, but Neena saw her in time. With a hasty step back, she clotheslined White Fox.

Neena and I made a good team – when White Fox crashed to the hull, I was right there to grab her head and slam it into metal. Another concussion, another person Johnny Dee couldn't reach.

Neena caught my eye and nodded. Then, without waiting for Johnny Dee to seize her or somebody else again, she turned and tackled Shoon'kwa.

The two of them rolled toward the side of the airship, and dropped to the sand below. I couldn't tell which of them, if either, were controlled by Johnny Dee. It could have been that neither of them were, and that Neena was making a preemptive strike.

I hoped Shoon'kwa had figured out what was happening. In one sense, it didn't really matter. But it made a difference to *me* that she knew her friends hadn't betrayed her.

I heaved in air. For the first time in minutes, the dark fringes around the edges of my vision receded. I jogged to the edge of the airship.

Whoever had been in control when they'd fallen, as soon as I saw them, I knew Johnny Dee had taken Shoon'kwa now. She scrambled away from Neena, hate frozen on her lips. She still held onto her ring blade. Neena stepped back, waiting for Shoon'kwa to make her move.

In a moment of terror that froze my voice in my chest, Shoon'kwa raised the blade toward her own neck instead. Neena wouldn't be able to reach her in time.

Johnny Dee had been trying to take us out all at once, as efficiently as possible. My stolen memory of that awful shock he'd gotten when he'd killed Milos still burned in my head. He couldn't kill all of us like that, not without stopping to recover between each death.

But he could get a head start on killing us one by one.

Shoon'kwa jerked, and stood rigid for a moment. Her weapon hand fell by her side. Then she dropped, still convulsing.

A few dozen feet behind her, Black Widow dropped to her knees. Her stunner pistol shook in her hand. Leave it to the super-spy to have an appropriate gadget.

I'd never been so grateful for her. Black Widow groaned, and fell facedown in the sand. Falling asleep was the last thing anybody with a head injury should have been doing, but I couldn't do anything for her at the moment.

Neena stepped over Shoon'kwa for the ugly, delicate work of giving her a concussion to protect her from Johnny Dee. I didn't watch. I couldn't bear it. I'd seen enough of my friends getting hurt today.

I grabbed onto the edge of the aircraft, and dropped to ground level. I landed in the sand.

"I think that's everybody with a head injury but you and me," Neena said.

"I'm already protected," I said. For a while.

"Then I need to–"

A fragment of loose hull plating, dangling from one of the airship's starboard wings by a sliver of metal, fell free. It was directly above Neena. I didn't even have time to wince.

After the impact, Neena's eyes widened, as if mildly surprised. She stepped forward, her balance faltering. Then, for a moment, she seemed fine.

"My lucky day," she said, and collapsed.

Then I was alone, at the bottom of a canyon strewn with wreckage, standing among the fallen bodies of enemies and friends. Panting for air, and waiting for all the pains I'd accumulated to catch up with me.

My lucky day, too.

EIGHTEEN

I couldn't let my friends stay unconscious. Not with head injuries. They might never wake up. Fortunately, they knew that as well as I did. As soon as I climbed back onto the wreck and shook White Fox into the world, she started struggling to stay in it. Pinching herself, and biting the inside of her cheek. She crawled over toward Shoon'kwa and Rachel to rouse them.

I hopped back to ground level. Neena hadn't woken the first time I'd shaken her. She did this time, and shoved my arm away like I was trying to get her to wake up and come to school. The second time, she punched me. Not very hard, but – still. Hurt my feelings a little. Also my nose. She kept stirring after that, though, so I moved on toward Black Widow, who was a little less ornery.

By the time I helped Black Widow wobble to her feet, Neena was gone.

My heart leapt to my throat. It didn't take long to find her again. She was staggering down the canyon, toward the bottom of an old rockslide. It would have been as much a climb as a hike, but the rockslide gave her a slope she could use to get out again.

I called, "Peaches!" She grumpily waved me off.

I had other work at the moment. I hoped she knew what she was doing – or that her luck would look out for her if she didn't.

Black Widow leaned on my good shoulder – without trying to make it *look* like she was leaning on me – as we three-legged-walked back to Josh.

Blood had soaked all the way through his impromptu bandage. It drooled over his side, into the sand. His eyes were open, but I wasn't sure he saw me. His pupils were wide and black, though he was staring directly into the sky. His breathing was shallow and rapid, and his forehead covered in sweat.

I kneeled beside him, and set my hands lightly on his shoulders.

"I don't know if he's going to pull through," Black Widow said. Even through the concussion-induced slur in her voice, I could tell that this was her trying to stay optimistic.

I didn't know Josh. Didn't know anything about him except the ways he was hurting, and the ways he'd tried to help me. I didn't care if he used to be with the Reavers. People can change.

I remembered the strange, cool feeling of his hands on my skin, and my skin mending. He could heal other people. He could change his own body, remold his bones. I hoped that meant that he could heal himself. But he seemed to have run out of energy. I hoped – desperately hoped – he hadn't spent the last of that energy on me.

I don't remember setting my forehead against his, but suddenly that was where I was. I kept remembering his body convulse against mine, that hateful moment of Wolfram's bullet ripping up his insides. I'd been too slow. I'd been trying to force my body to move, but couldn't make it happen in time.

I hadn't been good enough to stop it. *I hadn't been fast enough.*

If I survived this, I was going to leave this business. I couldn't hack it anymore. Nothing but blood and heartbreak left in it for me.

Combat used to come a lot more naturally to me. Right now, all I felt was lost and old. I couldn't forget the way Dad had looked when he'd wandered the fields, trying to remember his horses' names, or looking for a dog who'd died ten years ago. How sad he'd looked, how lost. Until now, I hadn't known what it was like to feel that old. That useless. Out of my element in a place that used to be my home. He had his ranch – I had my fights.

"He's gone," Black Widow slurred.

I looked up sharply. It took me half a moment too long to realize she wasn't talking about Josh.

She meant Wolfram. He'd left a streak of drying blood across the rock he'd been leaning on, but the man himself was gone.

"Huh," Black Widow said, audibly trying to railroad one muzzy thought into the next. "I would have thought he… I could have sworn he'd been kidney-shot. Shouldn't have been able to move far."

"*He* wouldn't have been." Not under his own conscious control. Not in as much pain as he should've been in. But Johnny Dee wouldn't care.

There was no sign of Wolfram in any direction along the canyon. If he'd started moving not long after the fight ended, and kept up a speed that paid no mind to either pain or exhaustion, he could have gotten just about anywhere.

I supposed this business did have one thing left for me besides blood and heartbreak. It tasted more and more bitter with every hour. But it was still a prize I would fight for.

Revenge was somewhere out there, if I could seize it.

I found one of my revolvers – no idea what had happened to the other – with three bullets. And Black Widow had kept hold of Dad's Beretta. It had bullets loaded, but I'd lost the spare magazines.

Wolfram had left his Desert Eagle behind, half-hidden under a rock. Funny thing was, it had no ammo. Strange that Johnny Dee had taken the magazines but not the gun. There must've been a reason for that I didn't understand. But it meant the Desert Eagle itself was useless to me.

No matter. I had enough killing tools for my purposes.

For a second, I'd debated taking Shoon'kwa's ring blade with me. But it didn't fit my grip and I hadn't trained in it. Besides, I still had the flip pocketknife. A bruise on my keister let me know it was very much still in my back pocket, and had been bouncing and rolling around with me all this time.

I left Black Widow with her stunner pistol. There was a good chance she'd need it. I didn't know how much time my friends' head trauma would buy. When Josh had hit his head earlier, Johnny Dee had gotten back into him after only a few minutes. But he'd had his healing factor, and I didn't think he'd been concussed as bad as my friends here. Still, Johnny Dee would only need to get his tentacles into one of them to bring the others down.

I told Black Widow what to watch for. She held her stunner ready, though her aim wavered. If Johnny Dee got into *her*... well... no use thinking about what would happen then.

Black Widow knew the clock was ticking, too. She wasted no time. "We got your message," she said. "From your brother." Her voice was thick, like listening to a drunk. "Came after you to help. Sensors picked up a couple signals before we crashed. You, in this canyon. And something else. Body heat source. Cavern entrance."

At that point, her train of thought derailed. She blinked several times. It was all I could do to keep from grabbing her shoulders and shaking her. "*Where?*"

She squinted into the sun, and then at the canyon walls. She started to wave to one of them, and then stopped and considered another. For a moment, I was afraid her injury hadn't left her up to the task of squaring the sensor map in her memory with what she saw.

But, even with her brain falling to pieces, she was still sharp. She wouldn't have been Black Widow otherwise. She pointed toward the same rockslide Neena had climbed.

"That way," she said, decisively.

I wasted no time on goodbyes, and started moving as fast as my battered bones would let me.

The slope was rougher going than I'd thought, and I hadn't expected it to be easy. Even the bottom was steep enough that I had to brace myself with my good hand to keep my balance. Cascades of sand trickled loose under my hand, falling into my boots. The top of the rockslide was part-climbing, part-slipping, and all-not-looking-down.

I wasn't the only person who'd been able to make it up. There was no sign of Neena on the way, and she'd had nowhere to go but up. Every once in a while, I came across a little splotch of blood. Something Wolfram had left behind him.

I paused close to the top and looked back. The vantage left little to the imagination as to how smashed-up Shoon'kwa's airship was. The ship's backbone had snapped when the nose had crumpled against the cliff. At least the smoke had stopped. Shoon'kwa, Rachel, and White Fox all clustered together atop the wreck. Black Widow sat upright near Josh. Nobody, except possibly Josh, was dead yet. If I couldn't finish this, it would only be a question of time.

All of it had happened because of me. Because I'd kept to myself how poorly I'd been feeling. If I'd fessed up earlier – told them how weak I was feeling – we might have figured out what was going on before Johnny Dee controlled my whole team. We would still have been in for a fight, but we'd have been in a lot better shape for it.

The last part of the climb was the hardest. I pulled myself over the lip, and onto my feet.

Hills crumpled the horizon, approaching the canyon in odd streaks, like some enormous beast had clawed them into the earth. Or Galactus's teeth had scraped the planet, given us a nibble. The terrain wasn't all that rough. But it did offer plenty of cover. And lots of places to hide.

Pillars of clouds towered over the western sky. The still air of morning had given way to a strange and intermittently wild breeze. It stirred the sand around my grit-filled boots.

That wind had erased any hint of tracks I could've followed.

I closed my eyes. I had been through too much recently to feel despair at this moment. But this was in the same zip code. They were unkind neighbors, eying each other through the window blinds. It left the same kind of hollowness in my chest.

I couldn't search this whole land. Hell, I probably didn't have time to make a beeline to Johnny Dee, assuming I knew where he was.

Somebody nearby snorted.

I cracked an eye open. I'd thought whoever snorted must have been right next to me, but this thing was still about a hundred feet away. I had to tilt my head before I saw, to my far left, a shape slide along the canyon rim.

The snort should have settled the source's identity. Nevertheless, for a variety of reasons, I did not credit my eyes when Wheezer ambled up in front of me.

She nickered as if making casual conversation. *Good afternoon. How've you been?* Nothing I had good answers for. By some lucky stroke, she looked as well-fed and watered as the hour I'd left her. I reached out and brushed my fingers across her mane, but she still didn't seem real.

It was not until my brain caught up with my eyes, and registered Neena slouched against Wheezer's neck, that I started to believe it.

Neena's involvement helped the coincidence make a little more sense.

"Hop on, bestie," Neena said. "We're going hunting."

NINETEEN

Even when Wheezer had been younger, she hadn't been built for hauling. The two of us on her back was more weight than she wanted to carry. Because I asked nicely and she was feeling generous, she allowed it. We still moved a lot faster than I could have alone. Enough that I could almost believe we were going to make it in time to save our friends.

Neena pointed the way forward. Like Black Widow, she'd seen the sensor screen right before the crash. There'd been a heat signature in a cavern somewhere ahead.

"Did I tell you recently that I love you?" I asked, knowing full well that I had. Not sure if she'd heard me with everything else going on, though.

"Not recently enough," she said.

My heart quailed as soon as I said it. I wanted to pull it back. I've never been good at confessing those kind of feelings. "I was talking to my horse."

"I don't think so," she said. "I try not to mix work and romance."

"Like hell you do." Not if even half the stories she told me were true.

I couldn't continue the conversation in this vein, not while she was struggling with a concussion. It wouldn't have been fair. Nor could I tell her that, no matter how this ended, I didn't figure I was going to be working with her much longer.

Her voice was getting clearer. The fog of her concussion was lifting. She knew it, too.

As soon as she saw our destination – a long horizontal scar of a shadow across the base of a steep hill – she looked like she made up her mind about something. She said, "I'm feeling better," like she really wished she wasn't. "I'm going to have to leave you here. I'll be a liability if he gets hold of me again."

A tightness squeezed my heart. "I don't know that I can do this alone."

"I know you can." Neena said it with such surety that, for a moment, I believed it, too.

I dropped off Wheezer's back when we were about half a minute's walk away from the cavern mouth. Wheezer blew air through her nose, as if in relief. I tried not to take that personally.

Wheezer could be a bear to control even with her reins, but she played nice for us today. It was like she knew how serious this was. Neena kept Wheezer's eyes off me. After a moment's struggle, Wheezer moved away at a canter. I felt lonelier than I ever had lost in the desert.

Hardly a few seconds after they were gone, a figure shambled out of the cavern mouth.

I tensed my hands above my weapons, but whoever it was

didn't seem to be armed. The figure stumbled forward, one disjointed step at a time. Their heels dragged against the sand.

It was Wolfram. He was in a bad way. Yellow, sweaty face. Deep red eyes. Those eyes didn't look much different than mine had after they'd been stippled with debris from his gunshot. His clerical collar was smeared with blood where he must have touched it with his gunshot hand. More blood ran in a 'T' across his shirt, as if, in the last moment he could have, he'd marked himself with the sign of the cross.

A dark streak ran down the inside seam of his jeans. At first, I took it to be something more embarrassing than it was. But it was blood. Blood from the bullet wound on his back had run down his pants.

Johnny Dee couldn't reanimate corpses. At least, I didn't think so. We would have been in a whole lot more trouble if he could. So Wolfram was, in some sense, still alive. But I doubted he was shambling under his own power.

At least while Wolfram was under Johnny Dee's control, Johnny Dee couldn't go after my friends. He could only puppet one person at a time. The clock, for now, wasn't ticking.

"I should have taken over that Domino earlier in the fight," Wolfram said, with Johnny Dee's sneer. "I didn't realize how dynamic that power of hers really was."

"Everybody makes mistakes," I said.

"Yeah, but I learn from mine. It's only a question of time before everything falls back into place."

"What the hell was your plan here, Johnny Dee? You obviously had DNA samples of your friends ready to go, no matter how careful they thought they'd been around you. How long were you figuring on betraying them?"

Wolfram scowled. "I knew what I wanted. I knew I'd need help to get there. I didn't figure I'd have to throw them away this soon."

"What you 'wanted' was to take some of the big names, the mutants most people would recognize, and use them to do terrible things. But *why*?"

"Mutants only survive because normal humans put up with us, Outlaw. The sooner more of them see that they'd be better off in a world without mutants… the sooner the world's going to come around."

The rage kindling inside me stoked hotter. "That's not true. On any count."

He hadn't just intended to kill the people whose bodies he stole, or use them to commit petty crimes. He wanted to do so publicly. The bigger the name, the better. Mutantkind was in bad enough shape already. Discredit the last few names that people unambiguously thought of as heroes, and mutantkind would lose our last protections against a hostile world. We'd survive, but… a lot more of us would get hurt and killed than needed to, and for what? Johnny Dee's bigotry? Making a little money off us? I ground my teeth.

"These idiots I was working with…" Wolfram said, and then trailed off, as if an idea had occurred to him. He held up his hand, as if to consider it.

As casually as if he were plucking a flower, he pulled his pinkie finger back until something in the knuckle snapped. Even I winced at the sound. Wolfram's mind was probably still in there, feeling everything. "They were thinking small. Banks. Fraud. Money. I needed their help to get started, get in with some organizations." He smirked. "They thought they were using *me*."

"Looks like all your plans crashed against each other. Now everybody's dead, and here you are… all on your pitiful lonesome again."

"Wolfram betrayed me, too, you know," Wolfram said. "Hid his gun right before I took him over. He knew. He *knew* I'd stolen some of his DNA. And he tried to get one over on me, right at the very end."

"Johnny Dee, if you actually manage to discredit mutantkind–" discredit us *more*, that was, "– then ordinary folk are just going to come down on you that much harder."

He looked at me dead in the eyes, and said the worst thing I think I'd ever heard him say: "We all have to make sacrifices to do the right thing, Outlaw."

He wasn't acting like a man with his back to a wall. That worried me. Wolfram had called Johnny Dee right earlier: he was a coward. That was why he'd belatedly tried to get back in Wolfram's good graces after trying to kill him. Like a coward, he was always second-guessing. Only he was acting pretty sure of himself now. Either it was just that, acting, or he knew something I didn't.

He wasn't moving to attack. He was content to trade barbs, trying to delay me. Maybe I'd been wrong about that clock not ticking.

I watched Wolfram's eyes carefully, looked one last time for the real Wolfram inside them. The cold, vicious criminal. The man who'd held Josh prisoner for days or weeks or months, forcing him to be Johnny Dee's puppet. The man who'd orchestrated, or thought he'd orchestrated, my own repeated bodysnatching.

He deserved every ounce of pain Johnny Dee was inflicting

on him now, no matter if he'd tried to help me near the end. I didn't know that I could forgive him enough to spare him this.

But I supposed I was going to have to forgive him. The same way he did.

Johnny Dee still thought I was listening. Wolfram said, "That's why I'm still going to get in good with the Blackguard Network, or something like it. They'll cover—"

I drew my revolver and shot him through the face.

I'd started running before Wolfram's body folded to the ground. I was past him before the pieces of his head had stopped skittering and dancing on the rocks. No more delays. No more stalling. Whatever Johnny Dee was trying to do, I'd given him too much time already. And now I was going to show him why, if he couldn't respect the rest of mutantkind, he would be better off fearing us instead.

I charged the cavern mouth like all the legions of Hell were behind me. I couldn't say whether they were chasing me or rallying behind me. Either would have felt about the same. Maybe it was both.

I was past seeing red. I saw flames.

That fire lit my path into the cavern, and grew brighter as my eyes adjusted. I was briefly surprised to find my path constrained by walls. Low, clay ones, about as tall as my shoulders. They bracketed the cavern just inside it. They were ancient. Built by the same people who'd made the cliffside village, perhaps. Or their enemies. They were far short of the cavern roof, but they would have been a formidable obstacle to a massed attack. Especially attackers without firearms.

Like the wall at the cliffside village, this one had a single entrance. Johnny Dee might have been expecting me to use it. I've always aimed to surprise.

One thing that isn't so obvious to outsiders about super-strength is that it applies to legs as much as arms.[18] I vaulted over the wall with space to spare, and landed tucked in a roll on the other side.

Johnny Dee was at the far end of the cavern mouth, maybe sixty feet away. All I could see of him was a pale orange silhouette, but that was enough to show me him holding his arm away like something had bitten him. Probably Wolfram's death. I saw no sign of the doll he must have used to control Wolfram. He'd probably tossed it away when it shocked him. He had the hunched look of a man who'd narrowly avoided electrocution.

Good. Let him hurt.

He spotted me the same instant I saw him. With a desperate lurch, he darted back into the shadows. There didn't seem to be any weapons in his hands, but that didn't mean he was defenseless.

The roll had left me disoriented and dizzy. I drew my revolver and fired. Too late. Johnny Dee disappeared behind a wall I hadn't seen in the darkness. Rock chips and dust blasted across the cavern floor.

I ground my teeth. I could have made that shot just a few years ago.

Too slow. Too old.

One bullet left in the revolver. An unknown number in Dad's Beretta. I chased Johnny Dee into the darkness.

---

18 Has to! With superstrength, if you're not braced against the ground as hard as you punch, Newton's Third Law will send you flying! –Ed.

The cavern was a lot larger than it looked outside. It sloped deeper into the earth. The cavern's prior inhabitants had raised roofless buildings of stone and packed dirt. Places to live and work during a siege or while under threat of invasion, maybe. It would have been a fascinating place to learn more about, in another time. I didn't see any archaeologists' placards. It could have been that Johnny Dee and I were the first human beings to set foot in here since the original builders had cleared out.

The complex had been even larger once. When my eyes finished adjusting, I saw that the back of the cavern terminated in an ancient rockfall. At least one of the buildings was half-crushed underneath it. That left about a dozen others that Johnny Dee could have taken cover in. A hiss of pain drew me to the east side of the cavern.

It had come from one of the buildings in the back. There wasn't enough overhead room for me to vault this one's wall. I charged through the door.

With a cry of rage, Johnny Dee crashed into my bad side.

He'd caught me in mid-stride, my foot off the ground. All the superstrength in the universe couldn't change the basic physics of that. He knocked me to the side. We crashed into the wall, shaking centuries of dust loose. It sprinkled all over us.

Johnny Dee slammed my revolver hand into the packed earth wall. One of us tripped the trigger. The gun went off. A shame. I still had Dad's Beretta, but, at this range, I wouldn't need it.

I didn't know what Johnny Dee had been thinking, trying to engage me in close combat. My strength versus his was about as fair a fight as an asteroid versus a cabin made of toothpicks.

As soon as I got my balance, I stomped hard on his boot. His foot broke in a satisfying *snap*. He yelled in shock, but not for long. I grabbed his neck in one hand.

From the angle I'd gotten him at, I couldn't quite snap his neck. But I could do a pretty good job of crushing his windpipe.

I lifted him off the ground in one hand. He grabbed at my arm with both of his, but couldn't shake me.

Something wet, warm, and slimy brushed my bare arm.

In the back of my head, distantly, I'd registered that I hadn't felt Johnny Dee's shirt collar as I was choking him. He'd taken his shirt off. Shadows writhed across his silhouette.

Oh God. The maw and tentacles.

One of the tentacles lashed across my arm. It wasn't all slimy and soft. Something hard and ridged, disconcertingly like fingernails or teeth, scraped across my skin. And then a searing pain drove into my muscles.

I let Johnny Dee go. I had no choice. The pain was incredible.

The muscles in my arm turned to liquid. I hadn't known before that Johnny Dee's tentacles could sting, but I'd never gotten that close to him. It made sense that he'd keep this secret close to his chest, so to speak, until the moment came.

I reached for my Beretta with my other hand. It wasn't my shooting arm, but, in these close quarters, even my left hand could score a hit. I only got as far as pulling the gun free. The pain forked through my body like lightning. All the muscles in my body – even my lungs, even my heart – were trying to lock. It took every ounce of strength I had to batter back the pain. The Beretta dropped through my twitching fingers.

It fell next to Johnny Dee, who'd collapsed the second I released him. He was gasping for air, in agony. He didn't stop to pick up my fallen gun. He couldn't think through his pain any more than I could think through mine. He pushed away from me as fast as his broken foot would let him.

My pain came in waves – growing and subsiding and then growing again. Blackness crawled along the side of my vision. I looked at my arm. Blood beaded from half a dozen puncture wounds in a neat little line. It didn't look *that* bad for all the agony pulsing through me.

Johnny Dee couldn't stand. He scrambled backward, fast as he could with his one good foot. In different circumstances, him scooting across the floor on his butt might've looked funny.

He hadn't chosen this building at random. He crawled over to a surface of raised packed earth in the corner, where something was waiting for him. There was just enough light to let me see what it was.

It was a little doll. Of me.

The face was no great resemblance – it looked like somebody had tried to sculpt it out of melting candle wax. But my long hair was distinctive.

Johnny Dee spat, breathing hard. "Been a while since I've tried to take you over, Outlaw," he said. "I bet that shield of yours is a lot weaker by now." This was why he'd been delaying me. He reached for the doll.

Panic surged through my gut. It pushed enough of the pain back to the point I could crawl toward him. His fingers clasped the doll.

His telepathic assault crashed into me like a tsunami wave. *Some* remnant of Magik's shield must have still been there, or I wouldn't have stood a chance – but it was plain that most of it was gone by now. It felt like I was forcing my way through a tidal wave at the same time the earth was shaking apart underneath my boots. The ground between Johnny Dee and me widened, and violently split apart. We were on opposite sides of an uncrossable chasm.

In the real world, all that had happened was that I'd stopped crawling, and cringed back from Johnny Dee. Some part of me was aware of that. The force of his telepathy felt more real than reality. It was like I was trying to keep upright while standing against a firehose.

But I've stood my ground against firehoses before. Firehoses are how you know a protest is drawing attention. Marching for mutants' rights had felt like pushing against an unmovable force. We'd faced worse than firehoses out there. I kept pushing against *this* unmovable force, and I succeeded. Inch by inch, I crawled toward Johnny Dee. The sides of the chasm drew closer. The drop disappeared.

I grabbed for the doll. He jerked it away. Something wet and pulpy slapped against my unstung arm. The needle-tips of stingers caressed my skin. I was ready this time. My hand was already in my back pocket.

I pulled out my knife, flicked the blade out, and swiped.

The tentacle's jellylike mass made for easy slicing. The tendril on my arm went limp. Then it fell away.

Half a second later, agony burned through my arm anyway. Some of the venom must have gotten in. It wasn't as bad as last time, but it was enough to keep me from capitalizing on Johnny Dee's distraction as he screamed.

Johnny Dee had talked about the maw and tentacles on his chest as if they were separate beings. I never figured out how literally to take that. But he certainly reared back like he'd felt its pain.

The thing was, his scream wasn't alone. Something else was shrieking, too. Right below his chest. A high, unearthly voice, that sounded like it had an echo built into it.

Johnny Dee still held onto the doll.

I locked my hand around his wrist and gripped him hard enough for my nails to draw blood, but that was all it could do. Between the venom and the telepathic battering, I no longer had the strength to break bones. The mental attacks were getting worse. His thoughts battered me down. They were tainted by rage and pain. I tasted his intentions, like gunpowder on the back of my tongue. He no longer intended to puppet me. He was going to kill me.

Another tentacle lashed out, caressed the base of my neck. Its teeth and stingers brushed over my carotid artery.

I could hardly think through all of this, but I made myself try. Johnny Dee's telepathy, however else it worked, was based on two things: the dolls he used as a focus, and the maw on his chest. The maw created the dolls. Feed it DNA samples of a person, and it would hatch out the dolls.

I had no idea what would happen if it were fed some of Johnny Dee's own DNA.

His blood ran underneath my fingernails, mixing with the sweat on his palms.

Sometimes, the wild card is the only choice you can make. I knew what would happen if I picked any other option. Nothing good.

I didn't have the leverage to peel Johnny Dee's fingers back. But, by bracing my knee on the ground, I wrenched his arm back. He almost fell onto me. He fought to keep his weight off his bad foot. Then, with what fading strength I had, I shoved his hand, together with mine, toward his chest.

Into the maw.

Layered rows of teeth sliced my wrist. Then my hand plunged into something sickeningly moist and hot, firm and dripping.

My hand, his hand. His blood. My blood. The little toy doll of me. All went in together.

A tight pressing feeling, like puckered lips, sealed over my forearm. With the ringing in my ears, I couldn't hear the wet gulping sound, but I could *feel* it. The maw squeezed painfully hard.

It was a proper blessing that my memory of events broke there.

TWENTY

On a dry, clear day at the ranch – which was most days – I could see the school bus coming from a mile away. Not the actual bus itself, though. Too many hills in the way. But the clouds of dust pluming up were unmistakable. By age five, I'd learned to recognize all different sizes of vehicles coming this way. I was twelve now. The dust Dad's big horse trailer kicked up looked a lot different than the school bus, even though they were about the same size.

On the mornings when I could see the dust, it was a countdown timer. I had a minute or two left to complete whatever homework assignment I'd put off until that morning. Once I got on, the other kids certainly weren't going to let me finish.

Most of them hadn't forgiven me for being so far from the rest of the route's stops and making their trip longer. And that was before we got into the whole mutant thing.

Elias came with me every day, but wasn't much help. He was younger than most of the kids, and couldn't face up to them. I'm not sure he would've if he could. He didn't want to have much to do with me. Half of the kids in his class already called him a mutie just because he was related to me.

If he'd had an X-gene, too, we figured it would have manifested by now. But – you know kids. The facts of it didn't really matter.

In a lot of ways, him being "normal" made him an easier target than me. He had fewer ways to defend himself.

Elias wasn't with me today, though. The bus was headed away. I didn't often stick around to watch the bus go. Usually, as soon as I was out of those folding doors, I had too much to do outside to pay it much attention.

The last thing I wanted to do was get any closer to home.

The school had yanked one of its bus drivers back on duty to give me a solo ride home. Usually, after suspending kids, the principal had them wait in her office staring at the wall until it was time for everyone else to go home, too. Under the circumstances, though, they didn't want me anywhere near other kids.

They'd had to pull a second bus driver, too, to take another kid to emergency dental surgery.

The kid deserved it. I had no regrets there.

I watched the bus's trail of dust dwindle for as long as I felt like, which turned out to be a while. Eventually, though, I had to start the long walk down our drive.

I wasn't terribly surprised when I rounded the next bend and found Dad walking toward me. He must've been out with the horses and seen the bus's dust come and go. The principal had said she'd called him. She'd been lucky to get a hold of him. His jeans and denim jacket, and even his mustache, were stained tan with dust. He would have been out working most of the day.

My chin trembled. I would have done anything other than have the conversation I knew we were bound to have. But I wouldn't let myself go in any other direction. I was no coward.

Dad set his big hand on my shoulder, and pointed to a grassy hill just off the drive. "Let's sit and chat."

My feet were leaden at the start of the climb. Strangely, though, they got lighter as we approached the top. I knew what I was going to have to say. I *didn't* know what I was going to face after that, but starting the battle was the hardest part. When we got to the top, I sat. This was one of the only places in the ranch, outside of the horses' pasture, where you *could* sit without getting sand in your pants.

"Do you know why you're here?" he asked.

"I'm not an idiot," I told him. "I know I'm stuck in some kind of mental combat with Johnny Dee."

He blinked. Opened his mouth and closed it. Of all the things I could have said, that seemed to have been last on his list of expectations. He didn't have anything prepared.

I'd said it with more vitriol than I ever would have used with my real dad, but I wanted the words to stick – and in me as much as him. All along, I felt this place, whatever was happening to me, tug me in a million directions. It was trying to tear me apart. Rip me into fragments, shreds of memory. Convince me I was *here* and not *there*. If I didn't keep myself rooted in the truth, I worried that I really would lose myself to the dream.

This place had power, like dreams usually did. I knew it wasn't real. But I wasn't in control, not even of myself. My memory was foggy. If I didn't keep reminding myself that this was a dream, I worried that I would forget it.

"Well," he said, "that's probably true–"

"Definitely true," I interrupted.

"–definitely true," he conceded. "I don't understand what you mean to do about it."

I shrugged. I was in a child's body, sitting on a Texas hilltop with my dad. My options here seemed limited.

White static fringed my vision. I smelled things I shouldn't have – nickels on the back of my tongue, citrus tickling my nose. Most of me was here, on this hill. But the rest of me was being spun in a dozen other places at once. It was like a crowd of people had each grabbed a limb and yanked in different directions.

All I could see, though, was that no one else was around. It was just me and Dad.

And he wasn't real.

I held up my arm, studied the shape and muscle mass. I really was twelve. Same age as I'd been when I really *had* sent another kid to dental surgery and been suspended for the rest of the school year. (The only reason I hadn't been expelled was that the administrators knew as well as I did that Marcos had it coming.)

But the other details were messed up. Dad and I hadn't had the hilltop conversation *then*. That had happened when we'd talked about whether I wanted to take a year off and home-school, just to let things between me and the other kids cool off. And the weather had been worse then. We'd actually just gone up to watch a storm roll in, and ended up talking about the other stuff, too.

Like a dream, as soon as I thought of the storm, the horizon grayed.

Shadows washed over us. Still, not all of my senses were working. The grass waved and flattened as a wind swept through, but I couldn't feel a thing.

When I looked up, clouds loomed over us, taller than mountains. Big and dark and tumorous. In this part of Texas, we were just outside tornado alley. We didn't have to worry about deadly storms as much as Oklahoma and Kansas, but they still came around sometimes. My first recurring nightmares used to be about tornadoes.

I knew right away that, if that storm hit me, I wouldn't be able to keep myself together. The storm would overwhelm me. My senses were being pulled in other directions already. In there, they would fly apart.

"Storm's a-brewin'," Dad intoned, because he thought he was funny. He enjoyed stating the obvious with as much folksy gravitas as possible, like he was understudying Sam Elliott.

"My God, Dad," twelve year-old me had said, back then. "Please don't be that embarrassing around other people."

Little brat. I didn't let her say that this time. But, somehow, Dad reacted as though I had. He raised an eyebrow to cover his hurt. "I don't see any other people around."

The twelve year-old in my memory wanted to answer again, but I blurted, "I do."

I'd said it without thinking about it, but I knew immediately that I was right. My instincts pointed the way, as usual. There *was* another person here. Overbearing. Thundering down.

The storm. The form had taken shape from my memories

and nightmares, but it had intent that didn't come from me. It wore a cloak of my dreams, but it hid a very real threat. It was a stranger's malice, boiling my way.

I sat on my haunches and stared.

The more I stared into the cloud, the more its contours unfolded. They expanded, enveloped me – became my world.

All at once, I was no longer on the hilltop. The storm boiled through me. Bilious clouds poured through my ears, into my nose and throat, and then into my breath and blood.

From inside, the cloud no longer looked like a cloud. It was just a dark, sullen mass of anger – all-encompassing and inescapable.

Johnny Dee, inside my mind. Come to kill me.

The storm boiled around me, but, somehow, I saw shapes in it. Figures. Figments, like my dad on the hilltop, but different forms. They resolved rapidly, gaining color and form.

These were Johnny Dee's memories.

The last thing I wanted to do was touch even more of him, but I had no choice. I couldn't let him keep crushing down on me. I had to push back.

A whirlwind of images tugged at my clothes and hair. I grabbed at the first thing that looked familiar. To my shock, I found myself in the control cabin of Shoon'kwa's airship.

Everything was silver, shiny, and clean. Not wrecked. Not on fire. The clouds outside the domed windshield were just as tall and energetic as the one in my dream, but, at this altitude, they were harmless little cotton balls. Brown Texas desert stretched endlessly underneath them. Black Widow casually leaned against the glass, a yawning eternity underneath her.

Johnny Dee was watching through Shoon'kwa's eyes.

265

Shoon'kwa glanced casually behind her. All of the others were there, too, standing or leaning. Extremely unsafe positions for a crash.

At the moment he'd been doing this, his physical self had been safely hidden in the cavern while the rest of Wolfram's gang ran to the canyon to deal with me.

"Anonymous employers are always trouble," Rachel was saying.

"Not *always*," Neena said.

"*Always*," Rachel answered.

"How the hell were we supposed to know Gifted Mind Technologies was a front for the X-Men?" Black Widow said. "Charles Xavier did everything he could to cover up the fact that he was on the board of directors."

"They wanted to turn a team led by a mutant against other mutants," Rachel said. "Damned anti-mutant fanatics. They figured if we could get in, mess up the company's work, good. If any of us got hurt or killed doing it, even better."

I knew it was a memory, and that I couldn't change things here any more than I could have made my twelve year-old self less of a brat, but none of that changed the flush of panic that surged through me. I had to warn them. Had to change things, if only in this dream.

I opened my – Shoon'kwa's – Johnny Dee's – mouth, but I couldn't make any sound. Everyone in the control cabin turned to look at me.

The windows darkened. A howl of rage split the sky. Johnny Dee had sensed my intrusion. The deck ripped away underneath me, and I fell into the screaming expanse.

Back into my own memories.

•••

Something had happened when I plunged our two hands into the maw on Johnny Dee's chest. The maw had gotten a gullet-full of both of our DNA – the blood on my hand, the blood on his hand. Plus whatever recursive feedback had come from shoving that doll of me back where it had come from. The result had been… some kind of telepathic shock, or overload. I didn't have the vocabulary to describe it.

"It's a psionic clash," Dad said, standing next to me as I hunched on the hilltop. "A crossed circuit of telepathic impulses, struggling to control a newly formed pathway."

"Hush," I said. "I'm not smart enough to piece that together."

"I'm a figment of your memory," he pointed out. "The words came from you."

I didn't know how to answer that. He did have a point. Also, even though I knew he wasn't real, it still hurt to hear him say so.

"You paid more attention to Magik and Triage than your conscious mind thinks you were capable of," Dad said. He sighed, wistful. "In a different lifetime, you could have been a doctor or a scientist."

"You're just saying that because you're my dad," I told him.

"I mean it," he said. "But you had to go a different course."

"Didn't feel like I had much of a choice at the time." Leave home, or let my family get hurt. Go into the merc business, or see my mutant abilities – and an identity I was proud of – matter less than nothing. The last thing I would ever let myself do was become just another anonymous Houston waitress.

Not that there was anything wrong with Houston waitresses. Just – wasn't me. Never had been.

"Well, it's too late now," Dad said. "Even if you wanted to change."

The pain of hearing that was almost physical, like a body slam. I gave him a look I hope expressed all that. "Too late?"

Before I could ask him what he'd meant, the wind picked up again. This time, I felt it.

I've been in a hurricane or two in my time. Not back home – we were too far inland to get much but the dregs of the monster storms that sometimes battered the state's coast. Some of my jobs had taken me into them, though.

The thing that's always hard to understand about these storms until you've lived through them is just how *wrong* they feel. The winds are warm in a way that few other storms are. It's hard to capture. On camera, to people who've mostly experienced inland storms, a hurricane looks like it should be freezing cold. It's not. It's so warm it might have blown in from an alien planet. All that charged, humid air is like the breath of a dragon. Like Thor's hammer is crashing down to Earth, but hasn't quite picked where to land yet.

Not to get all metal-album-cover on you, but that was how this wind felt. It bore down on us, mad as a cornered boar.

Dad disappeared under a sheet of driving fog. I could hardly see the grass under my legs. I thought I was lost to it, but an abrupt flash of lightning showed me where I was. I saw the hilltop – and other things, too. Shapes in the storm, things that hadn't been there before. Buildings. Smokestacks and streetlights. Just outlines at first – livid afterimages burned into my retina by lightning bolts. But they became more solid as I reached for them.

I hurled myself into the storm, raging at it as hard as it raged at me. I grabbed those images, assembled them one by one into a more coherent reality:

Cityscape. Nighttime. Bright yellow and orange streetlights, illuminated windows.

That was all of the New York skyline I had time to see. Most of the view was blocked off by anonymous brick walls. I got to know those bricks real well, close and personal-like, when someone's fist smashed into my face. The momentum of the blow wheeled me around and planted me lips-first into the masonry.

Something wet and squishy on my gut squealed its pain.

The maw. I was in Johnny Dee's body.

As soon as the thought occurred to me, my senses split from his, like a cell dividing. I was myself, in my own body and my own clothes, farther down the alley. But I could also feel everything the men who'd surrounded Johnny Dee did to him. The kick to his knee. The punch, aimed at his throat, striking his chin.

The Bronx. Shortly after M-Day. The number of mutants in the world had been winnowed from millions to less than two hundred. Mutants worldwide had been depowered, stripped of their identities – but not Johnny Dee. He'd had no idea how these three had divined what he was, but they'd cornered him, forced him into this alley, and were smashing his teeth right out of him.

All around the world, mutantkind's enemies had rallied, sensing weakness, and aiming to eliminate us for good. These men were all in their twenties, versus a scrawny Johnny Dee in his late teens. One of them had a jacket with a stylized "S" sewn onto it. The symbol of the Sapien League, a bunch of anti-mutant agitators who'd just marched on Central Park the day before. And they would do worse things in the future.

I hesitated, on the edge of intervening. Few people deserved what these toughs were dishing out, but maybe Johnny Dee did.

At the end of the day, though, I was going to be damned if I did anything to side with bigots. Against all my other instincts, I started running, barreling in to help.

Johnny Dee's vision was stained by tears. I could trace his thoughts as clearly as I felt each punch land. Those tears weren't tears of pain. They'd come from rage and betrayal, with a smidge of self-pity mixed in.

Johnny Dee knew these men. He'd been in Central Park with them yesterday. *He'd* joined their march. Shouted slogans with them. And he'd meant them.

Johnny Dee reached toward the waist of his shirt. He'd never killed anyone with his tentacles before. Not deliberately. But he'd dreamed of it. Made elaborate fantasies where he would have to. He'd just hoped for some different targets than his ideological brothers.

My momentum faltered. I stopped just short of entering the fray. But the memory took over. I'd become someone else in his eyes. No longer running, but falling. I was a shadow falling from the rooftops. Sweeping in on an impossibly thin silken strand.

Johnny Dee saw a blur of red and blue. The rearmost of his assailants went down.

The next in line had just started to turn when my gloved fist cold-cocked him in the jaw. He went down with no more sound than a grunt.

I fought to pull myself back into my own body, and shake off the twist of dream-logic that had made me someone else. It took effort to become Inez Temple again, but I managed. And just in time to get a better look at what was happening.

Johnny Dee's friendly, neighborhood Spider-Man looked to have about half the muscle mass of the last tough standing. That didn't stop him from picking the man up, and falling lithely onto his back while spinning the tough between his feet. Then, with a playful balletic twirl of his legs that belied the incredible strength behind it, hurled him down the alley. The tough crunched into the wall and fell on his head, unmoving.

I winced. But Spider-Man was a lot more adept than I was at making sure his opponents survived their vicious beat-downs. A lot kid-friendlier in general, really. A couple quick *thwips* of webbing stuck Johnny Dee's attackers in place, waiting for capture.

Spider-Man twisted onto his feet. "Usually you have to pay admission for a ride like that," he said. That man just could not help himself.

Johnny Dee was in no state to appreciate the line. He slumped toward the alley floor. Spider-Man caught him before he fell all the way over.

"Hey, hey, hey – stay with me now. Focus. I got here as fast as I could and I'm really hoping that was fast enough. Give me some sign it's safe to move you."

Johnny Dee was staring through those big, featureless white eyes, without seeing them. Blood streamed down his face. The pain had gone away, but not the rage. His world was rage and adrenaline. Johnny Dee's whole life had been a scream, trapped in his throat.

The scream was silent, but he couldn't hear anything else.

And he didn't really want to.

For years, he'd dreamed of getting this close to someone so powerful. Stealing a snip of their DNA. Now, in the moment, his plans evaporated.

All he heard was the scream between his ears. The rage. The hate. The urge to kill and kill and kill, and bring the rest of the world down with him.

His hand was still on the bottom of his shirt. Spider-Man was close enough for a sting.

Flashing lights danced across the front of the alley – red and blue to match Spider-Man's costume.[19]

Johnny Dee's tenuous courage evaporated.

When the EMTs got him into the back of the ambulance, it did not take them long to discover what Johnny Dee was, and from there to backtrace his identity. Soon enough, the police officers who'd responded to the call bracketed the back of the ambulance.

It wasn't that Johnny Dee was under arrest, though he did have warrants. Police across the nation had standing orders to "protect" the remaining mutants. The same thing was happening to mutants across the world, to heroes and villains and folks just trying to live as "regular" a life as they could. M-Day had, for now, wiped their slates clean. Everyone had new priorities.

Spider-Man lingered in the back of the ambulance, listening to the EMTs as they talked about this mutant refugee camp

---

19 Johnny Dee is remembering things a little differently than they happened in *Son of M #1*, but that's natural. Trauma fogs memory. –Ed.

being set up at the X-Mansion. Johnny Dee hardly heard them. There was too much blood roaring in his ears.

He was starting to realize this was a memory. We were somewhere between a dream, a shadow, and yesterday's reality.

That bolstered his courage where it had failed before. He shoved the EMTs aside and charged Spider-Man. It wasn't Spider-Man's arms that raised to block him, but my own.

The two of us crashed through the ambulance's back doors, my hand around his throat, and the tentacles from his exposed chest wrapped around my arm, stinging, stinging, stinging–

The burn of the stings and the venom never quite went away, even back on the hilltop.

The storm stretched across the horizon, so close that the front was almost a straight line. But it had gotten here already, hadn't it? Or had I beaten it back?

No – that was nonsense. I couldn't have pushed back a storm.

"I reckon we should mosey inside," Dad said, overdoing the folksiness, as usual.

"We'll never get back before the rain." Though I didn't actually see any rain under that storm.

No. Not a storm. *Johnny Dee.* I had to remember that. The knowledge kept slipping from me. In the centrifuge of this nightmare, I was losing everything but my center. Soon enough, even that would fly apart.

Johnny Dee kept battering me, over and over. I was losing to him.

Was this symbolism? I hated symbolism.

"Think you're right," Dad said, heedless. "We lost our chance a while ago."

I stood, having second thoughts. "Maybe if we run."

"No. We really are too late."

There was a sweetness and a sadness to him that I didn't think I'd seen before. Dad had not been the kind of man to broadcast his pain. Not even when we'd lost Mom.

Maybe, in this dream, he was becoming more like the man I always knew was there, rather than the one I saw most of the time.

Or maybe I was falling apart faster than I realized.

I didn't run. We waited to get rained on. I didn't have the nerve to ask him how he felt before the storm swept over us, and everything went dark.

The thing that stood out to me most in my memories of the mutant refugee camp were the high walls. Same thing in Johnny Dee's memory, too. They were the first thing to form out of the lightning and figments.

Enormously tall beige walls, and metal-skinned guards at their gates. We saw the same thing through different eyes.

We'd both been there. It was the first time we'd met. Though it would be a while, yet, before I discovered what a monster he was.

I wasn't going to let it happen the same way again.

As soon as I recognized the walls, I started running. I bolted past tents, past guards, and past mutants' startled faces – blue faces, violet faces, faces wreathed by fire.

I tried not to care about any of them. I had to find Johnny Dee. Had to stop him.

Something in the back of my head shouted that this was a memory inside a dream, that I couldn't change it in any way that mattered, but that voice had been growing increasingly distant. One of the many pieces of me that had spun away. What mattered was here, and now. And here and now I had a good idea where Johnny Dee was. I still remembered where his tent had been.

The towering walls were said to have been built to protect us. You didn't have to look closely, though, to see that the walls were sloped inward – to make them more difficult to scale on *this* side. The cannons on the walls could shred anything trying to get in, but they could also "deter" anyone flying, hovering, or floating out.

We were an endangered species. "For our security," it was important that we remained where we could be *protected*. And since this refuge had started under the aegis of the X-Men, we'd trusted them, the first few times they'd said that. By this point, it had been plain for a while that things were getting away from the X-Men. Unlike Johnny Dee, I hadn't needed to be coerced here. I'd come willingly. More fool me.

Our trust was exhausted by now. Jazz flinched as I ran past. Peepers and Mammomax, the squirt and the elephantine giant, had set up a table to play cards. Mammomax hunched over the table like he was having a tea party with a fairy. Half a second after I burst into view, Peepers had upended the table, and taken cover behind it. Everybody's nerves were keyed up, waiting for trouble to explode.

Everywhere I went, I was surrounded by people I hadn't seen in years. Some folks I would have given anything to catch up with. And plenty more I never wanted to see again.

In the back of my mind, I knew these people had never been farther away from me than they were right now. Some of them, like Mammomax and Jazz, were dead. But they felt real. I could look over and see them. Touch them. In Mammomax's case, smell him.

This must have been what Dad's life had been like right around his diagnosis, when he had still been himself enough to know what was happening. When, one minute, he thought he could walk down the hall and find his brother in his bedroom – and, the next, remembering that his brother had moved to New Jersey and had been dead for five years anyway. Oscillating between different frames of reality.

I knew this wasn't real. At the same time, I believed they were. The voice that said they weren't real kept getting smaller.

The moment that thought occurred to me, a blur launched from the shadows between the tents. It crashed into me, knocking me into the dirt. Johnny Dee. He'd been waiting for me. His eyes blazed, and his lips were curled into the snarl of a dog about to snap. That was all I saw of his face before I raised my arm to defend myself.

Johnny Dee was a lot bigger than I remembered him being. Stronger, too. But just as mean. He dug his fingers into my shoulder. That shoulder had been fine a minute ago, but now it was oozing blood. It bore the gunshot wound Wolfram had given me. The pain was paralyzing.

I tried to get him off me, but I couldn't find a good angle. I didn't have the strength. It wouldn't have gone like this in real life, but this, strangely, seemed more *real* to me than that. More honest.

Too old. Too slow. Too weak.

Until that moment, I'd thought that voice had been my own. Maybe most of it was. In the past, certainly, it had been.

But now there was a strange reverb to it. An echo. When I lowered my forearm, I caught Johnny Dee mouthing the words.

He was trying to tell me those things. Poison me with them.

Strength surged through my muscles. I swung my elbow upward, smashed it into his nose. It landed with a satisfying *crack* of breaking bone. The world fell away underneath us.

Dad and I had maybe a minute to ourselves, to contemplate what we had gotten into before the storm crashed down upon us. Again.

It had reached us before, but something had happened – I had beaten it back – I couldn't really remember. It wasn't anything I could count on happening again. Every time the storm found us could have been the last.

"When you got the diagnosis," I asked, "how did you take it? How could you stand it?"

I didn't know. I hadn't been living at home when he'd gotten it. True to his worst, most stubborn instincts, he hadn't told me for months afterward. He hadn't even told Elias, and Elias had been living with him at the time.

He gave me a little shrug, warding off emotional turmoil. That let me know that he *hadn't* been able to stand it. Not at first.

"After a point," he said, "there didn't seem to be any reason to dwell on it. I'd made my arrangements. Gotten my affairs in order. Any other thought I gave to it would have been taking away from the *now*. What will come, will come."

"You hadn't gotten your affairs in order if you hadn't told us," I muttered.

He shrugged, evasive. I dropped it.

"How could you go on with that looming over you?" I waved toward the storm as a convenient illustration. But what I meant was old age. Uselessness. Death.

"That was the future. Keeping it at the top of my mind all the time would have been like living in it ahead of time."

"But what did you do when that future started to become *now*?"

He chuckled, kindly. "Peaches," he said, "you don't think *you're* getting old, do you?"

"Well, like you've said, I've made a lot of my choices by now. There are lots of things I can't take back." I wasn't doing a very good job of hiding how what he'd said in our last conversation had hurt me.

He looked at me. For too long a moment, he said nothing. Then: "Like *I* said?"

I didn't have time to ask before the winds picked up, and the storm was upon us again.

TWENTY-ONE

I had never *not* been in combat with Johnny Dee. My hand had been locked around his throat, holding him back far enough that his tentacles couldn't reach me, for years. He'd been digging into the wound on my shoulder for longer. Any other kind of life was a distant memory.

But it was one of those memories that we crashed into now – rolling from the matted grass of the refugee camp outside the X-Mansion and onto clean, plush red carpet.

If I hadn't been so focused on murdering Johnny Dee, I would have felt bad for tracking our blood and filth onto it.

For the first time in eons, he forced himself away from me. I swiped at him, but he darted back. He paled. "*No.*"

I didn't see what there was to be panicked about (other than me, the woman trying to murder him). We'd landed in a fairly spacious living room, all nice and domestic-like. Tacky striped couch. Coffee table. Lamps. Big TV, a bigger picture window, and a beanbag chair.

Johnny Dee seemed a lot smaller here. He was three-quarters my height, and slenderer than he had been.

He gave me a look like I'd plugged in the game console underneath the TV, and deleted all his saved games while he watched. Pure anguish. With a full-throated child's howl of rage, he threw himself at me.

He might have seemed physically smaller, but he had all his unearthly strength. In the real world, I could have handled him easily, but, here, he knocked me off my feet. We crashed through a wall of memory.

I smashed shoulder-first into another carpet. A very different one. It was blue, short, and plainly hadn't been vacuumed in a while. And covered in white cat hair.

The shock of recognition was slow in coming. This place was the ramshackle headquarters of Agency X, the first real merc organization I'd joined. The apartment where Alex Hayden, Taskmaster, Sandi Brandenberg, and I had taken whatever work had come our way, and had much lower standards than I do now.

(Hell, don't tell anybody else this, but one of my first jobs with them had sent Alex and myself out to steal the Punisher's sidearms. Yeah. That hadn't ended well. Alex and I ended up crammed into a phone booth together, stripped to our underwear. Our employers, though, had their funerals the following week.[20])

All my old buddies were sitting around the kitchen table. Taskmaster, in his awful mask. Sandi, our agency's founder, gave me a look like she'd always known it would come down to me busting through the walls of my own memory, locked in a telepathic duel with a stranger. Alex, bald and goofy-looking as

---

20 You can find the shameful details in *Agent X #2*. –Ed.

ever, nodded sagely. Deadpool was with them, too. He was the first bigshot merc I'd met when I went into business for myself in New York.

They'd been playing cards. All of them turned to stare at us, except Deadpool, who remained fixated on his cards and was somehow failing to pull a poker face through his mask.

Johnny Dee's fist slammed into my stomach with the force of a pile driver.

He'd brought me here to distract me. Showing me my memories in revenge for seeing his. It worked.

His tentacles coiled around my arm, and I felt the stingers drive deep. Then I couldn't feel much besides pain.

I collapsed and Johnny Dee kicked me, over and over. I couldn't do anything. The floor quaked. Color bled from the walls. Everything became a little dimmer with each kick. Johnny Dee was dismantling me, blow by blow, thought by thought.

Not for the first time, the only thing that saved me was my friends.

One of Deadpool's katanas sliced into Johnny Dee's shoulder bone. The tip of the second emerged from his sternum. Brandi cracked a punch into the side of his face while he hung, suspended, from Deadpool's blades. They were figments, but they were *my* figments, and they packed a punch.

Damn, but I missed these folks. I didn't always. Times had been more bad than good, honestly, and I had some emotional scars that would never heal. Dad died while I was working with them. I'd come back to find that Alex, my then-boyfriend, had slept with Brandi while I was gone.

Right now, though? They were family. I hadn't seen them in years.

Those wounds looked vicious enough, but they weren't bleeding. They'd distracted him, not hurt him. They didn't have the emotional impact on him that they did on me.

I wondered if his memories would treat him any kinder than mine.

I grabbed his ankle and yanked. He fell forward, sliding off Deadpool's blades. When he hit the ground, it was no longer carpet – but a hard cement floor. Grimy and gritty.

Prison. His cell bars were painted bright red, but they were one of only two splashes of color in the place. The second was the dotted yellow line in the corridor outside, showing the guards just how far they needed to keep their distance from Johnny Dee.

This was where Johnny Dee had ended up the last time he'd tried to mess with mutantkind. I felt the cold squeeze his heart as clearly as if it had been my own.

He had no cellmates. He'd been deemed too much of a danger to – and in too much danger from – other prisoners. The guards never came near. Virtual solitary confinement. It was torture. He'd left it more unstable than when he'd gone in.

It wasn't the place itself that made him afraid, though. The cement floor and beige walls reminded him of something. Before he could recover his balance, I grabbed onto that dangling thought-thread and yanked. The cement floor cracked like eggshells underneath us, and we plunged into the darkness below.

Well, not so much dark as poorly lit. Where we landed, the thickly painted beige brick walls were the same. So were the unswept cement floors. But the bars were gone. This room was full of chairs and simple wooden desks, all facing one direction. A blackboard on a wheeled wooden frame stood at the front of the room.

One of the fluorescent lights over Johnny Dee's desk flickered dully. The other had gone out. That was why he sat here. He didn't need the other kids noticing him. He didn't want their stares. No matter how many times he'd begged, the institution would not give him shirts loose enough to cover the bulge underneath them. Nothing hid the tentacles' squirming.

Though this place didn't have guards or bars, it had the same aesthetics as Johnny Dee's cell for a reason. This was a prison. It wasn't fooling anybody, and never intended to.

Johnny Dee flinched back like he'd been struck. There was no one around him, though, and I hadn't hit him. Yet. When I listened to the roaring between his ears, I wasn't sure he would have felt it if I had.

He was in so much pain already. It boiled through his veins, into his head. It was a dull, constant background ache, leaving him both sensitive and lethargic. It curled in his stomach, turning it sour and clenched. He would have a stress ulcer at nineteen years old.

Every day, he was in some kind of pain. A migraine pounding between his temples. The skin on his chest and gut stretching and tearing as that horrible alien maw and tentacles grew. Those tentacles had bright red lines where he'd started to slice them off, but the pain had stopped him from finishing the amputation. The tentacles waved about, and the maw opened and closed, of their own volition. But he felt everything.

The healing scabs itched terribly. He couldn't scratch. Not without drawing attention to them, and to himself. He'd been well-trained to avoid that.

He hadn't had the maw all his life. It had only started growing when he was eight, and become unmistakable for what it was two years later. He'd been old enough to understand the doctors when they told him the maw and tentacles couldn't be removed without killing him (or rendering him quadriplegic and unable to digest his own food), but not old enough to believe them. He'd trusted his parents when, after the surgeons at the hospital had had that talk with them, they'd screamed and stomped and vowed to get a second opinion, and then a third, and so on.

He still believed them even when his dad had a breakdown, started drinking again, and went away. His dad didn't come back, didn't even call. And he *still* believed them when even his mom stopped contesting his juvie sentences after all the fights he kept getting into. And he still believed even after his mom had sent him here, to the institution. She hadn't visited in a month.

And, just like with the surgeons, he was old enough to understand he was being abandoned, but not old enough to believe it.

Until around age eight, he'd been, to all outside appearances, a normal suburban kid. Two parents. A cat. A dog. A video game console.

The pain of seeing this place again was like a frozen steel dagger sliding between Johnny Dee's ribs. I understood – almost *agreed* with – the fury in his yell when he charged and shoved me to the ground. His tentacles lashed at me. It took all my strength to hold him back while he snapped at me, trying to tear out my throat with his teeth.

The storm danced, livid, across the Texas sky. It didn't behave like any natural thing I'd ever experienced. It was not so much out of my memories as my nightmares.

The flash and afterglow of the lightning showed a slender finger of cloud sliding along the farthest hills. The strobing light made it impossible to tell which direction the twister was heading, but I already knew. This *was* a nightmare, after all.

Dad stared into the twister, unafraid. He let out a long breath like he'd been waiting for just this moment.

I had a hunch. One I didn't like very much.

I said, "It feels like I've already made most of the decisions I'll ever get a chance to. Like there are a lot more of them behind me than there are ahead."

"I think you've come to the crux of your problem," he said. "Facing facts that you don't want to."

A minute ago, he'd said he hadn't remembered this thread of our conversation. "You're not my dad."

He turned from the twister to look at me. His eyes were as dark and distant as the storm.

I felt frozen cold despite the warmth of the wind. Maybe he had been my real memory of Dad at some point. When he'd tried to be funny. When he couldn't remember the conversation where he'd essentially called me washed up. But it was plain that something awful had been worming its way into him, wearing his skin.

He'd been trying to hurt me. And he'd succeeded.

"And just when I was starting to feel bad for you, Johnny Dee," I said.

"You're such a cluster of neuroses I hardly needed to probe for them," Dad said.

"You're one to talk."

I tackled him, swinging punches, aiming for his stomach and to drive the breath out of him. I had no idea how much physical combat mattered in the dream, but it shut him up, and so already I felt much stronger than I had. My full mutant strength surged into my arms. My next punch hit just below his sternum, hard enough to crack a rib.

He shoved himself to the side. We tumbled down the hill, bouncing hard on our elbows and knees and asses, toward the tornado.

Lightning cascaded down the twister's face, and showed me Dad in flashes. I tried not to look at him. I didn't want to see Dad in him. But I couldn't help it. My head knocked against a rock. I let go of him and fell, dazed, into a heap. When I looked up, lightning sparked at just the right instant for me to see him striding toward me.

And all I saw, all I wanted to see, was Dad. The strength sapped right back out of my arms.

Dad's foot cracked into my nose.

At the same time I was losing the fight there, I fought on in his side of our dream.

His body had shifted to fit the scene. He was a kid. Ten or eleven years old. His eyes were dark and sad as Dad's had been. They glimmered with tears. But he fought with the power of an adult.

My ribs were bruised. It hurt to breathe. He'd bent back three fingers on my left hand, nearly broken them. And I didn't have my mutant strength here.

He smashed a punch into the side of my head. More and more of me was going dark. Just like my other self, at the ranch.

We weren't alone. Students sat at the other desks, watching us. They hadn't always been there, but they'd arrived without notice. There was a teacher, too – bald, silent, and judging.

Unlike my old friends at Agency X, none of these figments moved to help Johnny Dee. He didn't look to them for it, either. Even at this point in his memories, he'd been alone for a long, long time.

Those memories percolated through me. Every part of him hurt – so much so that anything I could do to help felt like stage punches by comparison.

He'd sat down with a dozen counselors over the years. None of them helped him find the words he'd needed to share that pain. He'd stopped trying. He was convinced that none of them would have listened if he'd found the words. All his anguish was trapped inside him. He couldn't process it. It had had nowhere to go but inward, and nothing to become except rage.

He couldn't manage to aim that rage at his parents. A big part of him had become convinced they'd been right to leave him. *He* wouldn't want to raise him. He'd turned the rage in the only direction he could: to the X-gene – to mutantkind at large – for taking away the life he'd thought he'd been given.

The voiceless scream I'd heard earlier, the first time I'd touched his thoughts, was in this memory, too. It had never ended, just kept getting louder. And he'd never been able to let it out. All the adults around him, his teachers and the few administrators who knew his name, always talked about how quiet he was.

As if summoned by my thinking of them, his teacher chose that moment to intervene.

His leathery, skeletal hand clamped around Johnny Dee's shoulder. He hadn't come to help, like my friends had come to help me. He yanked Johnny Dee off me. But that was all.

He did not act against *me* when I picked myself up, walked over to Johnny Dee, and slugged him in the jaw.

Johnny Dee's teacher just watched, owlishly, as I laid into Johnny Dee.

In this nightmare, I was the same size as Johnny Dee, and much shorter than the teacher. Johnny Dee had stopped seeing me as *me*, I realized. I'd become one of his classmates – beating him down while the only adult in the room encouraged it.

His tentacles hadn't developed their stingers or venom yet, and good thing, too – there would have been a lot more dead kids now otherwise. And it would be several more years before he figured out the maw's telepathic powers. But no one could deny what he was.

This was just the world he inhabited. He hardly thought about it anymore. He'd convinced himself of two contradictory things – things that, taken together, went a long way toward explaining the kind of monster he was.

The first was that he didn't deserve this. The second, though, was that the world was still *right* to work like this. *He* didn't deserve this treatment. But someone did. Mutants.

In the glimmer of his eyes, I caught glimpses of the person

he saw me as. It was hard to make out any detail in such tiny windows, but the reflection of the kid's blue skin was hard to miss.

I came back to my other self, under the unearthly and riven Texas sky, one scrap of my senses at a time. The psychic tug-of-war was dragging in my direction.

Johnny Dee gave me one last kick, square in the center of my forehead – and stopped.

Sight came back to me in stinging, watery blurs. Green-black clouds and strobing yellow-white lightning. And the shape of figures. In this half of our shared nightmare, Johnny Dee was being held back, too. Unlike the other side, though, it wasn't his figments and memories doing the work.

Neena held one arm tight. Rachel did the same thing on his other side. They both looked at me, tight-lipped. Waiting. They paid Johnny Dee no mind as he thrashed.

The twister howled behind them. It had crossed over our property line, and was impossibly huge – so big that I couldn't see all of it at once. In a way that was only possible in dreams, it hadn't touched us yet. The wind yanked on Rachel's violet hair, and tossed Neena's black and white mane all over, but that was all.

Johnny Dee was no longer wearing my Dad's guise. I was surprised by how bittersweet that felt. It had been good just to see him again.

There was no sign of him anywhere around us now. He'd left me alone.

Again.

But I didn't need him to figure out what the trick was. The

secret that was starting to see me come out on top in the fight between Johnny Dee and me.

He'd made an enemy of the world, and thought that made him stronger. I knew what strength actually was.

I almost hadn't. I'd been an idiot about it. Closed myself off. Tucked things away, dealt with them alone. I didn't want the answer to be as sappy as it was – but there it was, here *we* were, and I still almost hadn't made it.

I still might not. I thought I'd been opening up in that hotel room, when I'd told Neena about my symptoms. But I'd only done that because my back was against the wall. I'd been afraid of being kicked out of her posse. Take away the pressure, and I never would have said or done anything. That hadn't been opening up. That had been covering my ass.

I was still so closed up that, when I'd been struggling to tell Neena I loved her, I still hadn't been able to tell her I'd been thinking about leaving the posse. It seemed kinda pathetic, in retrospect.

But I knew these things about myself now. I wasn't sure that Johnny Dee ever would, or could, or wanted to.

There was a scream inside my head, too. I just hadn't heard it.

Neena and Rachel looked at me expectantly. I shook my head.

I didn't need to kick Johnny Dee into the twister. That would have just been cruel. The truth was that he had always been headed there on his own anyway.

They let go of his arms, and the dark wind took him.

I was the stronger person – inside and out. I didn't know if I had been before all this had started, or even before I'd gone inside his head, but I was now.

Finding this out didn't mean I was having any more fun than before, though.

These things are supposed to end in comfort – with me waking up cozy in a hospital bed, riding the good painkillers. Someone shouting, "She's coming around," and all my friends gathered at my bedside. All the hard parts of post-battle cleanup and travel and medical care already done. Much as I hated doctors and hospitals, that would've been nice.

I woke up bloodied, caked with dust and dirt and astonishingly itchy, on the floor of the cavern where I'd tangled with Johnny Dee.

My arms and legs tingled like I'd been laying on them. That was all I could feel. My limbs felt like somebody else's. I could only tell my fingers were moving when I looked at them. Whatever venom Johnny Dee had injected into me hadn't been fatal, but hadn't worn off, either.

Maybe it was better that I couldn't feel much: my right forearm, all the way up to my elbow, was coated in snotty yellow-white mucus. The skin underneath was scored with dozens of shallow cuts from the teeth of Johnny Dee's maw.

It would have been a hell of a thing if I were to have died of an infection after all this. But I wouldn't mind that so much if I got to do one little thing first.

I dragged myself to where Dad's Beretta had fallen. I plucked it off the ground, and crawled back to Johnny Dee.

He was lying flat on his back, arms spread wide, like he'd been blown back by an explosion. His eyes were slitted open and unfocused. His breathing was labored. I planted the Beretta's barrel on his temple.

For a long time, I waited and watched. His breathing never

changed. His forehead was clammy with sweat. What really caught my attention, though, were his maw and tentacles. They weren't moving.

From a scrap of memory I hadn't even realized I'd stolen from him, I knew they *always* moved on their own, even when he was asleep. The maw hung half-open, its scabrous tongue limp. The tentacles flopped lifelessly over his belly.

He looked like he was still in a dream. Trapped where I'd left him.

Gradually, I let the Beretta drop.

TWENTY-TWO

The hospital room reunion had to wait. Survival came first. For a while, that was still pretty dicey.

I forced myself to my feet, and out of the cavern. Judging from the position of the sun, I hadn't been in the telepathic duel all that long. I hadn't realized how thirsty I was until I came out. My tongue tasted like roadkill, a lizard left to desiccate in the desert sun. It was swollen and enormous in my mouth. I'd lost my canteens somewhere in the crash or the brawl afterward. It was a hard walk getting back to the canyon and the airship, but I made it.

Shoon'kwa's airship didn't look as bad inside as it did outside. The deck was slanted, and a lot of the windows were broken, but the ventilation systems had cleared out the smoke. Moving was a challenge. Every surface was slick with fire suppressant foam. The mess hall cabin was, well, a mess, but the sinks' water taps were still working. The water turned brown after only a second cupped in my dirty hands, but still – nothing had ever tasted so good. I must have sucked down half the ship's water tanks.

Then I helped my friends do the same. Some of them were in worse shape than others. Black Widow was her usual sharp-tongued self, except that she got dizzy when she helped me lift the others. White Fox had trouble speaking clearly, but she could move. Shoon'kwa and Rachel were deteriorating, though. They kept passing out. It was a full-time job just to keep them awake.

We got Josh inside, too. To my surprise, he seemed to have stabilized. But it was too early to feel relief. He was the only one of them without a recent head injury, and he could talk coherently, if raggedly.

Neena wasn't there when I got back, which was worrying. Wheezer's silhouette stood lonesome atop the canyon wall. But Neena found us not long after I arrived. She had the start of an awful sunburn, but, for someone as pale as her, it should have been a lot worse. I suspected that she'd found some shade to pass out in. Like Black Widow, she was doing better. Healing on her own. She spoke like herself.

While Black Widow went around to check on the others, Neena and I went searching for the airship's distress beacon. Shoon'kwa's slurred directions were hard to follow, but for every instruction we couldn't understand, Neena picked a random direction and it turned out to be the right one. I let Neena send the signal, in case her luck would help ensure that someone picked it up.

The airship's emergency beacon was housed in a compartment the size of a closet. Neena and I jarred elbows trying to get everything working.

She read more in my silences and expression than I'd intended to reveal. "Hey," she said, after the signal was sent.

"We're alive. The bad guys are dead. That's a good day in the merc business."

I snorted, affecting a laugh. I couldn't pretend any mirth in it.

"We're still doing good as a team," Neena said. "Aren't we?"

The answer was the hardest one I'd ever had to give, and saying it was the worst thing to happen today or yesterday. That put it at the top of a mighty long list. "No," I said. "We haven't been fine for a long time."

Sometimes being lucky, finding the right coincidences, can be awkward as hell. Neena's luck didn't care if it embarrassed her or not. She just pulls the lever on the slot machine and waits for things to fall into place.

Sometimes the symbols that come up are all butts. It just so happened that the first recipients of our distress beacon were Stark Industries surveillance drones.

Within half an hour, the area was swarming with transports, rescue and repair drones, and gleaming armor-suited helpers. I couldn't tell who was a robot and who wasn't. I didn't stay awake for the flight back to civilization. But I had enough energy to make sure that the rescuers sent someone for Wheezer, too.

"Tony Stark will never hire us again," Rachel groused when she found out who'd rescued us. "We botch his job, and then *the very next day* he has to drag us out of our own airship."

It was finally time for that hospital scene. I hated finding myself under the care of strange doctors as much as I knew I would, but I didn't have a choice in the matter. I needed help. These doctors weren't so bad, all told. Not one question about me being a mutant. Maybe Neena or the Stark people had given them a talking to while I hadn't been paying attention.

I healed up a lot faster than the others. But I also wasn't going to leave yet. Not while the rest of my team was here.

My brother was recovering at a different hospital. He'd ended up with a nasty infection and fever that put him out of commission for another few days. Outside of a quick video chat check-in, we hadn't spoken to each other much, but I knew that would be coming.

I still had a lot to come to terms with. A lot that I'd run away from.

But that particular thing was going to have to wait awhile. Neena and I were going around to see everybody. White Fox and Black Widow shared the room next door. Shoon'kwa and Rachel had this one.

I'd been at Shoon'kwa's and Rachel's bedsides the minute they woke up. Neither of them could remember anything that happened after the crash. Their concussions knocked the memories right out of them. Shoon'kwa turned a red-purple shade when we told her about her airship and tried to force her way past Neena and me. She only relaxed, a bit, when we told her that Stark Industries repair bots were piecing the thing back together.[21]

"We've lost plenty of employers before," Neena told Rachel with a shrug. "That's the merc business. If he's smart, he'll see how good we are."

"But… *Tony Stark.*" I didn't know how she did it, but – despite her mussed hair, the bandage on her forehead, and the

---

21 Wouldn't be the first time. Shoon'kwa remembers *Hotshots #3*. –Ed.

shadows under her eyes – Rachel made that hospital gown look good. Like she was lounging and would have been just as much at home beside a pool. Some folks just got it, I guess. "He has friends."

"You're not trying to get back in with Captain America, are you?" Neena asked. Fun fact: Rachel and Captain America used to date. Funnier fact: it hadn't ended well.

"My thoughts are one hundred percent business," Rachel said, indignantly. A pause. "Ninety-eight percent business."

Neena couldn't keep her smile up for long. "We've all got to talk."

"I hate that tone," Rachel muttered.

I didn't want to take my time telling the story of everything that had got me – and us – here. I would have knocked it out of the way and been done with it. But the fact was that it was a long story.

By the time I was done explaining everything, I'd moved from the foot of Rachel's bed to the window. I leaned against the pane, looking out. It was easier, at least for a while, to pretend I was talking to the El Paso streetlights.

The Stark jets had flown us directly to El Paso, and the University Medical Center. It wasn't all that far from the place I'd rented the Mustang. I didn't want to think about the conversation I'd soon have with insurance agents. I would hate to ask the posse for help paying off the bill. Mr Stark was probably going to charge us for the rescue, anyway.

These past few days had wiped out all the gains of the posse's last few jobs and then some. It was all one big, money-losing fiasco.

Johnny Dee was still holding onto life by a thread. If you

could call it life. He'd never woken up, not once. The maw and tentacles remained dormant. The few doctors who knew anything about mutants thought the tentacles might have been dead. If so, it wouldn't be long before they started rotting off. Johnny Dee wouldn't survive the septic shock.

That cruel, violent, idiot ball of anger. I wanted to pretend like I didn't understand him.

He was locked inside his own mind, an endless telepathic feedback loop. I didn't think he had the tools to pull himself out.

To do that, he'd have to face up to himself. See himself like he really was. I didn't think he had the strength. If he ever did, he'd wake up a different person.

Most of the time, though, I still think I should have shot him. Oh, well.

Josh had been flown to this hospital, too, but he wasn't here anymore. His healing factor meant his stay hadn't had to be a long one. Now he was in police custody.

Turned out he had more than a few warrants out for him. Breaking and entering, intimidation, accessory to assault and battery – all from when he was a part of the Reavers. We couldn't get much more information than that. The doctors kept the details private, as they should have. It was Josh's call to make if he wanted to contact us. For the past week, he hadn't seen fit to send us much. Seemed like he didn't want to share much with us.

His full name was Joshua Foley. The police had had to identify him from prints, and find out his story from Reavers already in custody.

Joshua Foley was a full-on anti-mutant bigot, driving

getaway cars for masked gangs ambushing suspected or former mutants. Or he *had* been, until his powers started manifesting.

He was a healer. He could reconfigure the inner workings of a human body – his own, or another's. It took energy, and, as I'd seen, he couldn't do it for very long without fainting, but he was powerful. He had the potential to be one of the more powerful mutants I'd ever met.

One day, he hadn't been able to resist healing one of his friends after they'd been hurt in a fight, and it was over for him. His old friends beat the hell out of him and took him prisoner. They'd been close to killing him as a mutant infiltrator when Wolfram swooped in and "bought" him instead. He'd paid cash for Josh, like Josh was a thing. With Johnny Dee to control him if he got out of line, Josh had effectively been Wolfram's slave.

I had no idea what happened now. Or what he was going to do. Become another Johnny Dee, maybe. I wanted to believe that people could change that much. But after seeing what Johnny Dee had done with his second chance, I was feeling pretty low about everyone and everything.

Rachel was a sharp cookie. When I finished telling the story, she asked, "So that's it, then? You're going to leave the posse?"

"I don't know," I said. "I'm still trying to make up my mind."

I'd softened on this a little bit since the wreck of the airship, when I told Neena that I was for-sure leaving. But, after everything that had happened, I couldn't just keep going on like I used to. Things had changed. *I* had changed. And one of the ways I'd changed was that I knew I needed to restock where I was going, what I'd done, and whether any of this was going to be worth it in the end.

Shoon'kwa pursed her lips and said nothing. Just listened.

Sooner rather than later, we were going to have to bring Black Widow and White Fox in on this, too. But they knew, like Shoon'kwa knew, that there was a different kind of bond between Neena, Rachel, and me. We'd been in the posse the longest. And we'd need to have this out among the three of us.

"You have to admit I've caused a lot of disasters for you all," I said. "I could have avoided them at any time." Looking out the window really did help me say this. "Because I was too stuck-up on myself."

"I don't understand," Rachel said. "You were tired and worn down, and you slipped up. But that was because of Johnny Dee's meddling. It's over now."

"It's also not the point," Neena told Rachel.

"It means you're not a danger to us, darling," Rachel said. "You're just like you always were."

"*Just like I always was* isn't good enough." The person 'I'd always been' was the same one who'd refused to tell her friends anything about how she was feeling until she endangered them on a mission.

"You talked to me," Neena pointed out. "When you got so bad you couldn't lie to yourself about what was happening."

"That's the thing I haven't been able to get across to you," I said. "That wasn't opening up. That was… desperation. When I knew I absolutely couldn't have done anything else to save things."

It was actually worse. It was the kind of thing *I had tricked myself* into believing was opening up, but it wasn't. It had been performance art. I was trying to escape the truth by giving away only a little part of it.

The truth about what I had really been afraid of. About growing old. About Dad. About being tired, and slow, and lost.

I wasn't sure all these things weren't true.

"I saw a lot of myself in that fight with Johnny Dee," I said. "And I really did not like what I saw."

"And you don't think you can change that?" Neena asked.

"Peaches," I said, "I don't think that's the right kind of question. It's not a question of change. It's just that – sometimes people are what they are."

All my life, Dad had been a big part of me. The biggest part, maybe. And I'd always been proud of that. It had been a real shock, looking back through my memories, finding out how much harm he'd done me, too.

That stupid, relentless stoicism of his. Even in the face of illness and death, he'd kept up the mask. For months, he hadn't even told Elias and me the diagnosis.

That hadn't been strength. That had been – dishonest. Covering up. And it had hurt all three of us more in the end.

There was still so much of him in me. It had put my friends in danger. In large part, it had led to everything that had just happened. I couldn't shake him.

The biggest part of my fear of growing old hadn't been about getting slow, or losing my reaction times. It had been in getting so old that I couldn't change.

Because that's what I was pretty sure I was.

"We all have days when we feel like quitting," Rachel said.

"Not me," I said. "Not like this." Until now.

A long silence followed. I wondered if Neena or Rachel were starting to understand what I was trying to tell them.

If I left, I'd probably stay in the business. Mercing was in my blood now. It wasn't a career so much as a lifestyle. But I'd been on my own before. Might be better that way.

These people were my friends. I'd never had better ones. Leaving them would hurt like ripping out my own heart. But... there was friendship, and there was business. The mercenary business didn't have much room for sentimentality. It hurt worse knowing that they'd come to harm because of my screw-ups.

Neena wanted me to stay. That was plain. But I had to wonder if sentimentality wasn't a chain, just keeping us leashed together. There was no reason we couldn't be friends even if we didn't stay in business together. Except we'd go long, long stretches without seeing each other.

But it wasn't just my problems making me feel this way, either. A whole lot of hate and bloodshed had come raining down on me and my brother, and I didn't know how long I could take it. It felt like nothing ever got better. Like I never accomplished anything that lasted. Johnny Dee was out for the count, sure. But I'd learned things about Josh that I'd rather not. Josh and Johnny Dee didn't seem all that different anymore.

Neena had a good sense for when following a train of thought would lead to a derailment. She changed the subject. "Josh sent you a letter," she said. "It arrived today, when you were out of our room."

I glanced at her. "Stealing someone else's mail is a federal crime," I said.

Neena didn't bite back. She didn't apologize, either. "He got an offer from New Charles Xavier School for Mutants. I guess they must have been keeping tabs on you after you visited.

They found out about him, paid his bail, and offered him a student slot. With some conditions – like if he screws up again or flunks anything, he's going right back to jail."

"Good for him," I snapped, and immediately felt awful – more awful – about being peevish. I wasn't ready for emotional whiplash.

"He said he wasn't sure about other mutants until he met you."

"I'm… glad for him," I said. "I really am."

"You don't sound very happy," Rachel said.

"He was hoping to have a chance to see you again," Neena said. "I think you should. It doesn't mean you have to forgive him."

I turned back toward the window so they couldn't see my face.

Once my lip started trembling, I couldn't stop it. I was so scared. I'd never let Neena, or Rachel, or Shoon'kwa see me like this before.

That was what I'd come to learn throughout all this, though. I *couldn't* keep hiding. Hiding how I was – or who I was – had made this whole mess worse from the start.

It was one thing to realize this, though, and another to do it. And I was finding that I still had a lot of barriers to break down. That wouldn't happen overnight. It was gonna take a lot of effort.

If I'd had any sense at all, I would have known that the next thing I'd feel was Neena's hands around my shoulders. Her cheek against mine. (Her damn hair getting up my nose, *snorfle snorfle*.) But I hadn't had any sense, though. Not, at least, when it came to this, and to her. I'd kept myself from learning.

It took more energy, more resolve – more cussedness – than I'd thought I'd had to turn around, let them see my face.

Not for the first time, I found myself wishing I'd stayed in Johnny Dee's nightmare for a little while longer, awful as it had been. Dad had been there. Johnny Dee had worn his skin, but my real memories of him had mixed in there, too. It had been a long time since I'd been that close to him. Felt his hands. Or heard his voice.

When Dad had died, because I was so much like him, I'd never really had a chance to grieve.

I must have blacked out. There was a hole in my memory.

I didn't remember Rachel struggling to stand and joining us. Shoon'kwa's hand grasped mine from around Neena's back.

I still don't know how much time passed like that.

"I'll stay on the team, if y'all will still have me," I said. "But I'm gonna need help. Keeping myself in check." Figuring out this stuff about myself was one thing. Changing it was going to be a long, hard road.

"We'd never do it without you, cowgirl," Rachel said.

"Yeah, you would," I said.

"OK, maybe," she admitted. "But we wouldn't want to. Wouldn't be the same."

"Funny. When I started in this business, I thought you weren't supposed to be sentimental. Never settle for less than the best for your team."

"Only problem with that assessment is that you *are* the best," Neena said. "Even if you weren't, I'm not in this business because I'm heartless. You need a heart to be a merc. We're not just a team. We're partners."

Of course. I'd told myself that – in the same words, even.

But learning to give myself the same kind of slack I gave other people was going to take time.

There was no one else in the world like Neena. And, just like a few minutes ago I hadn't been able to imagine staying on her team, now I couldn't imagine being anywhere else.

"You're a real peach, Peaches," I said.

"Yeah," she said. "You, too."

"That's us," I said. "Real peaches among peaches."

"This is very sweet," Shoon'kwa said, "but if you two keep talking like that, I will punch you."

TWENTY-THREE

Most big city police departments – and some of the more militant, paranoid, and bigoted small-town ones – had special holding cells for mutants and metahumans. But building those without a specific person in mind was a fool's game. The cops couldn't keep ahead of all the ways mutants and metahumans could outsmart or overpower them. They were still going to try.

The El Paso PD's metahuman cell was underground, where it was easy to seal off from the rest of the building. The cement walls had an interior lead lining to try to stop telepathy, telekinesis, and teleportation (it wouldn't work, but the police didn't know that). There were cameras in every corner, always being watched. And just in case they were dealing with someone who could tamper with electronics, there was a one-way window for the pair of guards outside.

Neena, bless her, was already out negotiating the contract for our next job. She never stopped looking for our next opportunity. Rachel and I went to the police station alone.

When we arrived, we were sent right down to Josh's cell.

Even though Josh was being released into our custody, the El Paso police didn't even want to bring him to the exit on their own. From the moment he stepped out of that cell, he was our responsibility.

Josh sat on his sheetless bunk, staring at the one-way window. The stark white lights robbed the room of any shadow. It must've been hell to sleep.

As soon as the two officers here caught the glower on my face, they pretended they weren't there. Good. My patience for everyday police bigotry had ended years ago. Neena, White Fox, and I were lucky we hadn't ended up down here ourselves, frankly. The police didn't have any charges they could pin on us.

The only reason Josh was here was because he was playing along. With a talent like his, he could have found some way to slip free. He could reconfigure his body. Handcuffs and restraints wouldn't hold him. I doubted a police officer could out-fight him.

By voluntarily staying here, he was making a point. He was on his best behavior.

The door was locked like a bank vault, with a heavy, mechanical bar blocking it. Nothing electronic for metahuman captives to mess with. I was told it usually took two officers to open. It was nothing that a big gal like me had any trouble with.

Josh looked up at the sound of the bar unlatching. He bolted upright when Rachel and I stepped inside. A flicker of a smile crossed his face. It didn't last.

For a second, he'd been glad to see us. Then he remembered everything else… like what else we must've heard about him, and the terms of the deal that was getting him out of here. He would stay with the X-Men for a couple months. He would get his training. After that, what happened next would be up to him.

He started to sit back down. I shook my head. "Up and at 'em," I told him. "You've got a big day ahead."

"I do? They don't even let me know what time it is here."

"Eight in the morning. Earliest they'd let this happen." As if because I'd reminded her, Rachel yawned hugely. "I'd say we're here to let you loose, but part of the agreement is that you do exactly what you're told for a little while."

Rachel was letting me take the lead here, but now she spoke. "If they've left you down here all this time, you must have had plenty of time to think."

"You mean about living as a mutie?"

"I mean about living as a *person*." I frowned. "You're a person. I'm a person. Mutants are people. I'm hoping you're a better person than someone who used to be in the Reavers."

"Also," Rachel added, "I wouldn't use the word you just did around other mutants if I were you."

"Right, right – sorry." Josh winced. "I'm still getting used to how to talk about this."

Notably, he'd let my challenge hang in the air. He didn't tell me that he was a better person. Good. That would have been a bad sign. That kind of change took a while.

The X-Men had done more than pay his bail. They'd gotten him the promise of a commuted sentence – attached, of course, to the conditions they'd laid out for him. The X-Men weren't popular, but they had connections, and some strings they could pull when they needed to. One of those strings was in the Texas governor's office.

"Have you heard much from the X-Men?" Rachel asked.

"Letters," he said. He had only been here for a few days, but, when the X-Men spotted a potential new student, they moved fast. "They've already given me a student code name."

That was a slight. Usually students picked their own code names. They were telling him that he wasn't free, not yet. I wondered if he'd picked up on that.

I still couldn't believe Triage had picked the name *Triage*. Whatever the Institute had picked for Josh must have been worse. "Let me guess. 'Bandage.' 'Antibiotic.' No – '*Ointment*.'"

He scowled. "'Elixir.'"

It was only a little more on-the-nose than I had been expecting. "Ooh," Rachel said. "Mysterious. A little bit magical."

I made an effort not to roll my eyes. Josh wasn't so polite.

"I can get used to it," Josh said. "I've gotten used to a lot. It could've been worse."

"Speaking of things you shouldn't bring up around other mutants," I said, "I wouldn't go mentioning the Reavers. Where you're going, people have lost friends to groups like that."

"I'm going to be around telepaths," he said. "You really think I can keep that to myself?"

Well, no, maybe not – having never been a student at that place myself, that hadn't occurred to me. "Fair point."

"It's going to come out anyway," he said. "If I manage to keep it hidden from the telepaths, some *dark figure from my past* will come back at just the wrong moment, or someone will open the wrong files, or… something even more dramatic that I can't think of. That's how it always works with you people. Keeping it to myself would just be asking for trouble." He chewed on his lip. "Might as well just get the pain over sooner. I'm going to be an outcast there, too."

"Yeah," I said. "You probably are."

He looked a little taken aback. "That was where you were supposed to comfort me and tell me I wouldn't be."

"Well, if what I've heard about you from those warrants is true, you've got a lot to make up for." I knew what that felt like.

And other people here knew it even more. Rachel shifted, uncomfortably. That was why she'd offered to come along with me. Her past as a member of the villainous Serpent Society still colored her interactions with just about everyone she worked with. Excepting the company of her current team, of course.

"Being against mutants made so much sense at the time," he said. "It was… it was like a gang. All of my friends were in. Everybody was so damn scared of mutants. We thought we were protecting ourselves. The rallies made everything seem so simple." He buried his head in his hands.

Rachel said, "Never trust anybody who makes the world seem simple."

"I was an awful human," he said, "and I'll be worse as a mutant. Outlaw, you helped turn me around on mutants, but do you know what the big push was? What made me regret being with the Reavers? It wasn't a change of conscience. It was finding out that I was a mutant. That *I* would be affected by all that hate. If I hadn't ever found out I was a mutant, I never would have changed. It was just… selfishness that shocked me out of it."

He must have been marinating in these thoughts the whole time he'd been in custody.

"Yeah," I said, "but you can *admit* you were awful. You're not making excuses. It's an important first step. You'd be surprised how many people can't do it."

I offered him my hand. He stared at it. For a long time, he didn't move to take it.

"Do you think this is going to be worth it?" he asked. "Getting involved? I'm already going to need years of therapy after what happened with Wolfram's gang, and I doubt life with the X-Men is going to get any easier. Even as a student. I don't know that I can hack it."

"I wouldn't join the X-Men myself," I said, "but I'm starting to think the X-Men and I can get along."

They were taking a big risk by doing this. It was the kind of thing they'd do only if they cared enough about him, without even having met him, to give him a chance. That was as brave as it was kind. I would have to reevaluate my opinion of them.

"That wasn't an answer to my question," he said. "You're not an X-Man, but you're a merc. You get into these kinds of fights all the time. *Is* that life worth it?"

If Josh and Rachel could change, so could I. Next to what they'd done, my problems were easy. I could lower my barriers. I could trust my friends. See? It sounded easy to say. With friends like mine at my side, I could do anything. If I let them help me.

And if *I* helped Josh continue turning around, then maybe all the trouble, heartache, and bloodshed of this job was worth the money after all. He didn't have to be another Johnny Dee. I'd help him find his way to being a better person.

Maybe someday, in return, he could do the same for me.

"Yeah," I told him. "You can make it worth it."

ACKNOWLEDGMENTS

Inez Temple wouldn't be in our lives without her creator, the mighty Gail Simone, and the many wonderful comics Gail wrote for Inez and her Posse. There's no world in which Inez or anyone like her exists without Gail. Anyone who would like to see more of Inez has dozens of comics with Gail's name on the cover to pick from. Go read!

Many enormous thank yous to my editor, Charlotte Llewelyn-Wells, both because this story wouldn't exist without her, and for putting up with me even more than usual. The "editorial" footnotes that appear throughout this book were written by me and not her. Any errors and oversights are my responsibility.

My first reader for this book and all my others has been my delightful partner and fellow writer, Dr Teresa Milbrodt, who I love more than Inez loves six-shooters.

The gorgeous cover art for this book and its predecessor, *Domino: Strays*, was done by Dale Halvorsen, aka Joey Hi-Fi. You can find his portfolio with more of his work at *dalehalvorsen.com*.

Tempus and Triage's appearance in this book was most directly inspired by their appearances in Carrie Harris's Xavier's Institute novel, *Liberty & Justice for All*, which takes place in the same continuity as *Outlaw: Relentless*.

Marc Gascoigne, Aconyte's publisher, and his continued faith in me has been astounding. Thank you to him and to everybody on the Aconyte Books team, including Anjuli Smith, Nick Tyler, Vanessa Jack, Vince Rospond, and Gwendolyn Nix.

We'll be seeing you around, cowgirls.

ABOUT THE AUTHOR

TRISTAN PALMGREN is the author of the critically acclaimed genre-warping blend of historical fiction and space opera novel *Quietus*, and its sequel *Terminus*. They live with their partner in Columbia, Missouri.

tristanpalmgren.com
twitter.com/tristanpalmgren

ACONYTE EXTRA!!

TRISTAN PALMGREN INTERVIEWS GAIL SIMONE, COMICS LEGEND AND CREATOR OF OUTLAW

GS: First, Tristan, I wanted to thank you both for inviting me to participate, but also for the excellent work you have done on the *Domino: Strays* and *Outlaw: Relentless* books. The writing is extraordinary, and just a pleasure to read. I am delighted that someone of your talents is writing those women I love so much![22] –Gail

TP: Just for the record, could you state which species you are? I've heard mixed reports, and some rumors that you may be a bear...

Heh. I was having a phone meeting about a very cool film project, it was something I'd really prepped for, and we live in the Oregon boonies on a quite remote lake, picture windows everywhere. I'm giving my presentation on the phone, and I look up from my notes and there's a huge *bear* outside my back window,

---

22 Aww shucks! –Ed

just staring right at me. Then it started trying to get onto my patio and I chased it away, all the while the execs on the other end probably were thinking I'd lost my mind.

Some really funny twitter folks decided the bear had eaten me and taken my job and ...

... human. Never mind, I'm human. Just human. Honest. Although I do love salmon. But human for *sure*.

Perfect. That question was just to calibrate our lie-detector equipment. Please keep that in mind while you answer the following questions.

Where were you on the day Inez Temple was created? What could possibly have motivated you to do such a thing? In short, Ms Simone – what were you thinking?

Probably something along the lines of, "Please don't let me mess this up". It was for my first issue of *Deadpool*, which was my first mainstream comics assignment, and I was told that if we couldn't raise the sales, it was likely to be canceled. No pressure, right?

But I had always told myself that if I ever did get a chance to write comics, I would try my best to add some kickass new female characters ... I didn't want to replace the older characters as I really love them. But I wanted there to be more characters who weren't just spin-offs.

Marvel is so much about New York. I'm from a small town, I'd never been to New York when I started writing comics. It might as well have been Atlantis or Latveria. So I started with the idea of someone who came from somewhere very different, and that got me thinking of Texas. And I wanted someone who could take care of herself in a scrap... not as an elite martial artist, just someone tough and durable, someone to really test Deadpool. And Inez was born, and to this day, she's still my favorite of the characters I have created at Marvel. I like that she's fierce, and fun-oriented, but with a hint of sadness underneath.

What about Inez, Neena, Rachel, and the Posse are special to you? No matter how many other projects you're working on, I see those three pop up in your social media a lot.

They do, and partly it's the joy of their chemistry. Marvel's had a ton of great writers but until recently, the vast majority have been guys, and it's hard not to see that inform the female characters a little. So, I wanted the Posse to be friends, like, those friends you discover late in life and somehow you can't believe you ever managed to live without them.

I mean, there have been, what, hundreds of super hero comics that have focused on a buddy friendship, or a mostly male dynamic, and that's great. I love those books. But it's still pretty new and fresh to present that with female characters. So I chose to pick some rowdy ladies in those three, and I dearly love the mix. The first goal is always entertainment, meaning, do you want to hang out with these characters? Do you want to learn more about them? If we don't have that, nothing else really matters.

If our fabulous audience wants to read more about Inez and the Posse, where can they start? What are your favorite stories with them?

Outlaw is pretty easy, most of her stories have been in the two recent Domino mini-series, which I wrote, and the Deadpool and Agent X stories collected in *Deadpool Classics* volumes nine and ten!

Your comics have a wide emotional range, but I think the thing that's most consistent across them is a sense of fun. How do you manage to keep that sense of levity, and keep it appropriate for the story being told?

I am not 100% certain that I do keep it appropriate, I think that's part of the fun, going right up the cliff and seeing if you fall over. I like comics that are safe and cozy sometimes, but the really memorable ones have a point of view, and some risk is being taken.

For me, that risk is often showing heroes in their less glamorous and charitable moments. I like showing them when things have gone hopelessly awry. I also like them to have flaws and needs.

Outlaw likes a drink and a fight and a roll in the hay, that already makes her a lot of fun to write.

You've worked with more iconic characters than I could count. What's your research process for starting with a character you haven't created? How do you make sure you get it right?

Oh, I promise, no one gets it right every time, that's why Marvel invented the No-Prize! But I do immerse myself in a character's lore before I start writing them. I tend to be drawn to the characters who have lost focus a bit, and I always find it delightful if you can sort of spotlight what made them great in the first place.

It's usually a matter of finding a key element, something that you love about them, and just… sharing it, illuminating it. It's easier with less iconic characters, but I find if you really dig, you can still find something new to say and do with the A-listers, which is very rewarding.

You've worked with plenty of established characters. You've also created plenty and set them loose in the world. Characters like Inez Temple. Is it exciting to see other people tell stories with them? Alienating? It sounds like it would feel tremendously weird, to be honest.

I love this question, Tristan. The truth is, I have never lost my sense of being a fan, even when I'm right in the middle of writing these books. I still love to read a great, beautifully drawn Spider-Man story, for example. I love when a new voice pops up and takes over some book I'd been overlooking. And the thing I love, love, love about the Marvel Universe is, it really is this incredibly luminous tapestry, it goes in every direction and on every timeline.

I was so thrilled the first time I got to write the Punisher or the Hulk, it felt like I was helping at the loom, you know? So to me, it's a big deal when a great writer, like yourself, cares enough about a character I created to carry on with the weaving. It means a lot.

Outlaw having a cardboard life-size standee in the second Deadpool movie, it just made me happy. That is part of my tiny contribution to this universe that meant so much to me. I am always thrilled.

You're a master of media. You've worked in comics and television, and from dark graphic novels to a delightful Princess-content-rich episode of My Little Pony: Friendship is Magic. That's astounding versatility. How do these different forms affect your writing style? How does the how of storytelling affect what gets told?

This is another great question… it's something I try to convey to new writers all the time. Winning the lottery as a writer for me is getting to do work that makes you happy. I have been so fortunate that way, and what makes me most happy is getting to tell a story with characters I love. Sometimes you have *one* great, say, Captain America story. I love that feeling, come in, do your story, put everything you have on the table, and then move on to another thing entirely.

I'll never forget, I was asked to do *Mortal Kombat* and *My Little Pony* stories at the same time, two different employers, and so all morning I would research Rainbow Dash, and all evening I'm decapitating ninjas.

I loved it. That's how I keep fresh, I don't want to stay on a book past where I can really keep surprising the readers.

Where can people find out more about you and your work?

Most of my social media is on Twitter, I talk about all subjects, including bear issues, and am happy to answer all questions.

I love this job, I am always delighted to talk about it! I'm @gailsimone on Twitter.

These words will be appearing in OUTLAW: RELENTLESS in September, 2021. What's up next for you?

I've always said that comics were my dream job, and it's true. But the past couple years I have signed on to some huge projects in other media and they make it difficult to keep doing regular monthly comics, although I hope to be doing some soon.

I am currently a consultant on the upcoming *Red Sonja* film, I am developing a couple series and some animated things, I have a novel in the works, some game projects... there's a lot and very little I can talk about.

I am busier than ever, which is a gift. The best thing is, a lot of these projects, I'm still working with the comics characters I love, they're just in new mediums, and that's a joy to be part of.

MARVEL HEROINES

Showcasing Marvel's incredible female Super Heroes in their own action-packed adventures.

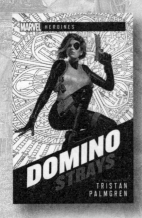

MARVEL XAVIER'S INSTITUTE

The next generation of the X-Men strive to master their mutant powers and defend the world from evil.

MARVEL UNTOLD

Discover the untold tales and hidden sides of Marvel's greatest heroes and most notorious villains.

MARVEL CRISIS PROTOCOL

Bring the action to life with the greatest heroes in the galaxy.

MARVEL LEGENDS OF ASGARD

Mighty heroes do battle with monsters of myth to defend the honor of Asgard and the Ten Realms.

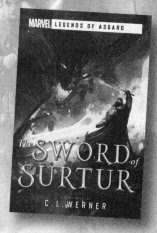

WORLD EXPANDING FICTION

Do you have them all?

MARVEL CRISIS PROTOCOL
- ☐ *Target: Kree* by Stuart Moore

MARVEL HEROINES
- ☐ *Domino: Strays* by Tristan Palmgren
- ☐ *Rogue: Untouched* by Alisa Kwitney
- ☐ *Elsa Bloodstone: Bequest* by Cath Lauria
- ☑ *Outlaw: Relentless* by Tristan Palmgren

LEGENDS OF ASGARD
- ☐ *The Head of Mimir* by Richard Lee Byers
- ☐ *The Sword of Surtur* by C L Werner
- ☐ *The Serpent and the Dead* by Anna Stephens
- ☐ *The Rebels of Vanaheim* by Richard Lee Byers *(coming soon)*

MARVEL UNTOLD
- ☐ *The Harrowing of Doom* by David Annandale
- ☐ *Dark Avengers: The Patriot List* by David Guymer *(coming soon)*
- ☐ *Witches Unleashed* by Carrie Harris *(coming soon)*

XAVIER'S INSTITUTE
- ☐ *Liberty & Justice for All* by Carrie Harris
- ☐ *First Team* by Robbie MacNiven
- ☐ *Triptych* by Jaleigh Johnson
- ☐ *School of X* edited by Gwendolyn Nix *(coming soon)*

EXPLORE OUR WORLD EXPANDING FICTION

ACONYTEBOOKS.COM
@ACONYTEBOOKS
ACONYTEBOOKS.COM/NEWSLETTER